He'd been shot.

He was still, too still. She could find no hint of life in him, and his skin was so cool… He'd been in the water for God knows how long.

It took every ounce of strength she had to roll him onto his stomach. She straddled his body and worked on him until she was rewarded by a choking cough and a stream of water gushing out of his mouth.

"There you go," she breathed, not ceasing her efforts. He went into a paroxysm of coughing, his body heaving beneath her; then he groaned hoarsely and shuddered before going limp. His eyes were closed, and his head rolled to the side when she shook him. He was unconscious.

"Don't you die on me," she ordered.

"Linda Howard knows what readers want, and dares to be different."
—*Affaire de Coeur*

LINDA HOWARD

DIAMOND BAY

ISBN 1-55166-480-1

DIAMOND BAY

Copyright © 1987 by Linda Howington.

All rights reserved. Except for use in any review, the reproduction or
utilization of this work in whole or in part in any form by any electronic,
mechanical or other means, now known or hereafter invented, including
xerography, photocopying and recording, or in any information storage or
retrieval system, is forbidden without the written permission of the publisher,
MIRA Books, 225 Duncan Mill Road, Don Mills, Ontario, Canada M3B 3K9.

All characters in this book have no existence outside the imagination of the
author and have no relation whatsoever to anyone bearing the same name
or names. They are not even distantly inspired by any individual known or
unknown to the author, and all incidents are pure invention.

MIRA and the Star Colophon are trademarks used under license and registered
in Australia, New Zealand, Philippines, United States Patent and Trademark
Office and in other countries.

Printed in U.S.A.

DIAMOND BAY

The clean golden sun still burned its heat into his flesh, all along his bare chest and long legs, even though it was near sundown. The lengthening rays threw dancing sparkles onto the tips of the waves, mesmerizing him as he stared at them. No, it wasn't the glittering water that mesmerized him, it was the fact that he had nothing more important to do than simply stare at it. He'd forgotten how peace sounded, how it *felt.* For a long, wonderful month of pure solitude he could relax and be only a man. He would fish when he felt like it, or cruise the warm, hypnotic waters of the Gulf if he felt restless. The water drew him on endlessly. Here it was midnight blue, there it was brilliant turquoise; over there it was a pale, shimmering green. He had money for fuel and provisions, and only two people in the world knew where he was or how to reach him. At the end of the month's vacation he would return to the gray world he'd chosen and lose himself in the shadows, but for now he could lie in the sun, and that was all he wanted. Kell Sabin was tired, tired of the endless struggle, the secrecy and maneuvering, the danger and deception of his job. It was a vitally important job, but for this month he would let someone else do it. This month was his; he could almost understand what had lured Grant Sullivan, his old friend and the best agent he'd ever had, to the quiet mystery of the Tennessee mountains.

Sabin had been a top agent himself, a legend prowling

the Golden Triangle and, later, the Middle East and South America, all the hot spots of the world. Now he was a department chief, the shadowy figure behind a group of crack agents who followed his directions and his training. Little was known about him; the security surrounding him was almost absolute. Sabin preferred it that way; he was a loner, a dark man who faced the hard realities of life with both cynicism and acceptance. He knew the drawbacks and dangers of his chosen career, he knew it could be dirty and vicious, but he was a realist and he had accepted all that when he took the job.

Still, it got to him sometimes, and he had to get away from it, live for a little while like a normal citizen. His private escape valve was his custom-made cabin cruiser. His vacations, like everything else about him, were highly guarded secrets, but the days and nights at sea were what kept him human, the only times when he could relax and think, when he could lie naked in the sun and reestablish his link with his own humanity, or watch the stars at night and regain his perspective.

A white gull soared overhead, giving its plaintive cry. Idly he watched it, free and graceful, framed against the cloudless blue bowl of the sky. The sea breeze brushed lightly over his naked skin, and pleasure brought a rare smile to his dark eyes. There was a streak of untamed savage in him that he had to keep under tight control, but out here, with only the sun and the wind and the water, he could let that part of himself surface. The restrictions of clothing seemed almost sacrilegious out here, and he resented having to dress whenever he went into a port for fuel, or whenever another boat pulled up beside him for a chat, as people were wont to do down here.

The sun had moved lower, dipping its golden edge into the water, when he heard the sound of another motor. He turned his head to watch the cabin cruiser, a little larger than his own, cut leisurely through the waves. That was the only way to get around out here: leisurely. The warmer the clime, the slower the time. Sabin kept his gaze on the boat, admiring the graceful lines and the smooth, powerful sound of the motor. He liked boats, and he liked the sea. His own boat was a prized possession, and a closely guarded secret. No one knew it belonged to him; it was registered to an insurance salesman in New Orleans who had no knowledge at all of Kell Sabin. Even the name of the boat, *Wanda*, had no meaning. Sabin knew no one named Wanda; it was simply a name that he'd chosen. But *Wanda* was completely his, with secrets and surprises of her own. Anyone who really knew him wouldn't have expected anything else, but only one man in the world had ever known the man behind the mask, and Grant Sullivan gave away no secrets.

The sound of the other boat's motor changed as it slowed and turned in his direction. Sabin swore irritably, looking around for the faded denim cutoffs he usually kept on deck for such situations. A voice drifted to him over the water, and he looked at the other boat again. A woman was standing at the forward rail, waving her arm back and forth over her head in a manner that held no urgency, so he guessed they were just looking for a chat and weren't having any sort of trouble. The afternoon sunlight glinted on her red hair, turning it into fire, and for a moment Sabin stared at it, his attention caught by that unusual, glowing shade of red.

A frown put furrows in his brow as he quickly stepped into his cutoffs and zipped them. The boat was still too far away for him to see her face, but that red hair had aggravated some hidden little memory that was trying to surface. He stared at her as the other boat idled toward him, his black eyes glittering with intensity. There was something about that hair....

Suddenly every instinct in Sabin shrilled an alarm and he hit the deck, not questioning that spine-tingling uneasiness; it had saved his life too many times for him to hesitate. He spread his fingers on the warm wood of the deck, acknowledging that he could be making a fool of himself, but he'd rather be a live fool than a dead wise man. The sound of the other motor dropped off, as if it had slowed even more, and Sabin made another decision. Still on his stomach, with the scent of polish in his nostrils and the scrape of wood on his bare flesh, he snaked his way over to a storage compartment.

He never went anywhere without some means of self-defense. The rifle that he pulled out of the storage compartment was powerful and accurate, though he knew it would be a temporary deterrent at best. If his instincts were wrong, then he would have no use for it at all; if his instincts were right, they would have far more firepower than this rifle, because they would have prepared for this.

Swearing under his breath, Sabin checked that the rifle was on full automatic fire and crawled back over to the rail. Coolly choosing his cover, he let the barrel of the rifle be seen, and he eased his head around just enough to let him see the other boat. It was still closing on him, less than a hundred yards away.

"That's close enough!" he yelled, not knowing if his voice would carry clearly enough to be understood over the noise of the motor. But that didn't matter, as long as they could tell he was yelling something.

The boat slowed, barely moving through the water now, seventy-five yards away. Suddenly it seemed to be swarming with people, and none of them looked like the ordinary Gulf fishermen or leisure boaters, because every one of them was armed, even the red-haired woman. Sabin scanned them quickly, his extraordinary eyesight picking up details of shape and size. He was able to identify the types of weapons without having to think about it, he was so familiar with them. It was the people he watched, and his eyes darted back to one man. Even at that distance, and even though he stood a little behind everyone else, there was something familiar about him, just as there was something familiar about the woman.

There was no doubt now, and icy, deadly calm settled over him, just as it always did in combat situations. He didn't waste time worrying about how badly outnumbered he was; instead he began weighing and discarding options, each decision made in the flash of a second.

A flat CRACK! split the twilight—the sound of rifle fire over open water. He caught the faint, warm percussion of the bullet as it split the air over his head and splintered the wood of the cabin behind him. With a motion as smooth as oiled silk Sabin took aim and fired, then pulled his head down, all in one continuous flow. He didn't need the involuntary sharp cry that pierced the air to tell him that he hadn't missed; Sabin would have been both surprised and furious if he *had*.

"Sabin!" The amplified voice echoed tinnily across the water. "You know you don't have a chance! Make it easy on yourself."

The accent was very good, but it wasn't quite American. The offer was only what he'd expected. His best chance was to outrun them; *Wanda*'s speed was just one of her unusual features. But to outrun them, he had to get to the controls up top, which meant exposing himself to their fire during the climb up the ladder.

Sabin weighed the situation and accepted that he had perhaps a fifty-fifty chance of reaching the top, maybe less, depending on how surprised they were by his move. On the other hand, he had no chance at all if he simply sat there and tried to hold them off with one rifle. He had a lot of ammunition, but they would have more. Moving was a risk he had to take, so he didn't waste time worrying about his diminishing chances. He took a deep breath, held it, then exhaled slowly, coiling his steely body in preparation. He needed to get as high up the ladder with the first jump as he could. Gripping the rifle firmly, he took another breath and leaped. His finger pressed the trigger as he moved, the automatic fire making the weapon buck in his hand and forcing everyone on the other boat to take cover. His outstretched right hand caught the top rung of the ladder, and his bare feet barely touched before launching him higher. Out of the corner of his eye he saw the white bursts even as he swung himself over the top and two red-hot sledgehammers slammed into his body. Only sheer momentum and determination carried him onto the deck, and kept him from falling to the lower one. Black mist almost obscured his vision, and the sound of his own breathing was loud in his ears.

He'd dropped the rifle. *"Goddammit." He'd dropped the rifle!* he thought furiously. He took a deep breath, forcing the black mist away, and summoned the strength to turn his head. The rifle still lay there, clutched in his left hand, but he couldn't feel it. The left side of his body was washed with his own blood, almost black in the dwindling light. His chest heaving with his rapid breathing, Sabin reached across with his right hand and got the rifle. The feel of it in his hand made things a little better, but not much. Sweat broke out and ran off him in rivers, mixing with his blood. He had to do something, or they'd be on him.

His left arm and leg wouldn't obey the commands of his brain, so he ignored them, dragging himself over to the side using only his right arm and leg. Bracing the rifle against his right shoulder, he fired at the other boat again, letting them know he was still alive and dangerous so they wouldn't come rushing in.

Glancing down, he took stock of his injuries. A bullet had gone through the outside muscle of his left thigh, another through his left shoulder; each was serious enough on its own. After the first burning impact his shoulder and arm had gone numb, useless, and his leg wouldn't support his weight, but he knew from experience that the numbness would soon begin to fade, and with the pain he would regain some use of his wounded muscles, if he could afford to wait that long.

He risked another look and saw that the other boat was circling behind him. The upper deck was open at the rear, and they would have a clear shot at him.

"Sabin! We know you're hurt! Don't make us kill you!"

No, they would much rather have him alive, for "questioning," but he knew they wouldn't take any chances. They would kill him if they had to, rather than let him escape.

Grinding his teeth, Sabin dragged himself over to the controls and reached up to turn the key in the ignition. The powerful engine coughed into life. He couldn't see where he was going, but that didn't matter, even if he rammed the other cruiser. Panting, he slumped back to the deck, trying to gather his strength; he had to reach the throttle, and he had only a few moments left. Hot pain was spreading over his entire left side, but his arm and leg were beginning to respond now, so he figured that was a fair trade. He ignored the growing pain and levered himself up on his right arm, forcing his left arm to move, to reach, until his bloody fingers touched the throttle and shoved it into forward gear. The cruiser began sliding through the water with slowly increasing speed, and he heard the shouts from the other boat.

"That's it, girl," he panted, encouraging the boat. "Let's go, let's go." He stretched again, every muscle in his body shaking from the effort, and managed to reach far enough to push the throttle wide open. The boat leaped beneath him, responding to the surge of power with a deep-throated roar.

At full speed he had to see where he was going. He was taking another chance, but those chances were getting better with every foot of distance he put between himself and the other boat. A grunt of pain exploded from his throat as he hauled himself to his feet, and salty sweat stung his eyes; he had to keep most of his weight on his right leg, but the left one didn't buckle beneath him, which was all he asked. He glanced over his shoulder at the other cruiser. He was rapidly pulling away from them, even though they were giving chase.

There was a figure on the top deck of the other boat, and he was settling a bulky pipe onto his shoulder.

Sabin didn't even have to think to know what it was; he'd seen rocket launchers too many times not to recognize them on sight. Only a second before the flash, and barely two seconds before the rocket exploded his boat, Sabin went over the right side, into the turquoise water of the Gulf.

He went deep, as deep as he could, but he had very little time, and the percussion rolled him through the water like a child's toy. Pain seared his wounded muscles and everything went black again; it was for only a second or two, but it was enough to completely disorient him. He was choking, and he didn't know where the surface was. The water wasn't turquoise now, it was black, and it was pressing down on him.

The years of training saved him. Sabin had never panicked, and now wasn't the time to start. He stopped fighting the water and forced himself to relax, and his natural buoyancy began carrying him to the surface. Once he could tell which direction was up, he began swimming as well as he could, though he could barely move his left arm and leg. His lungs were burning when he finally bobbed to the surface and gulped the warm, salt-scented air.

Wanda was burning, sending black smoke billowing into a pearlescent sky that held only the last few moments of light. Darkness had already spread over the earth and sea, and he seized it as his only available cover. The other boat was circling the *Wanda*, playing its spotlight over the burning wreckage and the surrounding ocean; he could feel the water vibrating with the power of the engines. Unless they found his body—or as much of it as they could realistically expect to remain—they would search for him; they'd have to. They couldn't afford to do anything else. His priority remained the same: he had to put as much distance as he could between himself and them.

Clumsily he rolled to his back and began a one-sided backstroke, not stopping until he was well away from the glare of the burning boat. His chances weren't good; he was at least two miles from shore, probably closer to three. He was weak from loss of blood, and he could barely move his left arm and leg. Added to that were the chances that the predators of the sea would be drawn to him by his wounds before he got anywhere close to land. He gave a low, cynical laugh, and choked as a wave hit him in the face. He was caught between the human sharks and the sharks of the sea, and damned if it really made any difference which one got him, but they would both have to work for it. He didn't intend to make it easy for them.

He took a deep breath and floated while he struggled out

of his shorts, but his twisting efforts made him sink, and he had to fight his way back to the surface. He held the garment in his teeth while he considered the best tactics to use. The denim was old, thin, almost threadbare; he should be able to tear it. The problem was in staying afloat while he did it. He would have to use his left arm and leg, or he'd never be able to manage it.

He had no choice; he had to do what was necessary, despite the pain.

He thought he might pass out again when he began treading water, but the moment passed, though the pain didn't lessen. Grimly he chewed on the edge of the shorts, trying to get a tear started in the fabric. He forced the pain out of his mind as his teeth shredded the threads, and he hastily tore the garment up to the waistband, where the reinforced fabric and double-stitching stopped his progress. He began tearing again, until he had four loose strips of cloth attached to the waistband; then he began chewing along the waistband. The first strip came loose, and he held it in his fist while he freed the second strip.

He rolled to his back and floated, groaning as his wounded leg relaxed. Quickly he knotted the two strips together to get enough length to wrap around his leg. Then he tied the makeshift tourniquet around his thigh, making certain that the cloth covered both the entrance and exit wounds. He pulled it as tightly as he could without cutting off circulation, but he had to put pressure on the wounds to stop them from bleeding.

His shoulder was going to be more difficult. He bit and pulled until he tore the other two strips from the waistband, then knotted them together. How was he going to position this makeshift bandage? He didn't even know if he had an exit wound in his back, or if the bullet was still in his shoulder. Slowly, awkwardly, he moved his right hand and felt his back, but his water-puckered fingers could find only smooth skin, which meant that the bullet was still in him. The wound was high on his shoulder, and bandaging it would be almost impossible with the materials he had.

Even tied together, the two strips weren't enough. He began chewing again, tore off two more strips, then tied them to the other two. The best he could manage was to sling the strip over his back, bring it around under his armpit and tie it in a tight loop over his shoulder. Then he folded the remnant of his cutoffs into a pad and slipped it under the loop, positioning it over the wound. It was a clumsy bandage at best, but his head was swimming, and deadly lethargy was creeping into his limbs. Grimly Sabin pushed both sensations away, staring fixedly at the stars in an effort to orient himself. He wasn't going to give up; he could float, and he could manage to swim for short periods of time. It might take a while, but unless a shark got him, he was damned well going to make it to shore. He rolled onto his back and rested for a few minutes before he began the slow, agonizing process of swimming to shore.

It was a hot night, even for mid-July in central Florida. Rachel Jones had automatically adjusted her habits to the weather, taking it easy, either doing her chores early in the morning or putting them off until late afternoon. She had been up at sunrise, hoeing the weeds out of her small vegetable garden, feeding the geese, washing her car. When the temperature soared into the nineties she moved inside and put a load of clothes in the washer, then settled down for a few hours of research and planning for the journalism course she had agreed to teach at night in Gainesville when the fall quarter began. With the ceiling fan whirring serenely overhead, her dark hair pinned on top of her head, and wearing only a tank top and an old pair of shorts,

Rachel was comfortable despite the heat. A glass of iced tea sat constantly beside her elbow, and she sipped at it as she read.

The geese honked peacefully as they waddled from one section of grass to the other, herded by Ebenezer Duck, the cantankerous old leader. Once there was an uproar when Ebenezer and Joe, the dog, got into a dispute over which one had the right to the patch of cool green grass beneath the oleander shrub. Rachel went to the screen door and shouted at her rambunctious pets to be quiet, and that was the most exciting event of the day. That was the way most of her days went during the summer. Things picked up during the fall, when the tourist season began and her two souvenir shops in Treasure Island and Tarpon Springs began doing a lively trade. With the journalism course her days would be even busier than usual, but the summers were a time for relaxing. She worked intermittently on her third book, feeling no great pressure to finish it, since her deadline wasn't until Christmas and she was well ahead of schedule. Rachel's energy was deceptive, because she managed to accomplish so much without ever seeming to hurry.

She was at home here, her roots deep in the sandy soil. The house she lived in had been her grandfather's, and the land had been in the family for a hundred and fifty years. The house had been remodeled in the fifties and no longer resembled the original frame structure. When Rachel had moved in she had renovated the inside, but the place still gave her a sense of permanency. She knew the house and the land surrounding it as well as she knew her own face in the mirror. Probably better, because Rachel wasn't given to staring at herself. She knew the tall pine thicket in front of her and the rolling grassland at her back, every hill and tree and bush. A path wound through the pines and down to the beach where the Gulf waters rolled in. The beach was undeveloped here, partly because of the unusual roughness of the shore, partly because the beachfront property was owned by people who had had it for generations and weren't inclined to see condominiums and motels rise in their faces. This was prime cattle country; Rachel's property was almost surrounded by a huge ranch, owned by John Rafferty, and Rafferty was as reluctant as she to sell any land for development.

The beach was Rachel's special haven, a place for walking and thinking and finding peace in the relentless, eternal surge of the water. It was called Diamond Bay because of the way the light splintered on the waves as they crashed over the underwater boulders that lined the mouth of the little bay. The water shimmied and glittered like thousands of diamonds as it rolled to shore. Her grandfather had taught her to swim in Diamond Bay; sometimes it seemed as if her life had begun in the turquoise water.

Certainly the bay had been the center of the golden days of her childhood, when a visit to Gramps's had been the most fun a young Rachel could imagine. Then her mother died when Rachel was twelve, and the bay became her permanent home. There was something about the ocean that had eased the sharpness of her grief and taught her acceptance. She'd had Gramps, too, and even now the thought of him brought a smile to her face. What a wonderful old man he'd been! He had never been too busy or too embarrassed to answer the sometimes awkward questions an adolescent girl could ask, and had given her the freedom to test her wings while still keeping her solidly grounded in common sense. He had died the year she'd finished college, but even death had met him on his own terms. He had been tired and ill and ready to die, and he'd done it with such humor and acceptance that Rachel had even felt a sort of peace at his going. She had grieved, yes, but the grief had been tempered by the knowledge that it was what he had wanted.

The old house had stood empty then, while Rachel pursued her career as an investigative reporter in Miami. She had met and married B. B. Jones, and life had been good. B.B. had been more than a husband, he had been a friend, and they had thought they had the world on a string. Then B.B.'s violent death had ended that dream and left Rachel a widow at the age of twenty-five. She quit her job and returned here to the bay, once again finding solace in the unending sea. She had been crippled emotionally, but time and the peaceful life had healed her. Still, she felt no urge to return to the fast-paced life she'd led before. This was home, and she was happy with what she was doing now. The two souvenir stores provided an adequate living, and she supplemented her income by writing an occasional article as well as the adventure books that had done so surprisingly well.

This summer was almost exactly like all the other summers she had ever spent at Diamond Bay, except it was hotter. The heat and humidity were almost stifling, and some days she felt like doing nothing more strenuous than lying in the hammock and fanning herself. Sundown brought some relief, but even that was relative. The night brought a light breeze from the Gulf to cool her heated skin, but it was still too hot to sleep. She had already taken a cool shower, and now she sat on the front porch swing in the dark, lazily keeping the swing moving with occasional movements of her foot. The chains squeaked in time with the chirping of crickets and the croaking of frogs; Joe lay on the porch in front of the screen door, dozing and dreaming his doggy dreams. Rachel closed her eyes, enjoying the breeze on her face and thinking of what she would do the next day: pretty much what she had done today, and the day before, but she didn't mind the repetition. She had enjoyed the old days of excitement, filled with the peculiar seductive power of danger, yet now she also enjoyed the peace of her present life.

Even though she wore only panties and a man's oversize white shirt, with the sleeves rolled up and first three buttons open, she could still feel small beads of sweat forming between her breasts. The heat made her restless, and finally she got to her feet. "I'm going for a walk," she told the dog, who flicked an ear at her but didn't open his eyes.

Rachel hadn't really expected him to join her; Joe wasn't a friendly dog, not even with her. He was independent and antisocial, backing away from an outstretched hand with his hackles raised and teeth showing. She thought he must have been mistreated before he'd shown up in her yard a few years before, but they had formed a truce. She fed him, and he filled the role of guard dog. He still wouldn't allow her to pet him, but he would come instantly to her side if a stranger drove up, and stand there glaring at the intruder until he either decided there was no danger, or the stranger left. If Rachel worked in her garden, Joe was usually close by. It was a partnership based on mutual respect, and both were satisfied with it.

He really had it easy, Rachel thought as she cut across the yard and took the path that wound down through the tall pines to the beach. He wasn't often called on as a guard; few people came to her house, except for the postman. She was at the dead end of an unpaved road that cut through Rafferty's property and hers was the only house. John Rafferty was her only neighbor, and he wasn't the type to drop in for a chat. Honey Mayfield, the local veterinarian, sometimes came by after a call at the Rafferty ranch, and they had developed a rather close friendship, but other than that Rachel was pretty much left alone, which was one reason she felt comfortable roaming around at night wearing only her underwear and a shirt.

The path sloped down a very gradual incline through the pine thicket. The stars were bright and heavy in the sky, and Rachel had walked the path since childhood, so she didn't bother with a flashlight. Even in the pines she could still see well enough to find her way. It was a quarter of a mile from the house to the beach, an easy walk. She liked walking the beach at night; it was her favorite time to listen to the ocean's power, when the waves were black except for their pearly foam tops. It was also low tide, and Rachel preferred the beach at low tide. It was at low tide that the ocean pulled back to reveal the treasures it had brought in to leave on the sand, like a love offering. She had collected a lot of sea treasures at low tide, and never ceased marveling at the wonders the turquoise Gulf brought to her feet.

It was a beautiful night, moonless and cloudless, and the stars were brighter than she had seen them in years, their light refracted on the waves like countless diamonds. Diamond Bay. It had been well named. The beach was narrow and uneven, with clumps of weeds growing along the edge, and the mouth of the bay was lined with jagged rocks that were especially dangerous at low tide, but for all its imperfections the bay created magic with its combination of light and water. She could stand and watch the glittering water for hours, spellbound by the power and beauty of the ocean.

The gritty sand cooled her bare feet, and she dug her toes deeper. The breeze gusted momentarily, lifting her hair away from her face, and Rachel inhaled the clean salt air. There was only herself and the ocean.

The breeze changed directions, flirting with her, blowing strands of hair across her face. She put up her hand to push her hair out of her eyes and paused in mid-motion, her eyebrows drawing together fractionally as she stared at the water. She could have sworn she'd seen something. Just for a moment there had been a flash of movement, but now her straining eyes picked up nothing but the rhythmic surge of the waves. Perhaps it had been only a fish, or a large piece of driftwood. She wanted to find a really good piece for a flower arrangement, so she walked to the edge of the waves, pushing her hair back so it wouldn't obscure her vision.

There it was again, bobbing in the water! She took an eager step forward, wetting her feet in the foamy surf. Then the dark object moved again and took on a funny shape. The sheen of the silvery starlight made it look just like an arm, flailing weakly forward, like a tired swimmer struggling for coordination. A muscled arm, at that, and the dark bulk beside it could be a head.

Realization burst, and Rachel's entire body tingled with electricity. She was in the water before she realized it, surging through the waves toward the struggling man. The water impeded her progress, the waves pushing her back with increasing strength; the tide was just beginning to come back in. The man sank from view, and a hoarse cry burst from her throat. Wildly she splashed toward him, the water up to her breasts now, the waves crashing into her face. Where was he? The black water gave no hint of his location. She reached the spot where she had last seen him, but her frantically searching hands came up empty.

The waves would wash him toward the beach. She turned and staggered back toward shore and saw him again for a moment before his head disappeared beneath the water once more. She struck out, swimming strongly, and two seconds later her hand closed on thick hair. Fiercely she jerked his head above the water, but he was limp, his eyes closed. "Don't you die on me!" she ordered between clenched teeth, catching him under the shoulders and towing him in. Twice the incoming tide knocked her feet out from under her, and each time she thought she would drown before she could struggle free of the man's confining weight.

Then she was in water to her knees, and he sagged limply. She tugged until he was mostly out of the water, then fell on her hands and knees in the sand, coughing and gasping. Every muscle trembling with reaction, she crawled over to him.

Chapter Two

He was naked. Her mind barely registered that fact before it was pushed aside by more urgent matters. She was still gasping for air herself, but she forced herself to hold her breath while she put her hand on his chest to detect a heartbeat, or the up and down movement of breathing. He was still, too still. She could find no hint of life in him, and his skin was so cool....

Of course it was cool! She brought herself up sharply, shaking her head to clear it of the cobwebs of fatigue. He'd been in the water for God only knew how long, but he'd been swimming, however weakly, the first time she'd seen him, and she was letting precious seconds tick past when she should be acting.

It took every ounce of strength she had to roll him onto his stomach, because he wasn't a small man, and the bright starlight revealed that he was solid muscle. Panting, she straddled him and began the rhythmic push-pull action that would stimulate his lungs. That was another thing her grandfather had taught her, and taught her well. Her arms and hands were strong from the gardening and swimming she did, and she worked on the man until she was rewarded by a choking cough and a stream of water gushing out of his mouth.

"There you go," she breathed, not ceasing her efforts. He went into a paroxysm of coughing, his body heaving beneath her; then he groaned hoarsely and shuddered before going limp.

Rachel quickly rolled him onto his back again, bending anxiously over him. His breathing was audible now. It was too rapid and too ragged, but he was definitely breathing. His eyes were closed, and his head rolled to the side when she shook him. He was unconscious.

She sank back on her heels, shivering as the ocean breeze went right through the wet shirt she wore, and stared at the dark head that rested on the sand. Only then did she notice the clumsy binding around his shoulder. She reached to pull it away, thinking that perhaps it was the remnants of the shirt he'd been wearing when he suffered whatever accident had cast him into the ocean. But the wet fabric beneath her fingers was denim, too heavy for a shirt in this weather, and it had been tied into a knot. She pulled at it again, and part of the fabric came away. It had been folded into a pad and shoved under the knot, and high on his shoulder was a wound, a round, obscene mouth where there shouldn't have been one, showing black in the colorless light.

Rachel stared at the wound, her mind jolting with realization. He'd been shot! She'd seen too many gunshot wounds not to recognize one, even in the pale light of the stars that reduced everything to silvery gleam and black shadows. Her head whipped around and she stared out to sea, straining her eyes to see the telltale pinpoint of light that would warn of a boat, but there was nothing. All her senses were alert, her nerves tingling, and she was instantly wary. People didn't get shot without reason, and it was logical to assume that whoever had shot him the first time would be willing to do so again.

He had to have help, but there was no way she could throw him over her shoulder and carry him up to the house. She stood, scanning the dark sea again to make certain she hadn't missed anything, but the expanse of water was empty. She would have to leave him here, at least for as long as it would take her to run up to the house and back.

Once the decision was made Rachel didn't vacillate. Bending, she grasped the man under his shoulders and dug her heels into the sand, grunting with the effort as she pulled him far enough out of the water that the incoming tide wouldn't lap around him before she could get back. Even in the depths of unconsciousness he felt the pain she caused him by tugging on his wounded shoulder and gave a low, hoarse moan. Rachel winced and felt her eyes burn momentarily, but it was something she had to do. When she judged that he was far enough up the beach she let his shoulders down on the sand as easily as she could, muttering a breathless apology to him even though she knew he couldn't hear her. "I'll be right back," she assured him, touching his wet face briefly. Then she ran.

Normally the path up the beach and through the stand of pines seemed like a fairly short one, but tonight it stretched endlessly ahead of her. She ran, not caring about stubbing her bare toes on exposed roots, heedless of the small branches that caught at her shirt. One such limb was strong enough to catch her shirt, halting her flight in mid-step. Rachel threw her entire weight against the fabric, too frantic to pause to untangle it. With a sodden ripping sound the shirt tore, and she was free to resume her wild plunge up the slope.

The welcoming lights of her small house were a beacon in the night, the house an oasis of safety and familiarity, but something had gone very wrong, and she couldn't shut herself inside its refuge. The life of the man on the beach depended on her.

Joe had heard her coming. He stood on the edge of the porch with his hackles raised and a low, rumbling growl issuing from his throat. She could see him silhouetted by the porch light as she sprinted across the yard, but she didn't have time to calm him down. If he bit her, he bit her. She would worry about that later. But Joe didn't even glance at her as she bounded up the steps and slammed the screen door back on its hinges. He remained on guard, facing the pines and the beach, every muscle quivering as he placed himself between Rachel and whatever had sent her flying through the night.

Rachel grabbed the phone, trying to control her breathing so she would be able to talk coherently. Her hands were shaking as she fumbled through the telephone book, looking for an ambulance listing, or a rescue squad—maybe the sheriff's department. Anyone! She dropped the book and swore violently, leaning down to grab it again. Rescue squad—they would have paramedics, and the man needed medical attention more than he needed a police report made out on him.

She found the number and was punching it out, when suddenly her hand froze, and she stared at the phone. A police report. She didn't know why, couldn't logically explain it to herself right then, but abruptly she knew she had to keep this quiet, at least for now. The instincts she had developed during her years as an investigative reporter were sending off steady warning signals, and she obeyed them now as she had obeyed them then. She slammed the receiver back onto its hook, shaking as she stood there and tried to force her thoughts into order.

No police. Not now. The man on the beach was helpless, no threat to her or anyone else. He would have no chance at all if this was more than a simple shooting, an argument that had gotten out of hand. He might be a drug-runner. A terrorist. Anything. But, dear God, he might not be any of those, and she was the only chance he had.

Even as she dragged a quilt from the top of her bedroom closet and bolted from the house again, with Joe right on her heels, jumbled scenes from her past kept skittering through her mind. Scenes of things that weren't quite right, where the glossy surface was accepted and neatly filed away, the real story forever hidden from view. There were other worlds beyond the normal, everyday life that most people lived, layers of danger and deceit and treachery that were never even suspected. Rachel knew about those layers. They had taken B.B.'s life. The man on the beach might be victim or villain, but if he was a villain she would have time to turn him in to the authorities long before he could recover from his wound; on the other hand, if he was a victim, the only time he had was what she could give him.

He was lying just as she'd left him, the tide swirling just inches from his feet. Gasping, Rachel fell to her knees in the sand beside him and put her hand on his chest, shuddering with relief when she felt the steady up and down movement that told her he was still alive. Joe stood beside her, his head lowered and his ears laid back as a low, continuous growl came from his throat, his eyes never leaving the man.

"It's all right, Joe," she said, automatically giving the dog a reassuring pat, and for once he didn't shy away from her touch. She spread the quilt on the sand, then knelt once again to brace her hands against the man's limp body. She rolled him onto the quilt. This time he didn't make a sound, and she was grateful he couldn't feel the pain she had to cause him.

It took her a few minutes to get him positioned; then she had to rest. She stared uneasily at the sea again, but it was still empty. There was no one out there, though it wasn't unusual to see the night lights of passing boats. Joe brushed against her legs, growling again, and she gathered her strength. Then she leaned down, gathered the two corners of the quilt nearest the man's head and dug her heels into the sand. She grunted with the strain; even with her entire weight thrown into the effort, it was all she could do to drag him a few feet. God, he was heavy!

Maybe when she got him off the beach and onto the slippery pine needles it would be easier. If it got much harder she wouldn't be able to budge him at all. She'd known it would be difficult, but she hadn't realized it would be almost beyond her physical capabilities. She was strong and healthy, and his life depended on her. Surely she could drag him up to her house, even if she had to do it an inch at a time!

That was almost what it amounted to. Even when she managed to get him off the beach, although the pine needles were slippery and the quilt slid over them more easily, her path was uphill. The incline wasn't steep, and she normally walked it easily, but it might as well have been vertical for the effort it took her to drag a two-hundred-pound man up it. She couldn't sustain her forward progress for any length of time at all. She lunged and lurched, falling to her knees several times. Her lungs were pumping and wheezing like bellows, and her entire body was one big ache before she had him halfway up the slope. She stopped for a moment and leaned against a pine, fighting the inevitable nausea of overexertion. If it hadn't been for the tree supporting her, she might not have been able to stand at all, because her legs and arms were trembling wildly.

An owl hooted somewhere close by, and the crickets chirped on undisturbed; the events of the night meant nothing to them. Joe hadn't left her side, and every time she stopped to rest he crowded against her legs, which was totally unlike him. But he wasn't pressing against her for protection; rather, he was protecting her, putting himself between her and the man. Rachel took a deep breath and steeled herself for another effort, patting Joe on the side and saying, "Good boy, good boy."

She reached down to take hold of the quilt again, and Joe did something extraordinary; he caught the edge of the quilt between his teeth and growled. Rachel stared at him, wondering if he'd taken it in his head to prevent her from dragging it any farther. Cautiously she braced her shaky legs, then leaned back and pulled with every ounce of strength left in her. Still growling, Joe braced his legs and pulled, too, and with his strength added to hers the quilt slid forward several feet.

Rachel stopped in amazement, staring at the dog. "Good boy," she said again. "Good boy!" Had it been a fluke, or would he do it again? He was a big, strong dog; Honey Mayfield had estimated that he weighed almost eighty pounds. If he could be coaxed into pulling with her, she could have the man up the slope in no time.

"Okay," she whispered, taking a better grip on the quilt. "Let's see if you'll do it one more time." She pulled, and Joe pulled, that low growl still rumbling in his throat, as if he disapproved of what she was doing, but would help her if she was determined to do it.

It was much easier with the dog's help, and soon they were out of the pine thicket, with only the dirt road and the small yard to cross before they reached the house. Rachel straightened and stared at the house, wondering how she would ever get him up the two steps to the porch. Well, she'd gotten him this far; she'd get him in the house, one way or another. Bending, she began tugging again.

He hadn't made a sound since that one groan on the beach, not even when they pulled him across exposed roots or the loose rocks on the dirt road. Rachel let the quilt drop and bent over him again, crouching on the cool, damp grass beside him. He was still breathing; after what she'd put him through, she didn't suppose she could ask for anything more. She stared at the two steps again, a frown puckering her forehead. She needed a conveyor belt to get him up those steps. A growing sense of urgency gnawed at her. Not only did he need attention, but the sooner she got him hidden inside, the better. She was isolated out here at Diamond Bay, so chance visitors weren't likely, but anyone who came looking for the man wouldn't be a chance visitor. Until he was conscious, until she knew more about what was going on, she had to hide him.

The only way she had of getting him up the steps was to catch him under the arms and pull him up them, just as she'd pulled him out of the sea. Joe couldn't help now. She would have to lift the man's head, shoulders and chest—the heaviest part of his body.

She'd gotten her wind back, and sitting there in the grass wasn't going to get anything accomplished. But she was so tired, as if her legs and arms were weighted down with lead; they were sluggish, and she staggered a little when she climbed to her feet. Gently she wrapped the quilt around the man, then positioned herself behind him and slid her hands under his shoulders. Straining, fighting for every bit of leverage, she raised him to a half-sitting position, then quickly propped him up on her legs. He started to fall over, and with a cry Rachel caught him around the chest, looping her arms tightly and locking her hands together. His head fell forward, as limply as a newborn's. Joe worried at her side, growling when he couldn't find a place to catch hold of the quilt.

"It's all right," she panted. "I've got to do it this way now." She wondered if she was talking to the dog or the man. Either was ridiculous, but both seemed important.

The steps were at her back. Keeping her legs under her and her hands tightly locked around the man's chest, Rachel thrust herself backward; her bottom landed on the first step with a jarring thud, and the edge of the top step scraped a raw strip down her back, but she'd managed to lift the man a little. Hot pain seared her back and legs from the strain she was putting on her muscles. "Oh, God," she whispered, "I can't collapse now. In a little while I'll rest, but not now."

Grinding her teeth, she got her feet under her again, using the stronger muscles of her thighs rather than her more vulnerable back muscles. Once more she lunged up and back, pushing with her legs, hauling the man up with her. She was sitting on the top step now, and tears of pain and effort were stinging her eyes. The man's torso was on the steps, his legs still out in the yard, but if she could get his upper body on the porch the rest would be easy. She had to do the agonizing maneuver one more time.

She didn't know how she did it, where she found the strength. She gathered, lunged, pushed. Suddenly her feet went out from under her and she fell heavily on her back on the wooden porch, the man lying on her legs. Stunned, she lay there for a moment, staring up at the yellow porch light with the tiny bugs swarming around it. She could feel her heart pounding wildly inside her rib cage, hear the wheezing sobs as she tried to suck enough oxygen into her lungs to meet the demand being made by overworked muscles. His weight was crushing her legs. But she was lying full-length on the porch, so if he was lying on her legs, that meant she'd done it. She'd gotten him up the steps!

Groaning, crying, she pushed herself into a sitting position, though she thought the planks beneath her made a wonderful bed. It took her a moment to struggle from beneath his confining weight, and then it was more than she

could do to stand. She crawled to the screen door and
propped it open, then scrambled back to the man. Just a
few more feet. Inside the front door, angle to the right, then
into her bedroom. Twenty, thirty feet. That was it, all she
would ask of herself.

The original method of catching the edge of the quilt and
pulling it seemed like a good idea, and Joe was willing to
lend his strength again, but Rachel had precious little
strength herself, and the dog had to do most of the work.
Slowly, laboriously, they inched the man across the porch.
She and Joe couldn't get through the door at the same time,
so she went first and knelt to reach for a new grip on the
quilt. Growling, his husky body braced, Joe pulled back
with all his strength, and man and quilt came through the
door.

It seemed like a good idea to keep on going while they
had him moving; she angled him toward her bedroom, and
a scant minute later he was lying on the floor beside her
bed. Joe released the quilt as soon as she did and immediately backed away from her, his hackles raised as he reacted to the unfamiliar confines of a house.

Rachel didn't try to pet him now; she'd already asked so
much of him, trespassed so far past the set boundaries, that
any further overtures would simply be too much. "This
way," she said, struggling to her feet and leading him back
to the front door. He darted past her, anxious for his freedom again, and disappeared into the darkness beyond the
porchlight. Slowly she released the screen door and closed
it, slapping at a gnat that had entered the house.

Methodically, her steps slow and faltering, she locked
the front and back doors and pulled the curtains over the
windows. Her bedroom had old-fashioned venetian blinds,
and she closed them. That done, the house as secure as she
could make it, she stared down at the naked man sprawled

on her bedroom floor. He needed medical attention, skilled medical attention, but she didn't dare call a doctor. They were required to report all gunshot wounds to the police.

There was really only one person who could help her now, one person she trusted to keep a secret. Going to the kitchen, Rachel dialed Honey Mayfield, keeping her fingers crossed that some emergency hadn't already called Honey out. The telephone was picked up on the third ring, and a distinctly drowsy voice said, "This is Mayfield."

"Honey, this is Rachel. Can you come out?"

"Now?" Honey yawned. "Has something happened to Joe?"

"No, the animals are fine. But…can you bring your bag? And put it in a grocery sack or something, so no one can see it."

All traces of drowsiness had left Honey's voice. "Is this a joke?"

"No. Hurry."

"I'll be there as soon as I can."

Two receivers were hung up simultaneously, and Rachel went back to the bedroom, where she crouched beside the man. He was still unconscious, and the handling he had received should have been enough to wake the dead, unless he had lost so much blood that he was in deep shock and near death himself. Sharp, piercing anxiety seized her, and she touched his face with trembling hands, as if she could pass the essence of life to him with her touch. He was warmer now than he had been, and he was breathing with slow, heavy movements of his chest. The wound on his shoulder was sullenly oozing blood, and sand clung to him, even matting his hair, which was still dripping seawater. She tried to brush some of the sand out of his hair and felt something sticky beneath her fingers. Frowning, she looked at the watery redness that stained her hand; then awareness dawned. He had a head injury, as well! And she had dragged him up that slope, then literally manhandled him up the steps and onto the porch! The wonder was that she hadn't killed him!

Her heart pounding, she ran to the kitchen and filled her biggest plastic mixing bowl with warm water, then returned to the bedroom to sit on the floor beside him. As gently as possible, she washed as much blood and sand out of his hair as she could, feeling the thick strands come unmatted between her fingers. Her fingertips found a swelling lump on the right side of his head, just past the hairline at his temple, and she pushed the hair aside to reveal a jagged tear in the skin. Not a gunshot wound, though. It was as if he'd hit his head, or been hit with something. But why was he unconscious now? He had been swimming when she'd first seen him, so he'd been conscious then, coming in on the surge of the tide. He hadn't lost consciousness until he was already inside the mouth of Diamond Bay.

She pressed the cloth to the lump, trying to clean sand out of the cut. Had he hit his head on one of the huge, jagged rocks that lined the mouth of the bay? At low tide they were just under the surface of the water and difficult to avoid unless you knew exactly where they were placed. Knowing what she did about the bay, Rachel decided that that was exactly what had happened, and she bit her lip at the thought of dragging the man around the way she had when he was probably suffering from a concussion. What if her imagination was running wild with her, and she caused the man's death with her fears and hesitation? A concussion was serious, and so was a gunshot wound. Oh, God, was she doing the right thing? Had he been shot by accident and fallen overboard at night, then lost his bearings from pain and confusion? Was someone frantically searching for him right now?

She stared blindly down at him, her hand moving to touch his shoulder as if in apology, her fingers stroking lightly over his warm, darkly tanned skin. What a fool she was! The best thing she could do for this man would be to call the rescue squad immediately and hope that she hadn't done any additional damage to him with her rough handling. She started to get to her feet, to forget her crazy fancies and do the sensible thing, when she realized that she had been staring at his legs, and that the left one had a knotted strip of denim tied around it. Denim. He'd had denim tied around his shoulder, too. Her spine tingled warily, and she left her position by his head to crawl down to his leg, already afraid of what she would find. She couldn't untie the knot; it was pulled too tightly, and the water had only tightened it.

She got a pair of scissors out of her sewing basket and neatly sliced the fabric. The scissors slipped from her suddenly nerveless fingers as she stared down at his thigh, at the ugly wound in the outer muscle. He'd been shot in the leg, too. She examined his leg almost clinically; there were both entry and exit wounds, so at least the bullet wasn't still inside him. He hadn't been so lucky with his shoulder.

No one was shot *twice* by accident. Someone had deliberately tried to kill him.

"I won't let it happen!" she said fiercely, the sound of her own voice startling her. She didn't know the man who lay on the floor, unmoving and unresponsive, but she crouched over him with all the protectiveness of a lioness for a helpless cub. Until she knew what was going on, no one was going to get a chance to hurt this man.

Her hands gentle, she began washing him as best she could. His nudity didn't embarrass her; under the circumstances she felt it would be silly to flinch from his bare flesh. He was wounded, helpless; had she walked up on him sunbathing in the nude, that would have been a different kettle of fish entirely, but he needed her now, and she wasn't about to let modesty prevent her from helping him.

She heard the sound of a car coming down her road and got hastily to her feet. That should be Honey, and though Joe normally wasn't as hostile to women as he was to men, after the unusual events of the night he might be on edge and take it out on the vet. Rachel unlocked the front door and opened it, stepping out on the front porch. She couldn't see Joe, but a low growl issued from beneath the oleander shrub, and she spoke quietly to him as Honey's car turned into the driveway.

Honey got out and reached into the back seat for two grocery sacks, which she clutched to her as she started across the yard. "Thanks for waiting up," she said clearly. "Aunt Audrey wants you to look at these quilting squares for your shops."

"Come on in," Rachel invited, holding open the screen door. Joe growled again as Honey walked up the steps, but remained beneath the oleander.

Honey sat the two grocery sacks on the floor and watched as Rachel carefully locked the front door again. "What's going *on*?" she demanded, planting her strong, freckled fists on her hips. "Why am I disguising my bag as quilting squares?"

"In here," Rachel said, leading the way to her bedroom. He still wasn't moving, except for the regular motion of his chest as he breathed. "He's been shot," she said, going down on her knees beside him.

The healthy color washed out of Honey's face, leaving her freckles as bright spots on her nose and cheekbones. "My God, what's going on here? Who is he? Have you called the sheriff? Who shot him?"

"I don't know, to answer three of those questions," Rachel said tensely, not looking at Honey. She kept her eyes trained on the man's face, willing him to open his eyes, wishing he could give her the answers to the questions Honey had asked. "And I'm not going to call the sheriff."

"What do you mean, you're not going to call?" Honey fairly shouted, shaken out of her usual calm capability by the sight of a naked man on Rachel's bedroom floor. "Did *you* shoot him?"

"Of course not! He washed up on the beach!"

"All the more reason to call the sheriff!"

"I *can't*!" Rachel lifted her head, her eyes fierce and strangely calm. "I can't risk his life that way."

"Have you lost your sense of reason? He needs a doctor, and the sheriff needs to investigate why he was shot! He could be an escaped felon, or a drug runner. Anything!"

"I know that." Rachel drew a deep breath. "But the shape he's in, I don't think I'm taking that much of a risk. He's helpless. And if things aren't that...cut and dried...he wouldn't stand a chance in a hospital where someone could get to him."

Honey put her hand to her head. "I don't understand what you're talking about," she said wearily. "What do you mean, 'cut and dried'? And why do you think someone would try to get to him? To finish the job they started?"

"Yes."

"Then it's a job for the sheriff!"

"Listen," Rachel said insistently. "When I was a reporter, I saw some things that were...strange. I was on the scene one night when a body was found. The man had been shot in the back of the head. The sheriff of that county did his report, the body was taken in for identification, but when the one-paragraph report appeared in the newspaper two days later it said that he had died of *natural causes*!

In a way, I suppose it is natural to die of a bullet in the brain, but it made me curious, and I poked around a little, looking for the file. The file had disappeared. The coroner's office had no record of a man who had been shot in the head. Finally the word filtered down to me to stop snooping, that certain people in government had taken care of the matter and wanted it dropped.''

"This doesn't make any sense," Honey muttered.

"The man was an agent!"

"What sort of agent? DEA? FBI? What?"

"You're on the right track, but go deeper."

"A spy? You're saying he was a spy?"

"He was an agent. I don't know for which side, but the entire thing was hushed up and doctored out of existence. After that I started noticing other things that weren't quite what they seemed. I've seen too much to simply assume that this man will be safe if I turn him over to the authorities!"

"You think *he's* an agent?" Honey stared down at him, her brown eyes wide.

Rachel willed herself to answer calmly. "I think there's a chance of it, and I think we'd be risking his life to turn him over to the sheriff. It would be a matter of public record then, and anyone hunting for him would be able to find him."

"He could still be a drug runner. You could be risking your life by protecting him."

"That's a possibility," Rachel admitted. "But he's wounded, and I'm not. He doesn't have any chance at all, except what I can give him. If the DEA has busted up a drug ring there'll be something about it on the scanner, or in the newspaper. If he's an escaped felon it'll be on the news. He's not in any condition to hurt anyone, so I'm safe."

"And if a drug deal has gone sour, and some other unsavory characters are after him? You wouldn't be safe then, from either him or the others."

"That's a chance I'll have to take," Rachel said quietly, her gray eyes level as she met Honey's worried gaze. "I know all the possibilities, and I know the risks. I may be seeing shadows where there aren't any, but think how terrible it would be for him if I'm right."

Honey drew a deep breath and tried again. "It just isn't likely that a wounded spy would wash up on your beach. Things like that don't happen to normal people, and you're still within the bounds of normalcy, even if you are a little eccentric."

Rachel couldn't believe what she was hearing, from Honey of all people, who was usually the most logical person in the state. The night's events were rattling everyone. "It isn't likely that a wounded man would wash up on my beach period, regardless of his occupation! But he did! He's here, and he needs help. I've done what I can, but he needs medical attention. He still has a bullet in his shoulder. Honey, please!"

If possible, Honey went even whiter. "You want *me* to take care of him? He needs a doctor! I'm a veterinarian!"

"I can't call a doctor! Doctors are required to report all gunshot wounds to the police. You can do it. No vital organs are involved. It's his shoulder and his leg, and I think he has a concussion. Please."

Honey glanced down at the naked man and bit her lip. "How did you get him up here?"

"Joe and I pulled him, on this quilt."

"If he has a severe concussion he may need surgery."

"I know. I'll handle that if it's necessary. I'll think of something."

They were both silent for a few minutes, looking down

at the man who lay so still and helpless at their feet. "All right," Honey finally said, her voice soft. "I'll do what I can. Let's get him up on the bed."

That was as difficult as getting him up from the beach had been. Because Honey was larger and stronger, she got him under the shoulders, while Rachel slid one arm under his hips and the other under his thighs. As Rachel had noted before, he was a big man, and roped with muscles, which meant that he weighed more for his size than a less muscular man would have. He was also deadweight, and they had to be careful of his injuries. "Good God," Honey panted. "How did you manage to get him up that slope and into the house, even with Joe's help?"

"I had to do it," Rachel said, because that was the only explanation she had.

Finally they got him on the bed, and Rachel slumped to the floor, totally exhausted by the night's efforts. Honey bent over the man, her freckled face intent as she examined him.

_____ *Chapter Three*

It was three o'clock in the morning. Honey had left half an hour before, and Rachel had held her weariness at bay long enough to take another much needed shower and wash the salt out of her hair. The heat of the day had finally abated enough that the air was comfortable, but soon it would be sunrise, and the heat would begin to build once more. She needed to sleep now, while she could, but her hair was wet. Sighing, she propped herself against the vanity and turned on the blow-dryer.

The man was still asleep, or unconscious. He was definitely concussed, but Honey hadn't thought it was severe, or that he was in a coma; rather, she'd decided that his continued unconsciousness was due to a combination of fatigue, loss of blood, shock and the blow to his head. She had taken the bullet out of his shoulder, stitched and bandaged his wounds and given him a tetanus injection and an antibiotic; then she and Rachel had cleaned him up, changed the bedding and made him as comfortable as they could. Once she had decided to help, Honey had become her usual capable, unflustered self, for which Rachel would be eternally grateful. Rachel felt that she'd strained herself to the limits physically, yet from somewhere she'd found the strength to help Honey during the nerve-racking operation to remove the bullet from the man's shoulder, then repair the damage done to his body.

Her hair dry, she put on the clean shirt she had brought

into the bathroom with her. The face in the mirror didn't look like her own, and she stared at it curiously, noting the colorless skin and the mauve shadows under eyes dark with fatigue. She was punch-drunk from weariness, and she knew it. It was time to go to bed. The only problem was: where?

The man was in her bed, the only bed in the house. She didn't have a regular-sized couch, only two matching love seats. There was always the possibility of making a pallet on the floor, but she was so tired that even the thought of the effort involved was almost beyond her. Leaving the bathroom, she stared at her neat bed with its snowy white sheets, and at the man who lay so quietly between those sheets.

She needed to sleep, and she needed to be close to him so she could hear him if he awoke. She was a thirty-year-old widow, not a trembling ingenue; the most sensible thing to do would be to crawl into bed beside him so she could rest. After staring at him for just a moment longer she made her decision and turned out the lights, then went around to the other side of the bed and slipped carefully between the sheets, trying not to jostle him. She couldn't prevent a low moan as her tired muscles finally relaxed, and she turned on her side to put her hand on his arm, so she would wake up if he became restless. Then she slept.

It was hot when she awoke, and she was drenched in sweat. Alarm flared briefly when she opened her eyes and saw the dark masculine face on the pillow next to hers; then she remembered and rose on her elbow to look at him. Despite the heat he wasn't sweating, and his breathing seemed a little too fast. Quick concern rose in her; she sat up and put her hand on his face, feeling the heat there. He moved his head restlessly, away from her touch. He was feverish, which wasn't unexpected.

Quickly Rachel got out of bed, noticing that it was past noon. No wonder the house was so hot! She opened windows and turned on the ceiling fans to get some of the hot air out of the house before she turned on the air conditioner to cool things even more. She didn't use it that much, but her patient needed to be cooled down.

She had to take care of him before anything could be done. She dissolved two aspirin in a teaspoon of water, then gently lifted his head, trying not to jar him. "Open your mouth," she crooned, as if he were a baby. "Swallow this for me. Then I'll let you rest." His head lay heavily against her shoulder, his black eyelashes still resting on his cheeks. His hair was thick and silky beneath her fingers, and warm, reminding her of his fever. She put the spoon against his mouth, noting the clear-cut line of his lips; the spoon pressed down on his bottom lip, opening it just a little. "Come on," she whispered. "Open your mouth."

How many levels of consciousness were there? Did he hear her voice? Make sense of the words? Or was it just the low, tender tone that got through to him? Was it her touch? The warm, sleepy scent of her flesh? Something reached him. He tried to turn toward her, his head nuzzling against her shoulder, and his mouth opened a little. Her heart pounded in her chest as she coaxed him to swallow, hoping that he wouldn't choke. It worked so well that she managed to get three more teaspoons of water down him before he lapsed back into deeper unconsciousness.

She wet a washcloth in cold water, folded it and placed it across his brow, then turned the sheet back until it was low across his hips and began sponging him down with the cold water. Slowly, almost mechanically, she drew the wet cloth over his chest and shoulders and down his powerful arms, then to his lean, hard belly, where the hair on his chest narrowed to a thin, silky line. Rachel drew a deep breath, aware of the slight trembling in her body. He was beautiful. She had never seen a more beautiful man.

She hadn't let herself think about it the night before, when it had been important to get help for him and tend to his wounds, but she had realized even then how attractive he was. His features were even and well formed, his nose thin and straight above the mouth she had just touched. That mouth was firm and strong, with a finely chiseled upper lip that hinted of determination and perhaps even ruthlessness, while his lower lip curved with disturbing sensuality. His chin was square, his jaw firm and darkened with a stubble of black beard. His hair was like thick black silk, the color of coal and without any blue shininess to it. His skin was darkened with an allover tan, a deep, olive-bronze hue.

He was very muscular, without having the off-putting bulk of a body-builder. His were the muscles of hard work and physical exercise, the muscles of a man trained for both strength and speed. Rachel picked up one of his hands, cradling it between both of hers. His hands were long fingered and lean, the strength in them apparent even though he was completely limp. His nails were short and well tended. Lightly she felt the calluses on his palm and fingertips; and she felt something else, as well: the hardness of his flesh on the outside edge of his hand. Her breath became shorter, and wariness prickled along her spine again. Cradling his hand against her cheek, she reached out tentatively and touched the scar on his flat belly, a curving, silvery line that almost glowed against the darkness of his tan. It went across his stomach and around his right side, curving down out of view. That wasn't a surgical scar. She went cold, visualizing the terrible ferocity and viciousness of a knife fight. He must have whirled away from the blade, leaving it to slice his side and back.

A man with a scar like that, and with those tell-tale calluses on his hands, wasn't an ordinary man working an ordinary job. No ordinary man could have swum to shore wounded the way he was; that had required incredible strength and determination. How far had he swum? She hadn't been able to see any lights at sea, she remembered. She looked at his hard, lean face and shivered at the thought of the mental toughness hidden behind his closed eyelids. Yet for all his toughness, he was helpless now; his survival depended on her. She had made the decision to hide him, so it was up to her to nurse and protect him as best she could. Her instincts told her that she had made the right decision, but the uneasiness wouldn't leave her until she had some hard facts to back up her intuition.

The aspirin and sponging had lowered his fever, and he seemed to be sleeping deeply, though she wondered how to tell the difference between sleep and unconsciousness. Honey had promised to come by again that day and check him, to make certain the concussion wasn't worse than she had first thought. There was nothing else Rachel could do, except go about her normal business.

She brushed her teeth and combed her hair, then changed into khaki shorts and a sleeveless white cotton shirt. She started to change in her bedroom, as she normally did, then cast a quick glance at the sleeping man in her bed. Feeling foolish, she went into the bathroom and closed the door. B.B. had been dead for five years, and she wasn't used to having a man around, especially a stranger.

She closed the windows and turned on the air conditioning, then stepped outside. Ebenezer Duck and his band of waddling followers rushed up to her, with Ebenezer squawking his displeasure at having to wait so long for the grain she usually scattered first thing in the morning. Ebenezer was the grouchiest goose living, she was sure, but there was a certain

majesty about him, so big and fat and white, and she liked
his eccentricities. Joe came around the back corner of the
house and stood watching as she fed the geese, keeping his
distance from them as he always did. Rachel poured Joe's
food in his bowl and filled his water dish with fresh water,
then stepped away. He never approached while she was still
near his food.

She gathered the ripe tomatoes from her small garden
and checked the bean vines; the green beans would need
gathering in another day or so. By that time her stomach
was rumbling emptily, and she realized that it was hours
past her normal breakfast time. Her entire schedule was
shot, and there didn't seem to be much point in trying to
regain it. How could she concentrate on writing when all
her senses were attuned to the man in the bedroom?

She went inside and checked on him, but he hadn't
moved. She freshened the wet cloth and replaced it on his
brow, then turned her attention to her growling stomach. It
was so hot that anything cooked seemed too heavy, so she
settled for a sandwich of cold cuts and slices from one of
the fresh tomatoes she had just picked. With a glass of iced
tea in one hand and her sandwich in the other, she turned
on the radio and sat down next to it to listen to the news.
There was nothing unusual: the standard political maneu-
verings, both local and national; a house fire; a trial of local
interest, followed by the weather, which promised more of
the same. None of that offered even a glimmer of an explanation for the presence and condition of the man in her
bedroom.

Switching to the scanner, she listened for almost an hour,
but again there was nothing. It was a quiet day, the heat
inducing most people to stay inside. There was nothing
about any searches or drug busts. When she heard a car
coming to a stop in front of her house she turned off the

scanner and got up to look out the window. Honey was just getting out of her car, carrying still another grocery sack.

"How's he doing?" she asked as soon as they were inside.

"He still hasn't moved. He was feverish when I woke up, so I managed to get two aspirin and a little bit of water down him. Then I sponged him off."

Honey went into the bedroom and carefully checked his pupil responses, then examined her handiwork on his shoulder and thigh and rebandaged the wounds. "I bought a new thermometer for this," she muttered, shaking it down and putting it in his mouth. "I didn't have one for humans."

Rachel had been hovering worriedly. "How does he look?"

"His pupil responses are better, and the wounds look clean, but he's a long way from being out of the woods. He's going to be a sick man for several days. Actually, the longer he stays quiet like this, the better it is for him. He's resting his head and not putting any stress on his shoulder or leg."

"What about his fever?"

Honey counted his pulse, then took the thermometer out of his mouth and read it. "A hundred and two. Not critical, but like I said, he's going to be very sick for a while. Give him aspirin every four hours and get as much water down him as you can. Keep sponging him off with cool water to keep him comfortable. I'll be back tomorrow, but I can't come too often or it'll look suspicious."

Rachel managed a tight smile. "Are you sure your imagination isn't running away with you, too?"

Honey shrugged. "I listened to the radio and read the newspaper. There wasn't anything to account for this guy. Maybe you're rubbing off on me, but all I can think is that only two scenarios are left. One is that he's an agent, and the other is that he's a drug runner hiding from his own people."

Looking down at him, at his tousled black hair, Rachel shook her head. "I don't think he's a drug runner."

"Why not? Do they have identifying tattoos, or something?"

She didn't tell Honey about his hands. "I'm probably just trying to reassure myself that I've done the right thing."

"For what it's worth, I think you have. Last night I didn't, but today I've thought about it, and I struck up a chat with a deputy this morning. He didn't mention anything unusual. If your guy is involved with drugs you'll have time to find out before he's in any shape to be dangerous. So, I guess you were right."

There was still another possibility, one that Rachel had thought of but had no intention of mentioning to Honey. What if he was an agent...for someone else? A drug runner, an agent—neither of those was very savory, considering what she had learned about both occupations while she'd been a reporter. Rachel had been a very good reporter, an ace, digging for the facts even in the face of danger. She knew, far more than Honey did, just how dangerous it was to hide this man, but there was something in her that was incapable of simply washing her hands of responsibility and turning him over to the sheriff, then letting events take their course. She had become responsible for him the second she had seen him feebly swimming in the Gulf, and turning him over to someone else wouldn't change that fact. As long as there was a possibility, however remote, that he was deserving of her protection, she had to offer it. It was a risk she had to take.

"How much longer will it be before he wakes up?" she murmured.

Honey hesitated. "I don't know. I'm a veterinarian, remember? With the fever, the loss of blood, the knock on his head...I just don't know. He should be hooked up to an IV, getting fluids. His pulse is weak and fast, he probably needs some blood and he's shocky, but he's coming out of it. He may wake up at any time, or it may be tomorrow. When he does wake up he may be disoriented, which isn't surprising. Don't let him get excited, and whatever you do, don't let him get up."

Rachel looked at him, at his powerfully muscled torso, and wondered if there was any way on earth she could prevent him from doing anything he set his mind on doing.

Honey was taking gauze and tape out of her bag. "Change his bandages tomorrow morning. I won't be back until tomorrow night, unless you think he's getting worse and call me, and in that case you'd be better off calling a doctor."

Rachel managed a taut smile. "Thanks. I know this hasn't been easy for you to handle."

"At least you brought some excitement into the summer. I've got to go now, or Rafferty will tear a strip off me for keeping him waiting."

"Tell John I said hello," Rachel said as they stepped onto the porch.

"Depends on his mood." Honey grinned, her eyes lighting with the pleasurable prospect of battle. She and John Rafferty had been warring ever since Honey had set up practice in the area; Rafferty had made plain his opinion that a woman wasn't strong enough to handle the job, and Honey had set out to prove him wrong. Their relationship had long since evolved into mutual respect and a continuous wrangle that they both enjoyed. Since Honey had a long-standing engagement to an overseas engineer, with plans to marry during the winter when he returned to the

States, she was also safe from Rafferty's legendary tom-catting, because one thing Rafferty didn't do was poach.

Joe stood just at the corner of the house, muscles tight as he warily watched Honey get in her car and drive off. Ordinarily Rachel would have spoken soothingly to him, but today she, too, was tense and wary. "Guard," she said softly, not knowing if he would understand the command. "That's a good boy. Guard the house."

She managed to work for a couple of hours on her manuscript, but she couldn't really concentrate on what she was doing when she kept listening for any sound from the bedroom. Every few minutes she went in to check on him, but each time he was lying just as he had been the time before. She tried several times to get him to drink something, but his head would loll against her shoulder whenever she lifted him, and he didn't respond at all. Late in the afternoon his fever began to rise again, and Rachel abandoned all attempts to write. Somehow she had to rouse him enough to give him more aspirin.

The fever seemed worse this time. His skin burned to the touch, and his face was flushed with hectic color. Rachel talked to him as she lifted his head, crooning and cajoling. With her free hand she stroked his chest and arms, trying to rouse him, and her efforts were rewarded when he suddenly groaned sharply and turned his face against her neck.

The sound and motion, from someone who had been still and silent, startled her. Her heart jumped wildly, and she was unable to move for a moment, simply holding him and feeling the scrape of his growing beard against her neck. It was an oddly erotic sensation, and her body quickened in remembrance. A hot flush colored her cheeks; what was she doing, reacting like that to the unconscious touch of a sick man? Granted, it had been a long time for her, but she'd never considered herself love starved, so hungry for the touch of a man that the most inadvertent contact could turn her on.

She reached for the teaspoon with the dissolved aspirin in it and held it to his mouth, touching his lips with the spoon as she had before. Restlessly he turned his head away, and Rachel followed the movement with the spoon. "No you don't," she crooned. "You aren't getting away. Open your mouth and take this. It'll make you feel better."

A frown puckered his straight black brows and he fretted, evading the spoon once more. Persistently Rachel tried again, and this time she got the bitter aspirin into his mouth. He swallowed, and while he was cooperating she spoon-fed him several ounces of iced tea before he began to sink back into a stupor. Following the routine she had begun that morning, she patiently sponged him down with cool water until the aspirin began to work and the fever subsided again, allowing him to rest.

His response, fretful as it had been, gave her hope that he would soon be waking up, but that hope died during the long night. His fever soared at intervals until she could give him more aspirin and bring it under control again. What rest she got that night came in brief snatches, because she spent most of the time bending over him, patiently wiping him with a cold wet cloth to keep him as cool as she could, and doing all of the other things that were necessary for a bedridden patient.

Toward dawn he groaned again and tried to turn onto his side. Guessing that his muscles were aching from lying in one position for so long, Rachel helped him to roll onto his right side, then took advantage of the new position and sponged his back with cold water. He quieted almost immediately, his breathing becoming deep and even. Her eyes burning and her muscles sore, Rachel continued to rub his back until she was convinced that he was at last resting, then crept into bed herself. She was so tired.... She stared at his muscled back, wondering if she dared go to sleep and how she could possibly stay awake a moment longer. Her eyelids drooped heavily, and she immediately fell asleep, instinct moving her closer to his warm back.

It was still early when she awoke; the clock told her that she had slept a little over two hours. He was lying on his back again, and had kicked the cover into a twisted heap around his left leg. Disturbed that his movements hadn't awakened her, Rachel got out of bed and went around to straighten the sheet and pull it back over him, trying not to jar his left leg. Her gaze drifted over his naked body and hastily she jerked her eyes away, flushing again. What on earth was wrong with her? She knew what naked men looked like, and it wasn't even as if this were the first time she'd seen him. She had been nursing him for almost two days now; she'd bathed him and helped sew him up. Still, she couldn't stop the warm feeling that swelled inside every time she looked at him. It's just lust, she told herself firmly. Plain, old-fashioned lust. I'm a normal woman, and he's a good-looking man. It's normal to admire his body, so I've got to stop acting like a giggly teenager!

She pulled the sheet up to his chest, then coaxed him into taking more aspirin. Why hadn't he awoken by now? Was the concussion more severe than Honey had thought? Yet his condition didn't seem to be getting worse, and in fact he was a little more responsive than he had been; it was easier to get him to take the aspirin and liquids now, but she wanted him to open his eyes, to talk to her. Until then she couldn't be assured that she hadn't harmed him by making the decision to keep him hidden.

Hidden from whom? her subconscious jeered. No one

had been looking for him. The jitters she had been suffering from seemed foolish on this bright, cloudless morning.

While he was quiet she fed the animals and worked in the garden, gathering the green beans and the few tomatoes that had ripened overnight. There were a few yellow squash ready to be picked, and she decided to make a squash casserole for dinner. She weeded the garden and around the shrubs, and by that time the heat had become stifling. Even the usual breeze from the Gulf was missing, and the air lay hot and heavy. She thought longingly of a swim, but didn't dare leave her patient unattended for that long.

When she checked on him again she found the sheet once again kicked down, and he was moving a little, his head turning fretfully. It wasn't time for more aspirin, but he was hot; she got a bowl of cold water and sat on the bed beside him, slowly sponging him with the cold water until he was cool and resting again. When she eased off the bed she glanced down at him and wondered if she would be wasting her time to cover him up. It was simply too hot for him, as feverish as he was, even though she'd left the air conditioning on and the house felt cool to her. Carefully she untangled the sheet from around his feet, her touch light and fleeting; then she paused and her hands returned to his feet. He had nice feet, lean and tanned, masculine and well tended, like his hands. He also had the same tough calluses on the outside ridges of his feet that he had on his hands.

He was a trained warrior.

Tears burned her eyes as she pulled the sheet up to his waist and left it there, deciding to compromise. She had no reason to cry; he'd chosen his life and wouldn't appreciate her sympathy. The people who lived on the edge of danger did so because that was what they wanted; she had lived there herself, and she knew that she had freely chosen to accept the perils that came her way. B.B. had accepted the danger of his job, counting it as the price to be paid for something he thought was worth doing. What neither of them had counted on was that it would be *her* job that would cost him his life.

By the time Honey came that night Rachel had long since controlled herself, and a fragrant squash casserole greeted Honey's nose when she came in the door. "Umm, that smells good," she breathed. "How's our patient?"

Rachel shook her head. "Not much change. He's moving around a little, fretting, when the fever gets high, but he hasn't woken up yet."

She had just twitched the sheet up over him again a few moments before, so he was covered when Honey went in to check on him. "He's doing good," Honey murmured after looking at his wounds and checking his eyes. "Let him sleep. It's just what he needs."

"It's been so long," Rachel murmured.

"He went through a lot. The body has a way of taking over and getting what it needs."

It didn't take much to get Honey to stay for dinner. The casserole, fresh peas and sliced tomatoes did a lot of convincing by themselves. "This is a lot better than the hamburger I'd planned on," Honey said, waving her fork for emphasis. "I think our boy is out of danger, so I wasn't going to come by tomorrow, but if you're cooking again I can always change my mind."

It felt good to laugh, after the tension of the past two days. Rachel's eyes sparkled. "This is the first meal I've cooked since it got so hot. I've been living on fruit and cereal and salad, anything to keep from turning on the stove. But since I've been running the air conditioning to keep him comfortable, tonight cooking didn't seem so bad."

After they'd cleaned the kitchen Honey checked her

watch. "It's not too late. I think I'll stop by Rafferty's and check on one of his mares that's due to foal. It may save a trip back out as soon as I get home. Thanks for feeding me."

"Anytime. I don't know what I'd have done without you."

Honey regarded her for a moment, her freckled face serious. "You'd have managed, wouldn't you? You're one of those people who do what has to be done, without fussing about it. That guy in there owes you a lot."

Rachel didn't know if he would see it that way or not. When she came out of the bathroom after showering she watched him intently, willing him to open his eyes and speak to her, to give her some hint of the man behind those closed lids. Every hour that passed increased the mystery that surrounded him. Who was he? Who had shot him, and why? Why was there nothing being mentioned in the news media that could apply to him? An abandoned boat found floating in the Gulf or washed up on shore would have made the news. A missing person's report would have been in the newspaper. A drug bust, a prison escape, anything, but there had been nothing that would explain why he had washed in with the tide.

She got into bed beside him, hoping for at least a few hours of sleep. He was resting better, she thought, the fever not climbing quite as high as it had at first. Her fingers closed over his arm, and she slept.

The shaking of the bed awoke her, startling her out of a sound sleep. She sat straight up in bed, her heart pounding. He was moving restlessly, trying to kick the cover away from him with only his right leg, and finally he succeeded in getting most of it off him. His skin was hot, and he was breathing too heavily. A glance at the clock told her that it was well past the time he should have had more aspirin.

She turned on the lamp beside the bed and went into the bathroom to get the aspirin and fresh water. He swallowed without fuss this time, and Rachel got him to drink almost a full glass of water. She eased his head down onto the pillow again, her fingers slow to move from his hair.

Daydreaming again! She jerked herself sharply away from the dangerous direction those daydreams were taking. He needed to be cooled down, and she was standing there fantasizing about him. Disgusted with herself, she wet a washcloth and bent over him, slowly wiping his torso with the cool cloth.

A hand touched her breast. She froze, her eyes widening. Her nightgown was loose and sleeveless, with a scooped neckline that had fallen well away from her body when she bent over him. His right hand moved slowly inside the neckline, and he brushed the backs of his lean, strong fingers insistently over her nipple, back and forth, until the small bud of flesh tightened and Rachel had to close her eyes at the sharp, unexpected pleasure. Then his hand moved lower, so slowly that her breath halted in her chest, stroking over the velvet underside of her breast. "Pretty," he murmured, his voice deep, the single word slurred.

The word echoed sharply in Rachel's mind, and her head jerked around, her eyes opening. He was awake! For a moment she stared into half-opened eyes that were so black it was as if light drowned in them; then his lashes slowly dropped and he was asleep again, his hand falling away from her breast.

She was so shaken that she could barely move. Her flesh still burned from his touch, and that instant when she had stared into his eyes was a moment that was frozen in time, so imprinted on her memory that she felt branded by his glance. Black eyes, blacker than night, without any hint of brown. They had been hazy with fever and pain, but he had seen something he liked and reached out for it. Looking down, she saw that the gaping neckline of the loose, comfortable cotton shift left her breasts completely exposed to his view, and his touch; she had unwittingly invited both.

Her hands trembled as she automatically continued wiping him down with the cool cloth. Her senses were reeling, her mind scrambling to adjust to the fact that he had been awake, that he had spoken, even if it had been only one word. Somehow during the long two days when he had lain motionless, even though she had longed for him to wake, she had stopped expecting him to. She had taken care of him as totally as one would an infant, and now she was as startled as if an infant had suddenly spoken. But he was no infant; he was a man. All man, if the frank appreciation in that single slurred word was any measurement. "Pretty," he'd said, and her cheeks heated.

Then the implications of that single word hit her, and she jerked upright. He was American! If he'd been anything else the first word he spoke, when he was only half-conscious and burning with fever, would have been in his native language. But that one word had been in English, and the accent, though slurred, had definitely been American. Part of the slur could have come from a natural accent, a southern or western drawl.

American. She wondered at the heritage that had given him his dark coloring, Italian or Arabic, Hungarian or American Indian, maybe even Black Irish? Spanish? Tartar? The high, chiseled cheekbones and thin, hawk-bridged nose could have come from any of those bloodlines, but he was definitely from the huge American melting pot.

Her heart was still hammering in her chest with excitement. Even after she had emptied the bowl of water, turned out the lamp and crawled into bed beside him, she was quivering and unable to sleep. He had opened his eyes and spoken to her, had moved voluntarily. He was recovering! A burden lifted from her shoulders with the knowledge.

She turned on her side and looked at him, barely able to see the outline of his profile in the darkness of the room, but every pore in her skin sensed his nearness. He was warm and alive, and an odd mixture of pain and ecstasy swelled inside her, because somehow he had become important to her, so important that the tenor of her existence had been irrevocably altered. Even when he left, as practicality told her he must, she would never be the same again. Diamond Bay had given him to her, a strange gift from the turquoise waters. She reached out and trailed her fingers lightly down his muscled arm, then withdrew her touch, because the feel of his skin made her heart lurch again. He had come from the sea, but it was she who had suffered the sea change.

Chapter Four

"He's dead, I'm telling you."

A slim man, with graying brown hair and a narrow, intense face that belied the self-imposed calmness and control of his manner, gave the speaker a look of contemptuous amusement. "Do you think we can afford to assume that, Ellis? We have found nothing—I repeat, nothing—to assure us of his death."

Tod Ellis narrowed his eyes. "There's no way he could've survived. That boat went up like a fuel tank."

An elegant red-haired woman had been silently listening to the two, and now she leaned forward to put out a cigarette. "And the report from one of the men that he saw something, or someone, go over the side?"

Ellis flushed angrily. These two had deferred to him when it came to setting up the ambush, but now they were treating him like a rank amateur. He didn't like it; he was far from an amateur, and they had damned well needed him when they were after Sabin. The plan hadn't worked out exactly as they'd wanted, but Sabin hadn't escaped, and that was the most important thing. If they had thought it would be easy to capture him, then they were fools, at best. "Even if he got into the water," he said patiently, "he was wounded. We saw him get hit. We were miles out. There's no way he could have gotten to shore. He either drowned, or a shark got him. Why take the chance on drawing attention to ourselves by searching for him?"

The other man's pale blue eyes looked beyond Ellis, into the past. "Ah, but this is Sabin we're talking about, not some ordinary man. How many times has he slipped away from us? Too many for me to trust that it was so easy to kill him. We found no remains on the boat, and if, as you say, he either drowned or was attacked by sharks, there still would have been *some* evidence. We've patrolled these waters for two days without finding anything. The logical thing to do is to move our search to shore."

"We'll be exposing ourselves if we do."

The woman smiled. "Not if we do it right. We must simply be discreet. Our biggest danger is the possibility that he was picked up by another boat and taken to a hospital. If he's had the opportunity to talk to someone, to make some calls, we won't be able to get near him. First we must find him, though. I agree with Charles. Too much is at stake for us to simply assume that he's dead."

Ellis's face was grim. "Do you have any idea how large an area we'll have to cover?"

Charles drew a map of Florida closer. "Our position was here," he said, marking the spot with an X. "Given the distance and the tides, which I've already checked, I think we should concentrate our efforts in this area." He drew a long oval on the map and tapped it with his pen. "Noelle, check all the hospitals in the area, and also the police blotters, to find if anyone has been treated for a gunshot wound. While you're doing that we'll be searching every inch of the coastline." He leaned back in his chair and surveyed Ellis with his arctic gaze. "Can you contact your people and find out without arousing suspicions if he's called anyone?"

Ellis shrugged. "I have a reliable contact."

"Then make it. We may have waited too long as it is."

He would make the call, Ellis thought, but he was sure

it would be a waste of time. Sabin was dead; these people persisted in acting as if he were some sort of superman who could disappear into thin air, then miraculously reappear. Okay, so he'd had a reputation when he was in the field; that had been years ago. He would have lost his edge since then, sitting around at a dull desk job the way he'd been doing. No, Sabin was dead; Ellis was certain of it.

Rachel sat on the front porch swing, a newspaper spread across her lap and heaped with green beans. A dishpan sat on the swing beside her, and she systematically broke the tips off the beans and peeled the string off them, then broke the pods into inch-long sections, which she dropped into the dishpan. She didn't like stringing green beans, but she liked to eat them, so it was a necessary evil. She kept the swing gently swaying and listened to a portable radio set on the windowsill. She was listening to an FM country station, but the volume was turned low because she didn't want to disturb her patient, who was sleeping peacefully.

She had spent the morning expecting him to finally wake up for good, but instead he was still alternating between periods of deep sleep, when the aspirin and sponging got his fever down, and restlessness, when his temperature soared. He hadn't opened his eyes or spoken again, though once he had groaned and held his shoulder with his right hand until Rachel loosened his grip and held his hand, soothing him with soft murmurs of reassurance.

Joe eased up from his position under the oleander bush, a rumble forming in his throat. Rachel glanced at him, then swept her gaze around the yard and toward the road, to the left, but could see nothing. It wasn't like Joe to pay any attention to squirrels or rabbits. "What is it?" she asked, unable to keep the tightness of apprehension out of her voice, and Joe responded to her tone by moving to stand directly in front of the steps. The rumble was a full-fledged growl now, and he was staring toward the pine thicket, toward the slope that led down to Diamond Bay.

Two men were coming out of the thicket.

Rachel continued to string and snap the beans as if she were totally unconcerned, but she felt every muscle in her body tense. She stared at them, openly, deciding that that would be the normal thing to do. They were dressed casually, in lightweight cotton canvas pants and pullover shirts, with loose cotton jackets. Rachel eyed the jackets. The temperature was ninety-nine degrees and it wasn't quite noon yet, so it promised to get hotter. Jackets were anything but practical—unless they were needed to hide shoulder holsters.

As the men crossed the road and approached the house Joe's growls became snarls, and he crouched, the hair along his neck lifted. The men halted, and Rachel caught the movement one man made beneath his jacket before he halted himself. "Sorry about that," she called, leisurely putting aside the beans and getting to her feet. "Joe doesn't like strangers in general, and men in particular. He won't even let the neighbor in the yard. Guess some man abused him once. Are you lost, or has your boat quit on you?" As she talked she came down the steps and laid a calming hand on Joe's back, feeling the way he shifted a little away from her.

"Neither. We're looking for someone." The man who answered her was tall and good-looking, with sandy brown hair and an open, college-boy smile that flashed whitely in his tanned face. He glanced down at Joe. "Uh, do you want to get a better hold on the dog?"

"He'll be all right, as long as you don't come any nearer to the house." Rachel hoped that was true. Giving Joe another pat, she walked past him and approached the men. "I don't think it's me he's protecting as much as his territory. Now what was it you said?''

The other man was shorter, slimmer and darker than Mr. All-American College Boy. ''FBI,'' he said briskly, flashing a badge in front of her nose. ''I'm Agent Lowell. This is Agent Ellis. We're looking for a man we think might be in this area.''

Rachel wrinkled her forehead, praying she wasn't overdoing it. ''An escaped convict?''

Agent Ellis's gaze had been appreciatively measuring Rachel's long, bare legs, but now his eyes lifted to her face. ''No, but prison is where we're trying to put him. We think he may have come ashore somewhere in this area.''

''Haven't seen any strangers around here, but I'll keep a sharp watch. What does he look like?''

''Six feet tall, maybe a little taller. Black hair, black eyes.''

''Seminole?''

Both men looked startled. ''No, he's not an Indian,'' Agent Lowell finally said. ''But he's dark, sort of Indian-looking.''

''Do you have a picture of him?''

A quick look passed between the two men. ''No.''

''Is he dangerous? I mean, a murderer, or anything like that?'' A lump had formed in her chest and was rising toward her throat. What would she do if they told her he was a murderer? How could she bear it?

Again that look, as if they weren't sure what to tell her. ''He should be considered armed and dangerous. If you see anything at all suspicious give us a call at this number.'' Agent Lowell scribbled a telephone number on a piece of paper and gave it to Rachel, who glanced at it before folding it and putting it in her pocket.

''I'll do that,'' she said. ''Thank you for coming by.''

They started to leave; then Agent Lowell paused and turned back to her, his eyes narrowed. "There are some strange marks on the beach down there, as if something has been dragged. Do you know anything about them?"

Rachel's blood froze in her veins. Fool! she told herself numbly. She should have gone down to the beach and obliterated all those marks. At least the tide would have washed away any blood and other signs that had been left where he had fallen. Deliberately she wrinkled her forehead, giving herself time to think, then let her face clear. "Oh, you must mean where I collect shells and driftwood. I pile them all on a tarp and haul it up here. That way I can get it all up the slope with just one trip."

"What do you do with them? The shells and driftwood."

She didn't like the way Agent Lowell was looking at her, as if he didn't believe a word she said. "I sell them," she said, and it was the truth. "I own two souvenir shops."

"I see." He smiled at her. "Well, good luck in your shell hunting." They turned to leave again.

"Do you need a lift?" she asked, raising her voice. "You look hot now, and it's going to get hotter."

Both of them looked up at the blistering sun in the cloudless blue bowl of the sky; their faces were shiny with perspiration. "We came by boat," Agent Ellis said. "We're going to check along the beach some more. Thanks, anyway."

"Anytime. Oh, watch out if you go north. It gets swampy."

"Thanks again."

She watched them disappear into the pines and down the slope, and chills prickled her skin despite the heat. Slowly she returned to the porch and sat down on the swing, automatically returning to the task of breaking the beans. Everything they had said swirled in her mind, and she tried to sort it all out, to get her thoughts in order again. FBI? It was possible, but they had flashed their badges so swiftly she hadn't been able to examine them. They knew what he looked like, but they didn't have any photographs of him; she thought it would be reasonable that the FBI would have some likeness, even if it was just a drawing of someone they were trying to find. And they had sidestepped the question when she asked what he had done, as if they hadn't anticipated that and didn't know how to answer. They had said he should be considered armed and dangerous, but instead he was naked and helpless. Didn't they know he'd been shot? Why hadn't they said something about that?

But what if she were harboring a criminal? That had always been one of the possibilities, though she had discounted it. Now it swarmed back into her mind, and she felt sick.

The beans were finished. She took the pan into the house and set it in the sink, then returned to gather up the paper with the strings and broken ends on it. As she carried it to the kitchen to stuff it in the trash can she cast an apprehensive look at her open bedroom door. She could just see the head of the bed and his black hair on the pillow...her pillow. When he woke up again, and she looked into those night-black eyes, would she be looking into the eyes of a criminal? A killer?

Swiftly she washed her hands and flipped through the telephone book, then punched the number. It rang only once before a harried male voice said, "Sheriff's Department."

"Andy Phelps, please."

"Just a minute."

There was another ring, but this time the answer was absentminded, as if the person had other things on his mind. "Phelps."

"Andy, this is Rachel."

Immediately his voice warmed. "Hi, honey. Everything okay?"

"Fine. Hot, but fine. How are Trish and the kids?"

"The kids are doing okay, but Trish is praying for school to start."

She laughed, sympathizing with Andy's wife. Their boys carried rowdiness to new heights. "Listen, two guys just stopped by the house. They walked up from the beach."

His voice sharpened. "They give you any trouble?"

"No, nothing like that. They said they were FBI, but I didn't get a good look at their badges. They're looking for some man. Are they legitimate? Has your department been notified of anything? I may be paranoid, but I'm out here at the end of the road, and Rafferty's miles away. After B.B...." Her voice trailed away with the sudden pain of the memory. It had been five years, but there were still times when the loss and regret seared her, when the emptiness got to her.

Like no one else on earth, Andy understood. He had worked with B.B. in the DEA. The memory roughened his tone. "I know. You can't be too careful, honey. Look, we've had orders come down to cooperate with some guys who are looking for a man. It's all hush-hush. They're not the local FBI people. I doubt that they're FBI at all, but orders are orders."

Rachel's hand tightened on the receiver. "And an agency is an agency?"

"Yeah, something like that. Keep quiet about it, but keep your eyes open. I'm not real comfortable with the feel of this."

He wasn't the only one. "I will. Thanks."

"Sure thing. Listen, why don't you come to dinner some night soon? It's been a while since we've seen you."

"Thanks, I'd love to. Have Trish call me."

They hung up, and Rachel drew a deep breath. If Andy didn't think the men were FBI, that was good enough for her. Going into the bedroom, she stood beside the bed and watched the man sleep, his deep chest slowly rising and falling. She had kept the blinds closed since the night she had brought him into the house, so the room was dim and cool, but a thin ray of sunlight crept between two of the slats and slanted across his stomach, making that long, thin scar glow. Whoever he was, whatever he was involved in, he wasn't a common criminal.

They played lethal games, the men and women who peopled the shadowy world of intelligence and counterintelligence. They lived their lives balanced on the razor's edge of death; they were hard and cold, intense but casual. They weren't like other people, the people who worked at the same job every day and went home to their houses, to their families. Was he one of those for whom a normal life was impossible? She was almost certain of it now. But what was going on, and who could she trust? Someone had shot him. Either he had escaped, or he had been dumped in the ocean to drown. Were those two men hunting for him to protect him, or to finish off the job? Did he possess some highly sensitive information, something critical to defense?

She trailed her fingers over his hand, which was lying limply on top of the sheet. His skin was hot and dry; fever still burned inside him as his body tried to mend itself. She had been able to spoon enough sweetened tea and water into him to keep him from becoming dehydrated, but he had to begin eating soon, or she would be forced to take him to a hospital. This was the third day; he had to have nourishment.

Her brow furrowed. If he could swallow tea, he could swallow soup. She should have thought of that before!

Briskly she went into the kitchen and opened a can of chicken noodle soup, ran it through the blender until it was liquified, then put it on the stove to simmer. "Sorry it isn't homemade," she muttered to the man in the bedroom. "But I don't have any chicken in the freezer. Besides, this is easier."

She watched him closely, checking on him every few minutes; when he began to stir restlessly, moving his head back and forth on the pillow and kicking at the sheet, she prepared a tray for his first "meal," such as it was. It didn't take her long, less than five minutes. She carried the tray into the bedroom and almost dropped it when he suddenly heaved himself up on his right elbow, staring at her with those piercing, fever-bright black eyes.

Rachel's entire body tensed as desperation flooded her. If he fell off the bed she wouldn't be able to get him back on it without help. He was weaving back and forth on his precarious prop, still staring at her with burning intensity. She plunked the tray down on the floor where she stood, sloshing some of the soup over the side of the bowl, then darted to the side of the bed to catch him. Gently, supporting his head and trying not to jostle his shoulder, she put her arm around his back and eased his head onto her shoulder, bracing herself against his weight. "Lie down," she said in the calm, soothing tone she always used for him. "You can't get up yet."

A frown laced his black eyebrows together, and he resisted her efforts. "It's time for the party," he muttered, his words still drunkenly slurred.

He was awake, but certainly not lucid, drifting in a fever-induced dream world. "No, the party hasn't started yet," she reassured him, catching his right elbow and pulling it forward so he wouldn't be able to prop himself up on it.

His weight fell heavily on her supporting arm as she lowered him back onto the pillow. "You have time for a nap."

He lay there, breathing heavily, his brow still furrowed as he stared at her. His gaze didn't flicker as she retrieved the tray from the floor and placed it on the bedside table; his attention was locked on her, as if he were trying to make sense of things, to fight his way out of the mists that clouded his mind. She talked quietly to him as she propped him up on her extra pillows; she didn't know if he understood what she was saying, but her voice and touch seemed to calm him. Sitting on the side of the bed, she began to feed him, talking to him all the while. He was docile, opening his mouth whenever she put the spoon to his lips, but soon his eyelids began to droop as he tired. Quickly she gave him aspirin, elated at how easy it had been to feed him.

As she supported his head and pulled the extra pillows from behind him so he could lie flat again, she had an idea. It was worth a try. "What's your name?"

He frowned, his head jerking restlessly. "Whose?" he asked, his deep voice full of confusion.

Rachel remained bent over him, her hand under his head. Her heart was beating faster. Maybe she could begin getting some answers! "Yours. What's your name?"

"Mine?" The questions were making him fretful, agitated. He stared hard at her as he tried to concentrate, his gaze slipping over her face, then moving lower.

She tried again. "Yes, yours. What's your name?"

"Mine?" He drew a deep breath, then said it again. "Mine." The second time it was a statement, not a question. Slowly he moved, lifting both hands, wincing at the pain in his shoulder. He molded his hands over her breasts, cupping them warmly in his palms and rubbing her nipples with his thumbs. "Mine," he said again, stating what he plainly considered to be his ownership.

For a moment, just for a moment, Rachel was helpless against the unexpected pleasure burning her flesh at his touch. She was frozen in place, her nerve endings going wild, her body flooding with warmth as his thumbs turned her nipples into hardened nubs. Then reality returned with a thud, and she jerked away from him, bolting off the bed. Exasperation at him—and anger at herself—filled her. "That's what you think," she snapped at him. "These are mine, not yours!"

His eyelids drooped sleepily. She stood there glaring down at him. Evidently the only things on his mind were partying and sex! "Damn it, you have a one-track mind!" she angrily accused, half under her breath.

His eyelashes fluttered open, and he looked at her again. "Yes," he said clearly, then closed his eyes and went to sleep.

Rachel stood beside the bed with clenched fists, torn between laughing and swatting him. It was doubtful that he had understood anything she'd said; that last provocative word could have been in answer to her accusation, or to some question that existed only in his own foggy consciousness. Now he was sleeping heavily again, totally relaxed and oblivious to the upheaval he had left behind.

Shaking her head, she picked up the tray and quietly left the room. Her insides were still quivering with mingled indignation and desire. It was an uncomfortable combination, uncomfortable because she wasn't one to delude herself, and she couldn't deny that she was attracted to him more powerfully than she could ever have imagined. Touching him was a compulsion; her hands wanted to linger on his warm skin. His voice made her shiver deep inside, and one look from those black eyes made her feel electrified. And his touch...his touch! Twice now he had put his hands on her, and each time she had turned molten with uncontrollable pleasure.

It was insane to feel so intensely about a man she didn't know, but no amount of self-lecturing could change her response. Their lives had become linked from the moment she had dragged him out of the surf; in assuming responsibility for his safety, she had committed herself to him on a level that went so deep she was only now beginning to realize its reaches. And he had become hers, as if that act of mercy had created a marriage of their lives, binding them together regardless of their wishes or wants.

Though he was a stranger she already knew a lot about him. She knew that he was hard and fast and well trained; he would have to be, to survive in the world he had chosen. He also possessed a tough-mindedness that was awesome in its intensity, a steely determination that had kept him swimming in the night-dark ocean with two bullet wounds in his body, when a lesser man would have drowned almost immediately. She knew that he was important to the people who were hunting him, though she didn't know if they wanted to protect him or kill him. She knew that he didn't snore and that he had an extremely healthy libido, despite his physical incapacitation. He was still when he slept, except when his bones and muscles ached from his flaring fever; that stillness had bothered her at first, until she realized that it was natural to him.

He also answered no questions, even in his delirium, not even one as elemental as his name. It could be the fever-induced confusion, but it was also more than possible that his training was so deeply ingrained in his subconscious that even illness or drugs couldn't override it.

Soon, tomorrow or the next day, or perhaps even during the coming night, he would wake up and be in full possession of his senses. He would require clothing, and answers to his questions. She wondered what those questions would be, and thought of her own questions, though she was beginning to wonder if he would provide any answers. She couldn't prepare for what he might or might not say, because she felt it would be useless to try to predict his actions. Clothing, however, was a problem she could do something about. She had nothing there that would fit him; though she often wore men's shirts she had bought them specifically for herself, and they would be far too small for him. She hadn't kept any of B.B.'s clothing, though that would have been useless in any case, as B.B. had weighed a good thirty pounds less than this man.

Mentally she made a list of the things he would need. She didn't like leaving him alone for the length of time it would take her to drive to the nearest discount store, but it was either that or ask Honey to do the shopping and bring the things out. She considered that. It was tempting, but the arrival of the two men that morning made her reluctant to involve Honey any deeper in the situation. It should be safe to leave him alone for an hour. She would do her shopping early the next morning, which would give those men time to move out of the immediate area.

She carefully locked the house when she left, and told Joe to stand guard. Her patient was sleeping quietly; she had just gotten him settled, so he should sleep for several hours. Her gun-metal Regal ate up the miles as she pushed her speed as fast as she could, anxiety gnawing at her. It should be all right to leave him alone, but she wouldn't breathe easy until she was back home and could see that for herself.

Though it had just opened for the morning, the local K mart was already swarming with customers who had all decided to do their shopping before the worst heat of the day was upon them. Rachel got a shopping cart and maneuvered it through the crowded aisles, dodging the darting preschoolers who had managed to escape their mothers and were headed, one and all, for the toy department. She steered around browsers, idled behind a frail white-haired woman who walked with a cane, then spotted a clear aisle and broke to the right.

A package of underwear, a few pairs of socks and a pair of jogging shoes, size ten, went into the cart. She had measured his feet that morning, so she was fairly certain the shoes would fit. Two button-up shirts and a cotton terry pullover shirt were piled on top of the shoes. She was uncertain of what size pants to get, but finally selected a pair of jeans, a pair of black denim cutoffs in case the jeans were too uncomfortable on his leg and a pair of khaki chinos. She was ready to head for the checkout counter when a tingle ran up her spine, and her head lifted. Glancing around, she saw a man casually examining some sale items, and the tingle became a full fledged chill. It was Agent Lowell.

Without breaking stride, she diverted her path to the women's section. The men's clothes, though androgynous enough that they couldn't be recognized as men's unless the sizes were examined, would be a dead giveaway under close scrutiny. Unfortunately Agent Lowell was exactly the type to subject everything to just such an examination. The undershorts, socks and shoes, beneath the pants and shirts, could have no logical explanation.

Ruthlessly she went through the underwear section. Several pairs of panties, all lace and satin, were thrown on top of the pile. A frothy confection of a bra and a matching half-slip were added; she hoped she could trust in the normal male's aversion to handling female lingerie in a public place to keep Agent Lowell from examining the contents of her shopping cart. Out of the corner of her eye she saw him casually moving closer, pausing every so often to examine certain items with absent interest. He was good; he slid through the crowds without attracting notice. He tracked, while giving no appearance of being a hunter.

A grim look entered Rachel's eyes. He would have to be determined indeed to get to the bottom of her cart. Wheeling around, she headed for the drug-and-health section. Intimate female items, some of which she never used but chose now for their conspicuous packaging, were thrown into the cart. If he dared reach for anything she would accuse him of being a pervert in a voice loud enough to bring every store security guard at a run.

He was closing in again. Rachel chose her moment, then turned her cart and all but rammed it into his knee.

"Oh, my goodness, I'm sorry!" she gasped in apology. "I didn't see you—oh," she said again, startled recognition in her voice. "Ag—" She stopped, looked around, then lowered her voice to little more than a whisper. "Agent Lowell."

It was an Academy Award-winning performance, but it might have been wasted on Agent Lowell, who was preoccupied with rubbing his knee. He straightened, a look of pain still in his eyes. "Hello again, Ms....I don't believe I got your name yesterday."

"Jones," she said, holding out her hand. "Rachel Jones."

His hand was hard, but his palm was a little moist. Agent Lowell wasn't quite as relaxed as he appeared.

"You're out early," he commented.

"With the heat the way it is, it's best to either get out early or wait until after sundown. You really should wear a hat if you're going to be walking around today the way you were yesterday." His face was already sunburned, so her advice was too late.

His expressionless eyes drifted down to the contents of the cart, then jerked back up abruptly. Rachel felt a moment's grim satisfaction at her choices. His presence could be pure coincidence, or it could be deliberate, but he was automatically curious; it was part of his job. She sensed that he had been less disarmed by her studied nonchalance and innocence than the other agent had been.

"You, uh, may have to float a loan to pay for all that," he said after a slight pause.

She ruefully examined the cart. "You may be right. Every time I go off on a trip it seems as if I never have what I need."

His eyes sharpened with interest. "You're going on a trip?"

"In a couple of weeks. I'm doing some research on the Keys, and it always helps to see an area firsthand."

"Research?"

She shrugged. "I dabble in several things. I have my souvenir shops. I do a little writing, teach a few night courses. It keeps me from getting bored with myself." Looking at the checkout counters, where the lines were growing, she said blithely, "I'd better get in line before everyone in the store gets ahead of me. Oh—did you find anything yesterday?"

His face was a blank mask, though his eyes were once again peering at her cart. "No, nothing. It may have been a false lead."

"Well, good luck. Remember to get a cap or something while you're here."

"Sure. Thanks."

She joined one of the lines at the row of checkout counters and selected a magazine to flip through while she waited, gradually nudging the cart forward. He had moved to the side and was looking at paperback books. Damn, would he never leave? When it came her time, she unloaded the cart and tried to keep her body between Lowell and the counter. The clerk picked up the package of undershorts and held them in front of her while she punched in the code number on the computerized cash register. Rachel shifted to that side, and when the clerk set the package down she pushed a shirt over it. Lowell was moving closer.

"One-forty-six eighteen," the clerk said, reaching for a large bag.

Rachel checked her wallet, inwardly grimacing. She seldom carried that much cash, and this was no exception. Disgruntled, she plunked down a plastic credit card and the clerk ran it through the imprinting machine, then called to get an okay on the amount. Lowell had walked around to the front of the store and was coming down in front of the checkout counters. Rachel grabbed the bag the clerk had laid on the counter and began shoving her purchases into it.

"Sign here," the clerk said, pushing the credit slip toward her. Rachel scribbled her name and a moment later the bag was stapled shut. She loaded it in the cart and began wheeling it out of the store.

"Need any help?" Lowell asked, falling into step beside her.

"No, rolling it in the cart is easier than carrying it. Thanks, anyway."

The humid heat settled on them like a suffocating blanket as soon as they left the cool confines of the store, and Rachel squinted her eyes against the almost painful brightness. After opening the trunk of the car she dumped the bag in and slammed the lid shut, agonizingly aware of Lowell's acute interest.

She pushed the cart to a buggy-return stand, then walked back to the car. "Goodbye," she said casually.

He was still watching as she drove out of the lot. Rachel wiped the perspiration off her face, aware that her heart was thudding in a panicky rhythm. She was out of practice for this! She only hoped he hadn't been too suspicious.

Chapter Five

The dreams were still so vivid that it was several minutes before he realized he was awake, but awareness did not necessarily bring understanding. He lay quietly, looking around the cool, dim, unfamiliar room and groping for any details in his mind that would give him a hint of what was going on and where he was. There seemed to be no connection between his only memories and this silent room. But were they memories, or dreams? He had dreamed of a woman, a warm and pliant woman, with eyes as clear and gray as a highland lake under cloudy skies, her hands tender as she caressed him, her velvety breasts swelling against his palms. His fingers twitched on the sheets; the dream was so real he almost ached to feel her under his hands.

Still, that had been only a dream, and he had to deal with reality. He lay there until certain things began to return, and he knew that *they* weren't dreams. The attack on his boat; the endless, agonizing swim in the dark, driven on by his own sheer inability to give up. Then, after that… nothing. Not even a glimmer of what had happened.

Where was he? Had he been captured? They would give almost anything, risk almost anything, to take him alive.

He moved cautiously, his mouth setting grimly at the amount of effort it took. There was pain in his left shoulder and lacing through his left thigh, and he had a dull headache, but both his leg and arm obeyed his mental command to move. Awkwardly using his right hand, he threw the sheet back and struggled to a sitting position. Dizziness assailed him, but he gripped the side of the bed until the feeling subsided, then he took stock once again. A pristine bandage was wrapped around his thigh, thickly padded over the wounds. The same treatment had been given to his shoulder; gauze had been wrapped around it, then anchored around his chest. He was totally naked, but that didn't bother him. His first priority was to establish his mobility; his second was to find out where the hell he was.

He stood, the wounded muscle in his thigh quivering in outrage at being forced into motion. He wavered, but didn't fall, merely stood there until the room stopped swaying and his leg was steady under him. Despite the coolness of the room a fine sheen of sweat began to form on his body.

There was no sound except for the gentle whir of a ceiling fan that hung over the bed and the distant mechanized sound of an air conditioner. He listened intently, but could detect nothing else. Keeping his right hand braced against the bed, he took a step toward the window, grinding his teeth together at the searing pain in his leg. The closed slats of the old-fashioned blinds drew him. Reaching the window, he used one finger to lift a slat and peer through the crack. A yard, a vegetable garden. Nothing unusual, but nothing in sight, either, human or animal.

An open door was in front of him, revealing a bathroom. Slowly he moved to the doorway, his black eyes taking note of the items on the vanity. Hair spray, lotions, cosmetics. A woman's bathroom, then. Perhaps the red-haired woman who had been on the boat? Everything was neat, impeccably clean, and there was a certain spare luxury to both the bath and bedroom, as if everything had been chosen for maximum comfort while still leaving a lot of what was simply bare space. The next door over was a closet. He pushed racks aside and checked sizes. Again, everything

was for a woman, or a small, very slender man of unde-
cided sexuality. The clothes ranged from remarkably ragged to sleekly sophisticated. A disguise?

Cautiously he opened the next door slightly, putting his
eye to the small crack to make certain there was no one
out there. The small hallway was empty, as was the room
he could see beyond it. He eased the door open, balancing
himself with a hand on the frame. Nothing. No one. He
was alone, and that made no sense at all.

Damn, he was weak, and so thirsty that the fires of hell
seemed to be in his throat. Limping badly, occasionally
staggering, he made his way through the empty living
room. A small, sunlit alcove was next, and the glaring sun
streaming through the windows made him blink as his eyes
adjusted to the sudden excess of light. Next was a kitchen,
small and sunny and extremely modern. A colorful array
of fresh vegetables lay on a counter, and there was a bowl
of fresh fruit sitting on the center work island.

Cotton lined his mouth and throat. He groped toward the
sink, then opened cabinet doors until he found the glasses.
Turning on the cool tap water, he filled a glass and turned
it up, pouring the water into his mouth so thirstily that some
of it spilled down his chest. With that first terrible urgency
satisfied, he drank another glass of water and this time managed to get it all in his mouth.

How long had he been here? The blanks in his memory
made him furious. He was vulnerable, uncertain of where
he was or what had happened, and vulnerability was one
thing he couldn't afford. But he was starving, too. The bowl
of fresh fruit beckoned, and he wolfed down a banana, then
half an apple. Abruptly he was too full to eat another bite,
so he tossed both the banana skin and the half-eaten apple
into the trash.

Okay, he could get around. Slowly, but he wasn't helpless. His next priority was to find some means of self-defense. The most available weapon was a knife, and he examined the kitchen knives before choosing the one with the sharpest, strongest blade. With that in his hand he began a slow, methodical search of the house, but there were no other weapons of any sort to be found.

The outside doors all had extremely strong dead-bolt locks on them. They weren't fancy, but they would damned sure slow down anyone trying to get in. He looked at them, trying to remember if he had ever seen any locks exactly like them, and decided that he hadn't. They were locked, but what sense did it make to put the locks on the inside, where he could get to them? He turned the lock, and it opened with a smooth, almost silent movement. Warily he reached for the knob and opened the door a little, again checking through the crack to see if anyone was in view. The door was heavy, too heavy to be an ordinary door. He opened it a little more, running his fingers along the edge. Steel reinforced, he guessed.

It was a snug little prison, but the locks were on the wrong side of the doors, and there were no wardens.

He opened the door completely, looking out through a screen door at a neat little yard, a tall pine thicket and a flock of fat white and gray geese searching for insects in the grass. The heat coming through the screen door was thick and heavy, hitting him like a blow. A dog appeared as if by magic from beneath a bush, leaping up onto the porch and staring at him with unblinking eyes as its ears went back and snarls twisted the canine muzzle.

Dispassionately he examined the dog, weighing his chances. A trained attack dog, German shepherd, weighing eighty or ninety pounds. In his weakened condition he didn't have a chance against a dog like that, even with a knife in his hand. He was effectively caged, after all.

His leg would barely support his weight. He was naked, weak, and didn't know where he was. The odds weren't in his favor, but he was alive and filled with a cold, controlled rage. Now he also had the advantage of surprise, because whoever had brought him here wouldn't be expecting him to be up and armed. He closed the door and locked it again, then watched the dog through the window until it left the porch and resumed its position beneath the bush.

He had to wait.

An enormous, purplish-black thunderhead was looming in the sky when Rachel turned into the driveway. She eyed it, wondering if it would dump its load of rain out at sea or hold it until it was over land. The rain would be torrential, and the temperature would drop sharply, but as soon as the cloud had passed the heat would rise again, and the rain would evaporate in a suffocating cloud of steam. Ebenezer Duck and his flock scattered, honking irritably, as she pulled the car under the shade of the oak tree where they had been lazily pecking at the grass. Joe lifted his head to look at her, then returned to his snooze. Everything was calm, just as it had been when she'd left. Only then did she feel an easing of the tight constriction in her chest.

She got the bag out of the trunk, unaware of the sharp black eyes that followed her every move. Holding the bag in one arm and the keys in the other hand, she climbed the steps to the porch, paused to shove her sunglasses on top of her head, then held the screen door open with her hip while she unlocked the door and pushed it open. The air-conditioned coolness was such a shocking contrast to the searing heat outside that goose bumps rose on her flesh, and she shivered. Taking deep breaths, she dropped the bag and her purse on one of the love seats and went to check on her patient.

Just as her hand touched the doorknob a hard arm circled her throat and she was jerked backward, her neck arched unnaturally. A brightly gleaming knife was held in front of her face. She had been too stunned to react, but now sheer terror flooded her as her gaze locked on the knife. How had they gotten in? Had they already killed him? The anguish that rose in her was wild and ferocious, consuming her.

"Don't fight and I won't hurt you," a deep voice murmured in her ear. "I want some answers, but I won't take any chances. If you make a wrong move—" He didn't finish the sentence, but he didn't have to. How calm the voice was, as cool and unemotional as stone. It made her blood congeal.

The arm under her chin was choking her, and she automatically raised both hands, clutching at him. The knife moved menacingly closer. "No, none of that," he whispered, his mouth close to her ear. Rachel shrank from the knife, her head digging into his shoulder, her body crowding frantically against his in an attempt to put distance between herself and that shining blade. Every detail of his body was imprinted against her, and suddenly her dazed senses realized what she was feeling. He was naked! And if he were naked, then it had to be...

Sharp, piercing relief, as painful in its own way as the fear and anguish had been, made her muscles suddenly tremble as the tension left them. Her hands relaxed on his forearm.

"That's better," the low voice growled. "Who are you?"

"Rachel Jones," she said, her voice breathless because of the pressure he was putting on her throat.

"Where am I?"

"In my house. I pulled you out of the surf and brought

you here.'' She could feel him hesitate, though perhaps it was simply that he was growing weaker. His strength was astonishing under the circumstances, but he had been very ill, and his stamina must be wavering. ''Please,'' she whispered. ''You shouldn't be out of bed.''

That was the truth, Sabin thought grimly. He was exhausted, as if he'd run a marathon; his legs felt as if they would give out on him at any moment. He didn't know her, and he couldn't trust her; he had only this one chance, and a wrong guess could cost him his life, but he didn't have much choice. Damn, he was weak! Slowly he relaxed his right arm from around her throat and let his left hand, the one holding the knife, drop to his side. His shoulder throbbed, and he doubted that he would be able to lift his arm again.

Rather than jerking away from him, she turned cautiously, as if afraid of startling him into an attack, and wedged her shoulder under his right arm, while her arms went around him and supported him. ''Lean on me before you fall,'' she said, her voice still a little breathless. ''It would be a mess if you tore all those stitches out.''

He didn't have much choice except to drape his arm over her slender shoulders and lean heavily on her. If he didn't either sit down or lie down—soon—he was going to fall, and he knew it. Slowly she helped him into the bedroom, supporting him as he virtually collapsed onto the edge of the bed, then holding his head in the crook of her left arm as she lowered him into a supine position while she reached around him with her other hand to arrange the pillow. Sabin drew a deep breath, his senses automatically reacting to her warm female scent and the softness of her breast against his cheek. He had only to turn his head to press his mouth against her nipple, and the image teased at him with a curious urgency.

He lay with his eyes closed, breathing rapidly in exhaustion, while she lifted his legs onto the bed and pulled the sheet up to his waist. "There," she said softly. "You can rest now." She stroked her hand over his chest, as she had done so many times in the past few days, an action that had become automatic because it seemed to calm his restlessness. He was much cooler; the fever had finally lost its grip on him. The knife was still clutched in his left hand, and she reached to take it, but his fingers tightened at her touch, and his eyes flew open, his gaze black and fierce.

Rachel kept her hand on the knife, levelly meeting his eyes. "Why do you need it?" she asked. "If I meant you any harm I've had a lot of opportunities to do something about it before now."

Her eyes were gray, completely so, without any hint of blue. They were almost charcoal in color, but warm, and with an utter clarity that made them seem fathomless. He felt a shock of recognition. The eyes, and the woman, had filled his recent dreams with a tender eroticism that made his loins tighten. But...were they dreams? The woman wasn't a dream. She was real, warm and firm of flesh, and her hands had moved over him with the ease of familiarity. She didn't act like a guard, but he couldn't afford to take the chance. If he relinquished the knife he might not be able to get it back. "I'll keep it," he said.

Rachel hesitated, wondering if she should press the issue, but there was something in his quiet, flat tone that made her decide to let it go. Even though he was weak and barely able to get around on his own, there was something about him that told her he couldn't be pushed. He was a dangerous man, this stranger sleeping in her bed. She moved her hand from his.

"All right. Are you hungry?"

"No. I ate a banana and an apple."

"How long have you been awake?"

He hadn't checked a clock, but he didn't need a clock to give him a sense of time. "Almost an hour." His gaze hadn't wavered from her. Rachel felt as if he could see through her, as if he were probing her mind.

"You woke up a couple of times before, but you were still feverish and talking nonsense."

"What kind of nonsense?" he asked sharply.

Rachel regarded him calmly. "No state secrets or anything like that. You thought you were going to a party."

Was there a double meaning to that crack about state secrets? Did she know anything, or had that just been a coincidence? Sabin wanted to question her, but he hardly had the upper hand at the moment, and his exhaustion was changing into acute sleepiness. As if she knew, she touched his face, her fingers cool and light. "Go to sleep," she said. "I'll still be here when you wake up."

It was, ridiculously, the reassurance he needed to let him relax into sleep.

Quietly Rachel left the room and went to the kitchen, where she leaned weakly against the work island. Her legs were shaking, her insides quivering like gelatin, in reaction to all that had happened to her already...and it wasn't even noon yet! Nor did she have any of the answers she had promised herself she would get as soon as he woke up; rather than asking questions, she had been answering his. She hadn't been prepared for the intensity of his gaze, so piercing that it was difficult to meet his eyes for any length of time. Warlock's eyes... She certainly hadn't been prepared for having a knife held to her throat! And she had been helpless, unable to do anything against a strength that was far superior to hers, even though he was undoubtedly weak from his wounds and illness.

The terror that had held her in its icy grip for those few

moments had been worse than she had ever imagined. She had been frightened before, but not to that degree. She was still shaking in reaction, and her eyes burned with tears that she refused to let fall. Now wasn't the time for tears; she had to get herself under control. He might sleep for half a day, or he might wake up in an hour, but she was going to be in complete command of herself whenever he woke. He would also need feeding, she thought, seizing gratefully on something practical to do. Banana and apple notwithstanding, his system would probably demand frequent feedings until he had recovered.

Her movements jerky, she set beef tips simmering for beef stew and began dicing potatoes, carrots and celery. Maybe the meal would be ready by the time he awoke; if not, he could settle for soup and a sandwich. When everything was in the pot she darted out to the vegetable garden and gathered the ripe tomatoes, then ignored the heat and began pulling up weeds. It wasn't until she finally fell to her knees on a wave of dizziness that she realized how erratically she had been behaving, spurred on by the overdose of adrenaline her system had absorbed that morning. It was insanity to work out in the broiling sun, especially without a hat!

She went inside and washed her face with cold water; she felt calmer now, though her hands were still trembling slightly. There was nothing to do but wait: wait until the stew was ready; wait until he woke up; wait until she got some answers…wait.

It was a tribute to her self-possession and concentration that she was actually able to do some research for the course she would be teaching in the fall. Like a manuscript, the course would require pacing and plotting to hold the students' interest, to make them stretch. Yet even though she was deeply involved in her reading and notes, she was so attuned to him that she heard the slight rustle made by the bedcovers when he moved, and she knew he was awake. Checking her watch, she saw that he had slept for a little over three hours; the stew would be ready, if he was hungry.

He was sitting up, yawning and rubbing his bearded face, when she entered the bedroom. Instantly she felt his attention settle on her like a beam of pure energy, tingling on her skin.

"Are you hungry now? You've slept for three hours."

He considered that, then gave a brief nod. "Yes. I need a bathroom, a shower and a shave first, though."

"Sorry, the shower is out while you still have stitches," she said, hurrying to his side as he threw back the sheet and eased his feet to the floor, wincing in pain and holding his left thigh. Rachel put a supporting arm around him until he was steady on his feet. "I'll put a new blade in my razor for you, though." Sensing that he preferred to get across the room on his own power, she let her arm drop and watched anxiously as he took each painful step. He was a loner; he wasn't accustomed to aid and didn't welcome it, though he had to know that he simply wasn't capable of some things right now. He would let her help him only when it was necessary. Still, she felt compelled to ask, "Shall I shave you, or do you think you're steady enough to do it yourself?"

He paused at the door to the bathroom and glanced over his shoulder at her. "I'll do it."

She nodded and started toward him. "I'll just put the new blade—"

"I'll find them," he said quietly, stopping her before she could reach him. Rachel accepted her dismissal, turning instead toward the other door.

It hurt to have him reject her help after the days he had

been totally helpless and dependent on her for everything, after the nights she had spent leaning over him, sponging him down to keep him cool, and especially after the mental strain she had endured. As she set the table she tried to deal with that hurt, to push it away. After all, she was even more of a stranger to him than he was to her, and it was only natural that he would try to regain control of himself as soon as possible. To a man like him, control would be vital. She had to stop hovering over him like a mother hen.

It was easy to tell herself that, but when at last she heard the water cut off in the bathroom she hesitated for only a moment before giving in to the compulsion to check on him. He was standing in the middle of the bedroom floor, looking around as if considering his options. A towel was knotted low on his lean hips, and contrary to logic it made him seem even more naked than when he had been completely unclothed. Rachel's pulse leaped. Even with the stark contrast of the white bandages on his leg and shoulder, he still seemed immensely powerful, and so male that she felt her mouth go dry.

He had shaved, and the clean line of his jaw made her fingers twitch with the urge to stroke it—another gesture he wouldn't appreciate.

"Is there anything I could wear, or do I just go around naked?" he finally asked, when Rachel made no move either to approach him or to speak.

She groaned as she remembered and hit the heel of her palm against her forehead. "I have something for you to wear. That's where I was this morning, picking up some things you would need." The shopping bag still lay where she had dropped it in the living room; she grabbed it and carried it into the bedroom, where she deposited it on the bed.

He opened the bag and a curious expression crossed his

face; then he pulled out a lacy pair of panties and held them up to examine them before Rachel could explain. "Size five," he commented, and looked at her as though measuring her for the fit. The scrap of lace and nylon dangled from one finger. "Nice, but I don't think they'll fit me."

"They weren't meant to," Rachel said calmly, still tingling from the once-over he'd given her. "They were camouflage, that's all. Anything you find in there that you don't ordinarily use, put back in the bag." She refused to be embarrassed, since she had only done what had seemed necessary. The "camouflage" had been darned expensive, too! Leaving him to dress in whatever he chose, she returned to the kitchen and popped buttered fresh bread into the oven, then ladled up the stew and poured tea into tall glasses full of ice.

"I need help with the shirt."

She hadn't heard him approach, and she whirled, startled by both his nearness and what he'd said. He was standing right behind her, clad in the black denim cutoffs and holding the terry-cloth pullover in his hand. His chest filled her vision, tautly powerful muscles covered with black, curling hair and the white bulk of the bandage wrapped around his left shoulder. How long had he struggled with the shirt before admitting that he couldn't manage it by himself? She was astonished that he hadn't simply exchanged it for one that buttoned, so he wouldn't have to ask for her help.

"Sit down so I can reach you better," she said, taking the shirt from his hand. He held the corner of the cabinets for support as he slowly limped to the table in the dining alcove and eased himself down onto one of the chairs. Rachel carefully worked the shirt up his arm, a look of intent concentration on her face as she tried not to jostle his shoulder. When she had it in place she said, "Put your other arm in the sleeve while I keep it from pulling on your shoulder.''

Without a word he did as she directed, and together they pulled the shirt over his head. Rachel tugged it into place, much as a mother would dress a toddler, but the man sitting motionless under her ministrations was no child in any sense she could imagine. She didn't linger over the chore, well aware of his dislike for having to rely on her aid. Briskly she got the bread out of the oven and put it in the napkin-lined breadbasket, then placed the basket on the table and took her own chair. ''Are you left-handed or right-handed?'' she asked, not looking at him, even though she could feel the burning energy of his gaze on her face.

''Ambidextrous. Why?''

''The spoon could be difficult for you to handle if you were left-handed,'' she replied, nodding at the stew. ''Would you like bread?''

''Please.''

He was very good at one-word sentences, she thought as she put the bread on his plate. Actually, she should have thought of asking him if he could handle the razor, too, but his clean-shaven face said that he evidently could. They ate in silence for a few moments, and he really did justice to the stew. She hadn't expected his appetite to be so good so early in his recovery.

The bowl was nearly empty when he put his spoon down and pinned her with the ebony fire of his eyes. ''Tell me what's going on.''

It was a demand that Rachel didn't feel like meeting. Carefully she put her own spoon down. ''I think it's my turn to ask a few questions. Who are you? What's your name?''

He didn't like the counterdemand. She sensed his displeasure, though his expression didn't flicker. The hesitation lasted for barely a second, but she noticed it and had the immediate impression that he wasn't going to answer. Then he drawled, "Call me, 'Joe'."

"I can't do that," she replied. "'Joe' is what I call the dog, because he wouldn't tell me his name, either. Make up another one." Driven by the electric surge of tension in the air she began clearing off the table, moving swiftly and automatically.

He watched her for a moment, then said quietly, "Sit down."

Rachel didn't pause. "Why? Do I have to be sitting down to listen to more lies?"

"Rachel, sit down." He didn't raise his voice, didn't change the calm, dead-level inflection of his tone, but suddenly it was a command. She stared at him for a moment, then lifted her chin and returned to her chair. When she merely waited in silence, looking at him, he gave a little sigh.

"I appreciate your help, but the less you know, the better it is for you."

Rachel had always hated it when anyone presumed to know what was best for her and what wasn't. "I see. Was I not supposed to notice that you had two bullet holes in you when I pulled you out of the surf? Was I supposed to turn my head when two men pretending to be FBI agents came looking for you, and just turn you over to them? Was it supposed to pass my notice that you held a knife to my throat this morning? I'm a little curious, I admit! I've nursed you for four days, and I really would like to know your name, if that isn't too much to ask!"

One level black brow lifted at her sarcasm. "It could be."

"All right, forget it. Play your little games. You don't answer my questions and I won't answer yours. Deal?"

He watched her for a little longer, and Rachel kept her gaze level, not backing down an inch. "My name is Sabin," he finally said, the words slowly drawn out of him, as if he begrudged every syllable.

She absorbed the name's sound, her mind lingering over the feel and form of it. "And the rest of it?"

"Is it important?"

"No. But I'd like to know, anyway."

He paused only a fraction of a second. "Kell Sabin."

She held out her hand. "Glad to meet you, Kell Sabin."

Slowly he took her hand, his callused palm sliding against her softer one and his hard, warm fingers wrapping around hers. "Thank you for taking care of me. I've been here four days?"

"This is the fourth day."

"Fill me in on what's happened."

He had the manner of a man accustomed to command; rather than requesting, he ordered, and it was clear that he expected his orders to be obeyed. Rachel pulled her hand from his, disturbed by his warm touch and the shivery way it affected her. Clasping her fingers together to dispel the tingling in them, she rested her hands on the table. "I pulled you out of the water and brought you here. I think you hit your head on one of the rocks that line the mouth of the bay. You had a concussion and were in shock. The bullet was still in your shoulder."

He frowned. "I know. Did you take it out?"

"Not me. I called the vet."

At least something could startle him, though the expression was quickly gone. "A veterinarian?"

"I had to do something, and a doctor has to report all gunshot wounds."

He eyed her thoughtfully. "You didn't want it reported?"

"I thought *you* might not want it reported."

"You thought right. What happened then?"

"I took care of you. You were out of it for two days. Then you started waking up, but the fever had you out of your head. You didn't know what was going on."

"And the FBI agents?"

"They weren't FBI. I checked."

"What did they look like?"

Rachel began to feel as if she were being interrogated. "The one who calls himself Lowell is thin, dark, about five foot ten, early forties. The other one, Ellis, is tall, good-looking in a toothpaste-ad sort of way, sandy-brown hair, blue eyes."

"Ellis," he said, as if to himself.

"I played dumb. It seemed the safest thing to do until you woke up. Are they friends of yours?"

"No."

Silence fell between them. Rachel studied her hands, waiting for another question. When none came she tried one of her own. "Should I have called the police?"

"It would have been safer for you if you had."

"I took a calculated risk. I figured the odds were more in my favor than yours." She took a deep breath. "I'm a civilian, but I used to be an investigative reporter. I saw some things in those days that didn't add up, and I did a little digging, found out some things before I was warned not to go any deeper. You could have been a drug runner or an escaped convict, but there wasn't any hint of anything like that on the scanner. You could also have been an agent. You had been shot twice. You were unconscious and couldn't protect yourself or tell me anything. If... people...were hunting you, you wouldn't have had a chance in a hospital."

His lashes had dropped, shielding his expression. "You've got quite an imagination."

"Haven't I," she agreed mildly.

He leaned back in his chair, wincing a little as he tried to get his shoulder comfortable. "Who else knows I'm here, other than the vet?"

"No one."

"Then how did you get me up here? Or did the vet help you? You're not Superwoman."

"I put you on a quilt and dragged you up here, with help from the dog. Maybe he thought it was a game." Her gray eyes darkened as she thought of the Herculean effort she had made to get him inside the house. "When Honey got here, we lifted you onto the bed."

"Honey?"

"The vet. Honey Mayfield."

Sabin watched her quiet face, wondering at what she wasn't saying. How far had she dragged him? How had she gotten him up the steps to the porch? He had carried wounded men out of battle, so he knew how difficult it was, even with his strength and training. He outweighed her by at least eighty pounds; there was no way she could have lifted him. She could be lying about not having anyone else help her, but there wasn't any reason for her to do so; all he could do was read between the lines. Almost anyone would have called the police immediately on finding a man unconscious on their beach, but she hadn't. Few people would ever have considered the options and circumstances that had occurred to her. People just didn't think about such things. It wasn't a part of their normal lives; it only happened in movies and books and therefore wasn't real. What life had she led that would make her so cautious, so aware of something that should have been beyond her experience?

They both heard the approaching car at the same time. Instantly she was out of her chair, her hand on his shoulder. "Go to the bedroom and close the door," she said evenly, not noticing the way his eyebrows lifted at her order. She went to the window and looked out; then the tension visibly left her body.

"It's Honey. Everything's okay. I guess she stayed away as long as her curiosity would let her."

Chapter Six

"**H**ow's the headache?" the veterinarian asked, peering into his eyes. She was a big, strong-boned woman with a friendly, freckled face and a light touch. Sabin decided that he liked her; she had a good bedside manner.

"Hanging in there," he grunted.

"Help me get his shirt off," she said to Rachel, and the two women gently and efficiently stripped him. He was glad that he'd chosen to wear the cutoffs, or they would have had his pants off, too. He didn't have any modesty to worry about, but it still disconcerted him to be handled like a Barbie doll. He dispassionately observed the purpled, puckered skin around the stitches in his leg, wondering about the extent of the muscle damage. It was essential that he be able to do more than hobble, and soon. The damage to his shoulder, with its complex system of muscle and tendons, was likely to be more permanent, but mobility was his greatest concern at the moment. Once he had decided what course of action to take he would need to move fast.

Fresh bandages were applied, and he was put back inside his shirt. "I'll be back in a couple of days to take out the stitches," Honey said, repacking her bag. It struck Sabin that not once had she asked his name or any other question that didn't deal with his physical well-being. Either she was remarkably incurious or she had decided that the less she knew, the better. It was a view that he wished Rachel shared. Sabin had always made it a rule not to involve innocent citizens; his work was too dangerous, and though he knew the risks of his job and accepted them, there was really no way Rachel could comprehend the extent of the risk she was taking in helping him.

Rachel went out with Honey, and Sabin hobbled to the door to watch as they stood by Honey's car, talking in low voices. The dog, Joe, took up a position at the foot of the steps, a low growl working in his throat as he turned first to watch Sabin at the door, then back to Rachel, as if he couldn't decide where to place his attention. His foremost instinct was to guard Rachel, but those same instincts couldn't allow him to ignore Sabin's alien presence at the door.

Honey got in the car and drove off, and after a final wave Rachel walked back to the porch. "Calm down," she admonished the dog softly, daring to give him a swift touch on the neck. His growl intensified, and she looked up to see Sabin coming out on the porch.

"Don't come too close to him," she warned. "He doesn't like men."

Sabin regarded the dog with remote curiosity. "Where did you get him? He's a trained attack dog."

Astonished, Rachel looked down at Joe, standing so close by her leg. "He just wandered up one day, all skinny and beat-up. We reached an understanding. I feed him, and he stays around. He's not an attack dog."

"Joe," Sabin said sharply. "Heel."

She felt the animal quiver as if he'd been struck, and blood-chilling snarls worked up from his throat as he stared at the man, every muscle in his big body quivering as if he longed to launch himself at his enemy but was chained to Rachel's side. Before she thought of the danger she went down on one knee and put her arm around his neck, talking softly to him in reassurance. "It's all right," she crooned. "He won't hurt you, I promise. Everything's all right."

When Joe was calmer Rachel went up on the porch and deliberately stroked Sabin's arm, letting the dog see her. Sabin watched Joe, unafraid of the dog, but not pushing him, either. He needed to have Joe accept him, at least enough to let him leave the house without attacking.

"He was probably abused by his owner," he said. "You're lucky he didn't have you for breakfast the first time you walked out of the house."

"I think you're wrong. It's a possibility that he was a guard dog, but I don't think he was trained to attack. You owe him a lot. If it hadn't been for him, I couldn't have gotten you up from the beach." Suddenly she realized that her hand was still on his arm, slowly moving up and down, and she let her arm fall to her side. "Are you ready to go back inside? You must be tired by now."

"In a minute." He slowly surveyed the pine thicket to the right and the road that curved away to the left, committing distances and details to memory for future use. "How far are we from a main road?"

"About five or six miles, I guess. This is a private road. It joins the road from Rafferty's ranch before it runs into U.S. 19."

"Which way is the beach?"

She pointed to the pine thicket. "Down through the pines."

"Do you have a boat?"

Rachel looked at him, her gray eyes very clear. "No. The only means of escape are on foot or driving."

The faintest smile lifted one corner of his mouth. "I wasn't going to steal your car."

"Weren't you? I still don't know what's going on, why you were shot, or even if you're a good guy."

"With those doubts, why haven't you called the police?" he returned, his voice cool. "I obviously wasn't wearing a white hat when you found me."

He was going to stonewall it to the end, the ultimate professional, alone and unemotional. Rachel accepted that she wasn't entitled to full knowledge of his situation, even though she had saved his life, but she would very much like to know that she had done the right thing. Though she had acted on her instincts, the uncertainty was gnawing at her. Had she saved a rogue agent? An enemy of her country? What would she do if it turned out to be that way? The worst part of it was the undeniable and growing attraction she felt for him, even against her own better judgment.

He didn't say anything else, and she didn't respond to his provoking mention of his lack of clothing when she'd found him. She glanced at Joe and turned to open the screen door. "I'm getting out of this heat. You can take your chances with Joe if you want to stay out here."

Sabin followed her inside, measuring the unyielding straightness of her back. She was angry, but she was also disturbed. He would have liked to reassure her, but the hard truth was that the less she knew, the safer she was. He had no way of protecting her in his present condition and circumstances. The fact that she was protecting him, willingly endangering herself even though her guesses ranged uncomfortably close to the truth, did something unwanted to his insides. Hell, he thought in disgust at himself, everything about her did something to his insides. He was already familiar with the scent of her flesh and the tender, startlingly intimate touch of her hands. His body still felt the press of hers against him, making him want to reach out and pull her back. He had never needed another human being's closeness, except for the physical closeness required for sex. He eyed her bare, slender legs and softly rounded buttocks; the sexual urge was there, all right, and damned strong, considering his general physical condition. The dangerous part of it was that the thought of lying in the darkness with her and simply holding her was at least as attractive as the thought of taking her.

He leaned in the doorway and watched as she efficiently finished cleaning the dishes. There was a brisk, economical grace to her movements, even while she was doing such a mundane task. Everything was organized and logical. She wasn't a fussy woman. Even her clothing was plain and unadorned, though her beige shorts and simple blue cotton shirt didn't need any adornment other than the soft feminine curves beneath them. Again he was aware of the tantalizing image of those curves, just as if he knew how she looked naked, had already had his hands on her.

"Why are you staring?" she asked without looking at him. She had been as aware of his gaze as she would have been of his touch.

"Sorry." He didn't explain, but, then, he doubted that she would really want to know. "I'm going back to bed. Will you help me with the shirt?"

"Of course." She wiped her hands on a towel and went ahead of him to the bedroom. "Let me change the sheets first."

Fatigue pulled at him as he leaned against the dresser to ease the strain of his weight on his left leg. His shoulder and leg throbbed, but the pain was to be expected, so he ignored it. The real problem was his lack of strength; he wouldn't be able to protect Rachel or himself if anything happened. Did he dare remain here while he healed? His brooding gaze remained fixed on her as she put fresh linens on the bed, his available options running through his mind. Those options were severely limited. He had no money, no identification, and he didn't dare call to be picked up, because he had no idea of the extent to which the agency had been compromised, or who he could trust. He wasn't in any shape to do anything anyway; he had to recuperate, so it might as well be here. The small house had its advantages: the dog outside was a damned good defense; the locks were strong; he had food and medical care.

There was also Rachel.

Looking at her was easy; it could become an uncontrollable habit. She was slim and healthy-looking, with a honey-eyed tan that made her skin look luscious. Her hair was thick and straight and shiny, a dark ash-brown so completely lacking in any warm highlights that it almost had a silvery sheen. It went well with her wide, clear, lake-gray eyes. She wasn't tall, less than medium height, but she carried herself so straight that she gave the impression of being a tall woman. And she was soft, with rounded breasts that nestled into his palms....

Damn! The image was so real, so strong, that it kept creeping back. If it was only a fever-induced dream, it was the most realistic he had ever known. But if it had really happened, when and how? He had been unconscious most of the time, and out of his head with fever even when he'd been awake. Yet he kept reliving the sensation of her hands on him, stroking gently, with the open intimacy of lovers, and he had either had his hands on her or his imagination had lurched into overdrive.

She plumped the pillows and turned to him. "Do you want to sleep in your shorts?"

For an answer he unsnapped the cutoffs and let them drop, then sat down on the bed so she could work the shirt off his shoulder. The warm, faintly floral scent of her enveloped him as she leaned close, and he instinctively turned his head toward it, his mouth and nose pressing into her shoulder. She hesitated, then quickly freed him from the shirt and moved away from his touch. The moist warmth of his breath had heated her skin through the fabric of her shirt and played havoc with the even rhythm of her heartbeat. Trying not to let him see how his nearness had affected her, she neatly folded the shirt and placed it on a chair, then picked up his cutoffs and placed them on top of the shirt. When she looked at him again he was lying on his back, his right leg bent at the knee and raised, his right arm resting across his stomach. His white briefs contrasted sharply with his bronzed skin, reminding her that he didn't have any tan lines on his body. She groaned inwardly. Why did she have to think about that now?

"Do you want the sheet over you?"

"No, the fan feels good." He lifted his right hand from his stomach and held it out to her. "Sit here for a minute."

Her mind told her that it wasn't a good idea. She sat down, anyway, just as she had done so many times since he'd been in her bed, her body angled to face him and her hip against his side. He draped his arm over her thighs, his hand cradling the curve of her hip as if to keep her nestled against him. His fingers, curving around to her buttock, began to move caressingly, and her heart started pounding again. She looked up to meet his eyes and was unable to look away, caught by the mesmerizing black fire.

"I can't give you all the answers you want," he murmured. "I don't know them myself. Even if I tell you I'm a good guy, you'd still only have my word for it, and why would I cut my own throat by telling you anything else?"

"Don't play devil's advocate," she said sharply, wishing she could find the will to break away from the seductive power of his gaze and touch. "Let's deal in facts. You were shot. Who shot you?"

"I was ambushed, set up by one of my own men—Tod Ellis."

"Bogus-FBI-agent Ellis?"

"The same, from the description you gave."

"Then make a call and turn him in."

"It isn't as simple as that. I'm on a month's vacation from the agency. Only two men knew my location, both of them my superiors."

Rachel sat very still. "One of them betrayed you, but you don't know which one."

"Perhaps both of them."

"Can't you contact someone higher up?"

Something cold and furious flashed in his eyes. "Sweetheart, you can't get much higher. I'm not even certain I can get through. Either one of them has the power to declare me an outlaw, and calling from here would endanger you."

Rachel felt the icy power of his rage and shivered inside, thankful that she wasn't the one who had crossed him. The look in his eyes was in direct contrast to the touch of his fingertips on her hip. How could his touch remain so gentle, while the wrath of hell glittered in his eyes?

"What are you going to do?"

His fingers trailed down her hip to her thigh and rubbed across the hem of her shorts, then gently glided beneath it. "Recuperate. I can't do a damned thing right now, including dress myself. The problem is that I'm putting you in danger just by being here."

She couldn't control her breathing, or her pulse rate. Heat was building inside her, destroying her ability to think and leaving her to operate purely on her senses. She knew she should move his hand, but the rasp of his rough fingertips on her thigh was so pleasurable that all she could do was sit there, quivering slightly like a leaf in a soft spring breeze. Did he normally treat women as if they were his to touch as he wished, or had he picked up on her uncontrollable responses to him? She thought she had disguised them well, kept them to herself, but perhaps his job had made his senses and intuitions more acute. Desperately she made herself move, putting her hand on top of his to prevent it from moving any higher.

"You didn't put me in danger," she said, her voice a little hoarse. "I made the decision without your help."

Despite her controlling hand, his fingers moved higher and found the edge of her panties. "I have a question that's been driving me crazy," he admitted in a low voice. He moved his hand again, delving beneath the elastic leg of her panties and curving his fingers over the cool bareness of her buttock.

A whimper escaped her before she bit her lip, controlling the wild little sound. How could he do this to her with just his touch? "Stop," she whispered. "You have to stop."

"Have we been sleeping together?"

Her breasts had tightened painfully, begging for that touch to be transferred to them, for him to claim them as he had before. His question destroyed what little concentration she had left. "This...there's only this one bed. I don't have a couch, only the love seats—"

"So we've been in the same bed for four days," he interrupted, stopping a flow of words that she had felt edging toward incoherency. His eyes were glittering again, but this time with a different fire, and she couldn't look away. "You've been taking care of me."

She drew a deep, shuddering breath. "Yes."

"All alone?"

"Yes."

"You've been feeding me."

"Yes."

"Bathing me."

"Yes. Your fever—I had to sponge you with cool water to keep it down."

"You did everything that had to be done, took care of me like a baby."

She didn't know what to say, what to do. His hand was still on her, his palm warm and hard against the softness of her flesh.

"You touched me," he said. "All over."

She swallowed. "It was necessary."

"I remember your hands on me. I liked it, but when I woke up this morning I thought it was a dream."

"You did dream," she said.

"Have I seen you naked?"

"No!"

"Then how do I know what your breasts look like? How they feel in my hands? It wasn't all a dream, Rachel. Was it?"

A hot, wild blush colored her face, giving him an answer even before she spoke. Her voice was stifled, and she looked away from him, her embarrassment at last freeing her from his gaze. "Twice, when you woke up, you... uh...grabbed me."

"Helped myself to the goodies?"

"Something like that."

"And I saw you?"

She made a helpless gesture toward her neck. "My nightgown drooped when I bent over you. The neckline was hanging open...."

"Was I rough?"

"No," she whispered.

"Did you like it?"

This had to stop, right now, though she had a feeling that it was already too late, that she should never have sat down on the bed. "Move your hand," she said, trying desperately to put some strength into her voice. "Let me go."

He obeyed without hesitation, triumph stamped on his hard, dark face. She shot up from the bed, her face on fire. What an utter fool she had made of herself! He probably wouldn't be able to sleep for laughing at her. She was at the door before he spoke, his voice momentarily freezing her to the spot.

"Rachel."

She didn't want to turn, didn't want to look at him, but the way he said her name was a command that pulled at her like a magnet. Lying down didn't diminish his power; being wounded didn't diminish it. He was a man born to dominate, and he did it effortlessly, with the sheer strength of his will.

"If I could, I'd come after you. You wouldn't get away."

Her voice was as quiet as his, rising only slightly above the whir of the ceiling fan in the cool, dim room. "I might," she said, and closed the door gently behind her as she left the room.

She wanted to cry, but she didn't, because crying never solved anything. She hurt inside, and she felt restless. Lust. She had identified it almost immediately, had properly labeled the source of her undeniable and, evidently, uncontrollable attraction to him. She could have handled it if it had remained merely lust, for lust was a human appetite, the perfectly normal reaction of one sex to another. She could have acknowledged it, then ignored it. What she couldn't ignore was the growing emotional impact he had on her. She had sat there on the bed and let him fondle her, not because she was physically attracted to him, though God knew that was the truth, but because he had rapidly become far too important to her.

Rachel's refuge was work; it had saved her when B.B. died, and she sought it instinctively now. Her study was small and cluttered with both her work and memorabilia: books, magazines, clipped articles and family photographs crowded together on every available space. It was comfortable for her; it was here that she immersed herself in her interests, and despite the clutter she knew where everything was. It wasn't until her eyes fell on her favorite picture of B.B. that she realized she wasn't going to find the comfort she sought in this room. There couldn't be any hiding from herself; she had to face it, and face it now.

Slowly her fingers traced B.B.'s smiling face. He had been best friend, husband and lover, a man whose cheerful manner had hidden a strong character and firm sense of responsibility. They had had so much fun together! There were still times when she missed him so much that she thought she would never get over the sense of loss, even though she knew that wasn't what B.B. would have wanted. He would have wanted her to enjoy her life, to love again with all the passion she was capable of, to have children, to pursue her career, to have everything. She wanted that, too, but somehow she had never been able to imagine having it without B.B., and he was gone.

They had both known and accepted the risks of their jobs. They had even talked about them, holding hands in the night and discussing the danger they faced, as if by bringing it out in the open they could hold it at bay. Her job as an investigative reporter had made it inevitable that she would step on toes, and Rachel was very good at anything she chose to do. B.B.'s job with the Drug Enforcement Administration was inherently dangerous.

Perhaps B.B. had had a premonition. His hand strong around hers in the darkness, he had once said, "Honey, if anything ever happens to me, remember that I know the possibilities and I'm willing to take the risks. I think it's a job worth doing, and I'm going to do my best at it, the same way you won't back down from a story that's getting too hot for comfort. Accidents happen to people who never take any risks at all. Playing it safe isn't a guarantee. Who knows? With the noses you put out of joint, your job may turn out to be more dangerous than mine."

Prophetic words. Within the year B.B. was dead. An investigation Rachel was making into a politician's background had turned up a connection with illegal drugs. She didn't have any proof, but her questions must have been making the politician itchy. One morning she had been late to catch a flight to Jacksonville and her car had been low on gas. B.B. had tossed her the keys to his. "Drive mine," he'd said. "I have plenty of time to get gas on the way to work. See you tonight, honey."

But he hadn't. Ten minutes after her flight left the ground B.B. started her car and a bomb wired to the ignition killed him instantly.

Haunted by grief, she had finished the investigation, and now the politician was serving a life sentence without parole for both his drug dealings and his part in B.B.'s death. Then she had given up investigative reporting and returned to Diamond Bay to try to find again some sense of life for herself. Peace, hard won but finally hers, had let her find pleasure in work again, and in the quiet tenor of life here on the bay. She had contentment, peace and pleasure, but hadn't come close to loving again; she hadn't even been tempted. She hadn't wanted to date, hadn't wanted a man's kiss, or touch, or company.

Until now. Her forefinger gently touched the glass that covered B.B.'s crooked grin. It was incredibly painful and difficult to fall in love. What an apt phrase it was! "Falling in love." She was definitely falling, unable to stop her whirling, headlong plunge, even though she wasn't certain she was ready for it. She felt like a fool. After all, what did she know about Kell Sabin? Enough for her emotions to go wildly out of control, that was for certain! She had somehow started loving him from the first, her intuition sensing that he would be important to her. Why else had she fought so desperately to hide him, to protect him? Would she have taken the risk of caring for any other stranger? It would be romantic of her to assume that it was predestination; another explanation was an ancient one, that a life belonged to the one who saved it. Was it a primitive predilection, a sort of bonding forged by danger?

At that point in her thoughts Rachel gave a wry laugh at herself. What difference did it make? She could sit there all night thinking of plausible and implausible explanations, but they wouldn't change a thing. She was, regardless of will and logic, already half in love with the man, and it was getting worse.

He was trying to seduce her. Oh, he wasn't in any physical shape for it, but given his superb conditioning and strength he would probably recover much faster than an ordinary person. Part of her shivered in excitement at the thought of making love with him, but another part, more cautious, warned her not to let herself become that involved with him. To do so would be to take an even larger risk than hiding him and nursing him back to health had been. She wasn't afraid of the physical risk, but the emotional price she might have to pay for loving such a man could be crippling.

She took a deep breath. She couldn't limit her emotions and responses to carefully measured dollops, like following a recipe. Her nature wasn't that controlled and unemotional. All she could do was accept the fact that she loved him, or was growing to love him, and deal with it from there.

B.B.'s photographed gaze looked back at her. It wasn't a betrayal to love someone else; he would want her to love again.

It was wrenching to accept the idea; Rachel didn't love lightly. When she gave herself it was with all the passion of her emotions, which wasn't an easy or casual way to love. The man in her bed wouldn't welcome her devotion; it didn't take a crystal ball to tell that he was one of those men who combined icy unemotionalism with fiery sensuality. He lived for the danger of his job, and it was a job that didn't encourage emotional ties. He could take her with raw, hungry passion, then calmly walk away and return to the life he had chosen.

Wryly she looked around the study; she wasn't going to be able to work, after all. Her emotions were too turbulent to allow her to sink into either planning her class or working on her manuscript. She had gotten her hero into a sticky situation, but could it be any stickier than the one she found herself in? Actually, she could use some practical advice. A smile suddenly lit her face. She had an expert in her bedroom; why not use his knowledge while he was there? If nothing else, it would help occupy his time. To occupy her time, she could finish weeding the garden now that it was late afternoon and the sun's ferocious heat had abated somewhat. She might as well do something practical.

The twilight was rapidly fading and she had almost finished her chore, when she heard the simultaneous creak of the screen door at the back steps and Joe's explosive, furious spring from his position at the end of the row where she was working. Rachel screamed Joe's name as she jumped to her feet, knowing that she'd never be able to reach the dog in time to stop him.

Sabin didn't retreat. Joe hesitated when Rachel screamed at him, his attention momentarily split, and Sabin used the interval to ease himself down into a sitting position on the steps. It left him vulnerable, but it also took him out of a threatening position. Joe stopped four feet away, his face contorted, the fur on his neck raised as he crouched.

"Stay back," Sabin said evenly as Rachel approached from the side, trying to put herself between Sabin and the dog. She was far too willing to use herself as a shield; he didn't think the dog would intentionally hurt her, but if the dog attacked and Rachel tried to protect him... He had to reach an understanding with Joe, and it might as well be now.

Rachel stopped as he'd directed, but she spoke softly to the dog, trying to calm him. If he attacked she wasn't strong enough to wrestle him off of Sabin. What was he thinking of, coming out like that, when he knew Joe didn't like men?

"Joe, heel," Sabin said firmly.

Just as it had earlier, the command sent Joe into a paroxysm of rage. She edged closer, ready to leap if Joe made any move to attack. Sabin gave her a warning glance.

"Joe, heel." He repeated the command over and over, always in a quiet, level voice, and Joe made a lunge that brought his sharp teeth within inches of Sabin's bare foot. Rachel gasped and threw herself at the dog, wrapping her arms around his neck. He was quivering in every muscle of his body. He ignored her, his attention locked on the man.

"Turn him loose and back away," Sabin instructed.

"Why don't you just go back in the house while I hold him?"

"Because I'm a prisoner as long as he doesn't accept me. I may need to leave in a hurry, and I don't want to have to worry about the dog."

Rachel crouched by Joe, her fingers buried in his fur and gently rubbing. Already Sabin was planning to leave, but, then, she had known how it would be. Slowly she released the dog and stepped back.

"Joe, heel," Sabin said again.

Rachel held her breath, waiting for another violent reaction. She could see Joe shake, and his ears went back. Sabin repeated the command. For a moment the dog quivered on the verge of attack, then, abruptly, he went to Sabin's side and took up the heeling position.

"Sit," Sabin said, and Joe sat.

"Good boy, good boy." Stiffly he moved his left arm to pat the dog's head. For a moment Joe's ears went back and he snarled softly, but he made no move to bite. Rachel slowly released her pent-up breath, relief making her legs wobble.

Sabin slanted her a quick glance from his midnight eyes. "Now you come sit beside me."

"Just like the dog?" she quipped, sinking gratefully onto the step beside him. At her action Joe sprang up and moved to stand in front of them, his ears going back again.

Sabin put his right arm around her shoulders and hugged her against his bare chest, carefully watching the dog. Joe didn't like it at all; a growl began rumbling in his chest.

"He's jealous," Sabin observed.

"Or he thinks you might hurt me." His arm around her was interfering with her breathing, and to take her mind off it she held her hand out to Joe. "It's all right. Come here, boy. Come on."

Warily Joe came closer. He sniffed at Rachel's outstretched hand, then Sabin's knee. After a moment he dropped to the ground at their feet and put his head on his paws.

"It's a shame someone abused him. He's an intelligent, expensive animal, and he isn't old. He's about five."

"That's what Honey thinks."

"Have you always had a penchant for taking in strays?" he asked, and she knew he wasn't just talking about Joe.

"Only the interesting ones." She could hear the tightness creeping into her voice and wondered if he could hear it, too, if he could guess what caused it. His right hand was lightly rubbing her bare arm, an innocent touch if it hadn't been for the warm pleasure it gave her. A flash of lightning in the darkening sky made her look up, glad for an interruption.

"It looks like there's a chance of rain. A thunderhead passed right over us this morning and didn't leave a drop." Right on cue, thunder rumbled and a few fat drops of rain splashed down on them. "We'd better go in the house."

Sabin let her help him to his feet, but he negotiated the steps on his own. Joe got up and took shelter under the car. Just as Rachel latched the screen door thunder cracked deafeningly directly overhead, and the heavens opened to release a deluge of rain. The temperature plummeted while they stood there, the rain fresh and cool, and the wind blew a fine mist through the screen door. Laughing, Rachel shut the wooden door and locked it, then turned to find herself in Sabin's arms.

He didn't say anything. He simply closed his fist in her hair and held her head back, and his mouth came down on hers. Her world shuddered, then tilted off-balance. She stood there, her hands on his bare chest, and let him have her mouth as he pleased, unable to do anything except give him what he wanted. His mouth was hard, as she had known it would be. Hungry, as she had known it would be. He kissed her with the slow, hot skill of experience, his tongue on hers, the roughness of his faint beard scraping her softer skin.

The exquisite pleasure stunned her, and she jerked her mouth from his, her eyes wide as she stared up at him.

His fist tightened in her hair. "Are you afraid of me?" he asked roughly.

"No," she whispered.

"Then why did you pull away?"

She couldn't do anything but give him the truth, staring up at him in the growing darkness while the storm raged over their heads. "Because it was too much."

There was a storm in his black eyes, glittering and snapping with hot fire. "No," he said. "It wasn't enough."

Tension was coiling tightly inside Rachel; it had been increasing as the night wore on. He hadn't kissed her again, hadn't touched her again, but he had watched her, and in some ways that was worse. The power of his gaze was like a physical touch, stroking and burning. She couldn't make small talk to lessen the tension, because every time she looked up at him, he was watching her. They ate; then she turned on the television for diversion. Unfortunately the programs weren't very diverting, and he watched her, instead, so she turned the set off again. "Do you want something to read?" she finally asked in desperation.

He shook his head. "I'm too tired, and this damned headache is worse. I think I'll go back to bed."

He did look tired, but that wasn't surprising. He had been on his feet a lot, considering that he had just recovered full consciousness that morning. She was tired, too, the events of the day having sapped her energy. "Let me take a shower first. Then I'll help you get settled," she said, and he nodded in agreement.

She hurried through her shower and pulled on her most modest nightgown, then belted a light robe around her. He was waiting in the bedroom when she left the bath, and the rest of the house was dark. "That was fast," he said, smiling faintly. "I didn't know a woman could get out of a bathroom in less than half an hour."

"Chauvinist," she said mildly in reply, wondering if his smiles ever reached his eyes.

He unfastened the cutoffs and let them drop, then stepped out of them and limped into the bathroom. "I'll wash what I can reach, then call you to do the rest, all right?"

"Yes," she said, her throat tightening at the thought of feeling his body under her hands again. It wasn't as if she hadn't washed him before, but he was awake now, and he had kissed her. It was her own response to him that was making her nervous, not worrying over anything he might do. He was still too much of an invalid to make any serious advances.

There was no need for her to sleep with him now; it would be easier on both of them if she didn't make a big deal out of it and simply made a pallet before he came out of the bathroom. Thinking that, she took a couple of quilts from the top of the closet and unfolded them on the floor, then dragged a pillow from the bed and tossed it down. She wouldn't need a cover; her robe would be enough.

After twenty minutes he opened the door. "I'm ready for the reinforcements."

He wore only a towel knotted around his lean waist, and he was literally weaving on his feet. Rachel looked at him closely, concern driving away her nervousness. He was pale, the skin stretched tautly over his high cheekbones, but his lips were very red. "I think you're feverish again," she said, laying her hand against his cheek. He was too warm, but the fever wasn't nearly as high as it had been before. Quickly she lowered the lid on the toilet and helped him to sit down, then gave him two aspirin and a glass of water before she finished washing his torso, working as fast as she could. The sooner he was in bed, the better. She should have been looking for the fever to flare again after the way he'd pushed himself that day.

"Sorry about this," he muttered as she dried him. "I didn't intend to give out on you this way."

"You're not Superman," Rachel told him briskly. "Come on, let's get you in bed."

She helped him to stand, and he said, "Wait." Removing his right arm from around her shoulders, he tugged the towel loose from his waist and draped it over one of the towel racks. Totally and unconcernedly nude, he put his arm back around her shoulders and leaned on her heavily as she helped him walk to the bed. Rachel didn't know if she should laugh or get huffy with him, but in the end she decided to ignore his lack of clothing. It wasn't as if she hadn't seen him before, and if it didn't bother him, it shouldn't bother her.

Even though he was feverish and exhausted, nothing escaped his notice. He saw the pallet at the foot of the bed, and his dark, level brows lowered as his eyes narrowed. "What's that?"

"My bed."

He looked at it, then at her. His voice was quiet. "Get that damned thing up from there and get in bed with me, where you belong."

She gave him a long, cool look. "You're presuming a lot on the basis of one kiss. You're a lot better now. I won't need to get up with you during the night, so I don't need to sleep with you."

"After sleeping with me that many times, why stop now? God knows it can't be modesty at this stage, and sex is out of the question. Any pass I made would be false advertising, and you know it."

She didn't want to laugh, didn't want him to know that his logic seemed very...logical. It wasn't the thought of what he might do that made her wary of sleeping with him now, but rather the knowledge of what it would mean to her to lie beside him in the night, to feel his weight and warmth in the bed next to her. She'd gotten used to sleeping alone, and it was painful to rediscover the subtle but powerful pleasure of sharing the dark hours with a man.

He put his hand on her throat, his callused thumb rubbing the sensitive tendons running down to her shoulder and making her shiver. "There's another reason why I want you to sleep with me."

She didn't know if she wanted to hear it. That cold, lethal expression was in his eyes again, the look of a man for whom there were no illusions, who had seen the worst and not been surprised. "I'll be right there, at the foot of the bed," she whispered.

"No. I want you at hand, so I'll know exactly where you are at all times. If I have to use the knife, I want to make certain you don't accidentally get in the way."

She turned her head and looked at the knife, still lying there on the table beside the bed. "No one can break in without waking us."

"I'm not taking that chance. Get in the bed. Or we'll both sleep on the floor."

He meant it, and with a sigh she gave in; there was no use in both of them being uncomfortable. "All right. Let me get my pillow."

His hand dropped to his side, and Rachel retrieved her pillow, tossing it into place on the bed. Gingerly he eased between the sheets, and a low groan escaped him as he lay back, putting strain on his shoulder. She turned out the light and got into bed on the opposite side, pulling the sheet up over both of them and curling up in her usual position, just as if they had done this for years, but the casual pose was completely superficial. She was tightly knotted inside; his caution was catching. She doubted that he really expected

the men who were hunting him to break into the house in
the middle of the night, but he prepared himself, anyway.

The old house settled around them with comfortable
squeaks and groans; in the evening silence she could hear
the crickets chirping outside the window, but the familiar
noises didn't reassure her. Her thoughts roamed restlessly,
trying to piece her snippets of information into a coherent
picture. He was on vacation, but he'd been ambushed? Why
were they trying to get rid of him? Had he learned something they wanted suppressed? She wanted to ask him, but
his quiet, even breathing told her that he had already gone
to sleep, worn out from the day.

Without thinking, she reached out and put her hand on
his arm. It was a purely automatic gesture, left over from
the nights she had needed to be aware of his every movement.

There was no warning, only the lightning-fast strike of
his right hand as his hard fingers clamped around her wrist
with a force that bruised and twisted. Rachel cried out, in
fear as much as pain, every nerve in her jolted by his attack.
The hand that held her wrist slackened a little, and he muttered, "Rachel?"

"You're hurting me!" The involuntary protest was
wrung from her, and he released her completely, sitting up
in the bed and swearing softly under his breath.

Rachel rubbed her bruised wrist, staring up at the faint
outline of his body against the darkness. "I think the pallet
would be safer," she finally said, trying for lightness. "I'm
sorry. I didn't mean to touch you. It just…happened."

His voice was rough. "Are you all right?"

"Yes. My wrist is bruised, that's all."

He tried to turn toward her, but his injured shoulder
stopped him, and he swore again, halting the movement.

"Climb over on this side, so I can sleep on my right side and hold you."

"I don't need holding, thank you." She was still feeling a little shaken by the way he'd reacted, as violently and swiftly as a snake striking. "You must have a hard time keeping bed partners."

"You're the only woman I've slept with, in the literal sense, in years," he snapped. "Now do you want to take your chances on startling me again, or are you going to crawl over here?"

She got out of bed and walked around to the other side, and he slid over enough to make room for her. Without a word she lay down, turned her back to him and pulled the sheet up to cover them. In equal silence he positioned himself against her like a spoon, his thighs against the backs of hers, her bottom snuggling his loins, her back against his hard, broad chest. His right arm went under her head, and his left one curved around her waist, anchoring her in place. Rachel closed her eyes, branded by his heat and wondering how much of it was fever. She'd forgotten how it felt to lie like this with a man, to feel his strength wrapped around her like a blanket. "What if I bang against your shoulder or leg?" she whispered.

"It'll hurt like hell," he replied dryly, his breath stirring her hair. "Go to sleep. Don't worry about it."

How could she not worry about hurting him, when she would rather die than cause him pain? She nestled her head into the pillow, feeling the iron hard strength of his arm beneath it; her hand slid beneath the pillow and lightly closed over his wrist, a touch that she had to have now. "Good night," she said, sinking into his warmth and letting drowsiness take over.

Sabin lay there, feeling her softness in his arms, the female sweetness of her scent in his nostrils and the remembered taste of her on his tongue. It felt too good, and that made him wary. It had been years since he'd actually *slept* with anyone; he had trained to such a fine, sharp edge that he hadn't been able to tolerate anyone close to him while he slept, including his ex-wife. Even while he'd been married he had still been essentially alone, both mentally and physically. It was odd that he could feel so comfortable now, with Rachel sleeping in his arms, as if he didn't need to be distant with her. He was innately cautious and solitary, on guard with everyone, including his own men; that trait had saved his life more than once. Maybe it was because he was already subconsciously accustomed to sleeping with her, to touching her and being touched by her, though that light touch on his arm had startled him into a violent reaction before he could catch himself.

For whatever reason, it felt good to hold her, to kiss her. She was a remarkably dangerous woman, because she tempted him in ways he'd never been tempted before. He thought of having sex with her. Every muscle in his body tightened, and he began to harden. Too bad he wasn't able to roll her onto her back and do all the things to her he wanted to do, but that would have to wait. He would have her, but he'd have to be very careful that it didn't become anything more than a good time. He couldn't afford to let it be anything else, for both of them.

Rachel woke slowly, so completely comfortable she was loath to open her eyes and start the day. She was normally an early riser, wide-awake as soon as her feet hit the floor, and she really liked the morning. But on this particular morning she had burrowed deeply into her pillow, her body warm and relaxed, and she was aware of having slept better than she had in years. But where was Kell? She was immediately aware that he wasn't in the bed; her eyes popped open, and she was out of bed before the thought was even completed. The bathroom door was open, so he wasn't in there. "Kell?" she called, hurrying out of the bedroom.

"Out here."

The answering call came from the back, and she almost ran to the rear door, which was standing open. He was sitting on the steps, wearing only the denim shorts, and Joe was lying on the grass at his feet. Ebenezer Duck and his faithful flock were waddling around the backyard, peacefully hunting insects. The rain the night before had left everything so fresh it almost hurt to look at it, and now the sun lit a dark-blue sky that didn't have a cloud in sight. It was a remarkably peaceful morning, warm and sweet.

"How did you get out of bed without waking me?"

Bracing his hand on the step, he pushed himself to a standing position; she noticed that he seemed to be moving more easily than he had the day before. He faced her through the screen. "You were tired after taking care of me for four days."

"You're getting around better."

"I feel stronger, and my head isn't hurting." He opened the screen door and hesitated for a moment, his black eyes swiftly running down her body. It was all she could do to keep from folding her arms across her chest, but she knew that the gown she'd chosen didn't reveal anything, so the gesture would have been futile. She probably looked a mess, with her hair uncombed, but she'd seen him at his worst, so she wasn't going to worry about that, either.

"I'm too used to playing mother hen," she said, laughing a little. "When you weren't in the bed I panicked. But since you're all right, I'll go get dressed and make breakfast."

"Don't get dressed on my account," he drawled, a comment she ignored as she walked away. Kell watched until she was out of sight, then slowly made his way back up the steps and inside. He latched the screen door behind him. She didn't play games by wearing slinky nightgowns and then pretending to be embarrassed by what was revealed, but she didn't have to. With that pink flowered nightgown and her tousled hair, she looked warm and sleepy and so damned soft a man could sink into her. That was exactly what he'd wanted to do when he awoke to find that her nightgown had ridden up during the night and he was pressed against her bare thighs, with only the thin nylon of her panties keeping him from her. He'd become so aroused that he'd had to get out of bed, to remove himself from the temptation of her body. He swore impatiently at his own physical disability, because it kept him from taking her the way he wanted to take her, hard and fast and deep.

In only a few minutes she came back into the kitchen, her hair brushed out and pulled up on each side of her head with a wine-red butterfly clip. She was still barefoot, and she wore denim shorts so old that they were almost white, along with an oversize maroon jersey with the tail knotted at her waist. Her tanned face was completely free of makeup. She was comfortable with herself, he realized. She could probably stop traffic when she did deck herself out in silk and jewels, but she would do so only when she felt like it, not for someone else's benefit. She was self-assured, and Kell liked that; he was so dominant that it took a strong woman not to be completely overpowered by him, not to shrink from him both in bed and out.

Working with an economy of motion, she put on the coffee and started the bacon frying. Until those twin aromas started filling the air he hadn't been aware of how hungry he was, but abruptly his mouth began watering. She put biscuits in the oven, whipped four eggs for scrambling, then peeled and sliced a cantaloupe. Her clear gray eyes turned toward him. "This would be easier if I had my best knife."

Sabin seldom laughed or was even amused, but the dry, chiding tone of her voice made him want to smile. He leaned against the work island to take the weight off his injured leg, unwilling to argue. He needed a means of self-defense, even if it was just a kitchen knife. Both logic and instinct insisted on it. "Do you have any sort of gun around here?"

Rachel deftly turned the bacon. "I have a .22 rifle under the bed, and a .357 loaded with ratshot in the glove compartment of the car."

Swift irritation rose in him; why hadn't she said anything about them the day before? Then she gave him another of those long, level looks, and he knew she was just waiting for him to say something. Why should she give a gun to a man who had held a knife on her? "What if I'd needed them during the night?"

"I don't have any shells for the .357 other than ratshot, so I discounted it," she replied calmly. "The .22 was within reach, and I not only know how to use it, I have two good arms as opposed to your one." She felt safe at Diamond Bay, but common sense dictated that she have some means of protection; she was a woman who lived alone, without close neighbors. Both the weapons she had were for what her grandfather had called "varmints," though anyone looking down the barrel of the .357 wouldn't know that it was loaded with ratshot. She had chosen both for self-protection, not for killing.

He paused, his black eyes narrowed. "Why tell me now?"

"One, because you told me who you are. Two, because you asked. Three, even without the knife, you weren't unarmed. Handicapped, but not helpless."

"What do you mean?"

She looked down at his hard, brown bare feet. "The calluses on the outside edges of your feet, and on your hands. Not many people have them. You work out barefoot, don't you?"

When he spoke his voice was quiet and silky, and it raised a chill along her spine. "You notice a lot, honey."

She nodded in agreement. "Yes."

"Most people wouldn't think anything about calluses."

Just for a moment Rachel hesitated, her gaze turned inward, before she resumed setting the table and checking the food. "My husband took extra training. He had calluses on his hands, too."

Something tightened inside him, twisting, and his fingers slowly curled. He darted a quick glance at her slim, tanned, ringless hands. "You're divorced?"

"No. I'm a widow."

"I'm sorry."

She nodded again and began dishing up the eggs and bacon, then checked the biscuits in the oven. They were just right, golden brown on top, and she quickly turned them out into the breadbasket. "It's been a long time," she finally said. "Five years." Then her voice changed and became brisk again. "Wash up before the biscuits get cold."

She was, he reflected a few minutes later, a damned good cook. The eggs were fluffy, the bacon crisp, the biscuits light, the coffee just strong enough. Homemade pear preserves dripped golden juice over the biscuits, and the yellow cantaloupe was ripe and sweet. There was nothing fancy about it, but it all fit together, and even the colors were harmonious. It was simply another facet of her competent nature. Just as he was savoring his third biscuit she said serenely, "Don't expect this every day. Some mornings I have cereal and fruit for breakfast. I'm just trying to build up your strength.'' Her manner hid the satisfaction she felt in watching this coldly controlled man eat with such obvious enjoyment.

He leaned back in his chair, taking his time as he examined the twinkle in her eyes and the smile that was barely hidden by the coffee cup she held in her elegant hands. She was teasing him, and he couldn't remember the last time anyone had actually dared to tease him. Probably back in high school, some giddy, giggling teenage girl trying out her newfound powers of seduction and daring to use them on the boy even the teachers considered "dangerous." He'd never actually done anything to make them think that; it had simply been the way he looked at them, with that cold, level gaze as black as a night in hell. Rachel dared to tease him because she was certain of herself, and because of that certainty she met him as an equal. She wasn't afraid of him, despite what she knew, or had guessed.

In time. He'd have her, sooner or later.

"You're going about it the right way," he said, finally responding to her teasing statement. Rachel wondered if he did it deliberately, waiting so long before answering. He could either be thinking about what he wanted to say, or those long pauses could be designed to tilt the other person a little off-balance. Everything he did was so controlled that she didn't think it was a habit; it was a deliberate tactic.

There could be a double meaning to his words, but Rachel chose to take them at face value. "If that's a bribe to keep me cooking like this, it won't work. It's too hot to eat a big meal three times a day. More coffee?"

"Please."

As she poured the coffee she asked, "How long are you planning to stay?"

He waited until she had set the pot back on its warming pad and returned to her seat before he answered. "Until I get over this, and can walk and use my shoulder again. Unless you want me gone, and then it's up to you when you throw me out."

Well, that was plain enough, Rachel thought. He'd stay while he was recuperating, but that was it. "Do you have any idea what you're going to do?"

He leaned his forearms on the table. "Get well. That's the first item on the list. I have to find out how deeply we've been compromised. There's still one man I can call when I need him, but I'll wait until I've recovered before I do anything. One man alone won't stand much of a chance. I have three weeks left of my vacation. Three weeks that they'll have to keep this quiet, unless my body just 'happens' to wash up somewhere. Without my body they're stalled. They can't make any moves to replace me until I'm officially dead, or missing."

"What happens if you don't turn up at work in three weeks?"

"My file will be erased from all records. Codes will be changed, agents reassigned, and I will officially cease to exist."

"Presumed dead?"

"Dead, captured, or turned."

Three weeks. At the most she would have three weeks with him. The time seemed so pitifully short, but she wasn't going to ruin it by moaning and sulking because things weren't turning out just the way she wanted. She had learned the hard way that "forever" could be heartbreakingly brief. If these three weeks were to be all she had with him, then she would smile and take care of him, even argue with him if she felt like it, help him in any way she could...cherish him... then wave goodbye to this dark warrior and keep her tears for herself, after he had gone. It didn't give her much comfort to know that women had probably been doing that exact thing for centuries.

He was thinking, his lashes lowered over his eyes while he stared into his coffee cup. "I want you to make another shopping trip."

"Sure," Rachel said easily. "I meant to ask you if the pants were the right size."

"Everything's the right size. You have a good eye. No, I want you to get hollowpoint ammunition for that .357, a good supply of it. The same for the rifle. You'll be reimbursed."

Being reimbursed was the last of Rachel's worries, and she felt a flare of resentment that he'd even mentioned it. "Are you sure you don't want me to buy a couple of deer rifles while I'm at it? Or a .44 Magnum?"

To her surprise he took her sarcasm seriously. "No. I don't want you on record as having purchased any type of weapon since the date I disappeared."

That startled her, and she leaned back. "You mean records of this sort that are likely to be checked?"

"For anyone in this area."

Rachel looked at him for a long, long time, her gray eyes drifting over the hard planes of his face and the closed expression in his eyes, eyes that were older than time. At last she whispered, "Who are you, that anyone would go to such lengths to kill you?"

"They'd rather take me alive," he replied dryly. "It's my job to make certain that never happens."

"Why you?"

One corner of his mouth quirked upward in what passed for a smile, though it was totally humorless. "Because I'm the best at what I do."

It wasn't much of an answer, but then he was good at

answering questions without giving any information. The details that he'd told her had been carefully considered, chosen to exact the response from her that he wanted. It wasn't necessary; Rachel knew that she would do whatever she could to help him.

She drained the last of her coffee and stood up. "I have chores to do before it gets too hot; the dishes can wait until later. Do you want to come outside with me, or stay in here and rest?"

"I need to move around," he said, getting up and following her outside. He slowly limped around the yard, taking in every detail, while Rachel fed Joe and the geese, then set to work gathering the ripe vegetables from the garden. When he tired, Kell sat down on the back steps and watched her work, his eyes narrowed against the sun.

Rachel Jones had a comfortable way about her that made him feel relaxed. Her life was peaceful, her small house cozy, and that hot Southern sun burned down on his skin.... Everything here was seductive, in one way or another. The meals she cooked and shared with him brought up stray thoughts of what it would be like to have breakfast with her every day, and those thoughts were more dangerous to him than any weapon.

He'd tried to have a normal private life once, but it hadn't worked out. Marriage hadn't brought the intimacy he'd expected; the sex had been good, and regular, but after the act was finished he'd still been solitary, set apart by nature and circumstance from the rest of the world. He'd been fond of his wife, as far as it went, but that was it. She hadn't been able to scale the barriers to reach the inside man; maybe she'd never even realized he existed. Certainly she either hadn't realized or hadn't wanted to face the true nature of his job. Marilyn Sabin had looked on her husband as merely one of the thousands of men who held civil service desk jobs in Washington, D.C. He went to work in the mornings and he returned—usually—at night. She was busy with her own growing law practice and often had to work late hours, so she understood. She was a fastidious woman, so Kell's cool, distant character had suited her perfectly, and she'd never made any effort to see beyond the surface to the complicated man beneath.

Kell turned his face up to the sun, feeling everything in him loosen up and slow down. Marilyn...it had been years since he'd even thought of her, an illustration of how shallowly she had touched him. The divorce hadn't elicited any response from him other than a shrug; hell, she would have been crazy to have stayed with him after what happened.

The attempt on his life had been clumsy, not well planned or well executed at all. He and Marilyn had been out to dinner, one of the few times in their married life that they had been out together socially, and never to one of the ritzy in places that Marilyn loved so dearly. Kell had seen the sniper as soon as they left the restaurant and acted immediately, shoving Marilyn down and rolling for cover himself. His action had saved Marilyn's life, because she had kept walking and ended up between Kell and the sniper, who had fired almost simultaneously with Kell's shove, wounding Marilyn in the right arm.

That night had forever changed the way Marilyn viewed her husband, and she hadn't liked the new view at all. She'd seen the cool way he had tracked and cornered his assailant, seen the short, vicious fight that left the other man unconscious on the ground, heard the biting authority in Kell's voice as he gave orders to the men who arrived shortly and took over. One of those men took her to a hospital, where she was treated and kept overnight, while Kell spent the night piecing together how the sniper had learned where he would be that evening. The answer, obviously, had been

Marilyn. She saw no reason to be secretive about her movements or the fact that she would be dining with her husband that night, or where; she'd truly had no idea how dangerous and highly classified her husband's job was, nor had she been interested in learning.

By the time Kell collected her at the hospital the next day their marriage was over in every way except legally. The first words Marilyn had said to him, very calmly, were that she wanted a divorce. She didn't know what it was he did, didn't want to know, but she wasn't going to risk her own life being married to him while he did it. It might have piqued her vanity a bit when Kell agreed so easily, but he'd been doing some thinking during the night, too, and had reached basically the same conclusion, though for different reasons.

Kell didn't blame her for getting a divorce; it had been the wise thing to do. The close call had shaken him, because it had illustrated how easily he could be reached through the very person who was supposed to be closest to him. It had been a mistake for him even to attempt to have a normal private life, considering who he was and what he did. Other men could manage it, but other men weren't Kell Sabin, whose particular talents put him on the leading edge of danger. If there was any one man in intelligence whom other agencies wanted to take out of commission, it was Kell Sabin. Because he was a target, anyone close to him was automatically a target, too.

It had taught him a lesson. He had never again let anyone get close enough to him that they could be used against him, or hurt in an effort to get to him. He had chosen his life, because he was both a realist and a patriot, and he was willing to pay whatever price he had to, but he was determined to never again involve an innocent, a civilian, one of the very people whose lives and freedom he was sworn to protect.

He'd never been tempted to marry again, or even to take a mistress. Sex was casual, never on a regular basis with the same woman, and he always carefully limited the number of times he saw anyone in particular. It had worked out well.

Until Rachel. She tempted him. Damn, how she tempted him! She was nothing like Marilyn; she was comfortable and casual, where Marilyn had been fastidious and chic. She knew—somehow, she *knew*—too much about his way of life in general, while Marilyn hadn't realized even a fraction that much about him in the years they were married.

But it simply wouldn't work. He couldn't allow it to work. He watched Rachel as she worked in her small garden, content with her chores. Sex with her would be hot and long, writhing on that bed with her, and she wouldn't worry if he mussed her hair or smeared her makeup. To protect her, he had to make certain that sex was all it ever was. When he walked out of her life it would be for good, and for her own good. He owed her too much to risk any harm coming to her.

She straightened from her bent position and stretched, reaching her arms high in the air; the movement thrust her breasts upward against the thin fabric of her shirt. Then she picked up her basket and picked her way across the rows of vegetables toward him; Joe left his position at the end of the row and followed her to find shade under the back steps. There was a smile on Rachel's face as she approached Kell, her gray eyes warm and clear, her slim body moving gracefully. He watched her approach, aware of her in every cell of his body. No, there was no way he'd endanger her by staying any longer than was necessary; the real danger was that he was so hungry for her that he might be tempted to see her again, something he couldn't let happen.

Chapter Eight

The next few days were slow, hot and peaceful. Now that Kell was on the mend and didn't require her constant attention Rachel resumed her normal work schedule; she finished planning her course and began working on her manuscript again, as well as tending the garden and doing all the other small chores that never seemed to end. She got the requested hollowpoint bullets for Kell, and the .357 was never far from his hand. If they were inside he sometimes placed it on the table in the bedroom, but usually he kept it stuck into his waistband at the small of his back, instantly accessible.

Honey came to take the stitches out of his wounds and professed to be amazed at how well he had healed. "Your metabolic rate must be something else," she said admiringly. "Of course, I did a terrific job on you. The muscle in your leg was a mess, but I did some repair work, and I think you're going to come out of this without even a limp."

"You did a helluva job, doc," he drawled, smiling at her.

"I know," Honey returned cheerfully. "You were just plain lucky on your shoulder. You may lose some of your rotation ability, but not much, I don't think. Take it easy on both the leg and shoulder for another week or so, but you can start working the stiffness out if you're careful."

He had already been working the stiffness out; Rachel

had seen him exercising his shoulder and arm carefully, as though testing the limits of the stitches. He hadn't put any weight on either his leg or shoulder, but he had been doing exercises to ease his movements, and as a result his limp was much better, no worse than if he'd had a sprained ankle.

Honey hadn't even blinked when he removed the pistol from his waistband and placed it on the table while he took off his khaki pants and blue cotton shirt. Wearing only his briefs, he'd sat at the table and observed expressionlessly while she removed the stitches and Rachel leaned over to watch. Then he put his clothes back on and returned the heavy pistol to its accustomed place at the small of his back.

"Stay for lunch," Rachel invited. "Tuna salad and fresh tomatoes, light and cool."

Honey made it a practice never to refuse one of Rachel's invitations. "Done. I've been craving a fresh tomato."

"Southerners serve tomatoes with almost everything," Kell observed.

"That's because almost everything tastes better with a tomato," Honey defended. She was from Georgia, and passionately fond of tomatoes.

"Love apples," Rachel said absently. "Tomatoes, that is. Though I don't know why they were called that, since most people thought they were poisonous because they're a member of the nightshade family, like belladonna."

Honey chuckled. "Oh, ho! You've been reading up on old poisons, haven't you? Is someone in one of your books going to kick the bucket from an overdose of belladonna?"

"Of course not. I don't write whodunits." Not at all perturbed by Honey's teasing, Rachel glanced at Kell as she set the table. "You're not a Southerner, are you? You have a drawl, but it isn't Southern."

"Most of it comes from spending a lot of time with a man from Georgia. We were in Vietnam together. I was born in Nevada."

That was probably the limit of the personal information he would give about himself, so Rachel didn't ask any more questions. They ate the simple meal, with Kell sitting between the two women, and though he ate well as always and kept up with the conversation, she noticed that he sat where he could watch both the window and the door. It was habit with him; he did it at every meal, even though he knew no one could approach the house without Joe giving warning.

As Honey was leaving she smiled at Kell and held out her hand. "If I don't see you again, goodbye."

He took her hand. "Thanks, doc. Goodbye." Rachel noticed that he made no pretense about staying.

Honey eyed him consideringly. "I'm literally bursting with questions, but I think I'm going to follow my own good advice and not ask them. I don't want to know. But be careful, you hear?"

He gave his crooked half smile. "Sure thing."

She winked at him. "If anyone asks, I don't know a thing."

"You're a smart woman, doc. After I'm gone Rachel can fill you in on the details."

"Maybe. But maybe I'll just make up my own answers. That way I can get as wild and romantic as I want but still play it safe."

Probably Honey's outlook *was* the best, Rachel thought after she and Kell were alone. Honey allowed herself to be wild and romantic in her fantasies, but in real life she opted for safety. Honey would never do anything as risky as falling in love with a man like Kell Sabin. She would clean the kitchen, just as Rachel was doing, and forget about the rest. Rachel turned and found him watching her in that steady, unnerving way of his. Her chin lifted. "What is it?"

For answer he walked up to her and cupped her chin in his hand, then bent and covered her mouth with his. Surprise held Rachel motionless for a moment; he hadn't kissed her after that first time, though she sometimes thought there was a touch of possessiveness in the way he held her at night. She hadn't betrayed the pleasure she felt in sleeping in his arms, but there was no way she could hide the heavy surge of desire that made her respond to his mouth, her lips parting at the pressure of his, her hands sliding up the hard, warm wall of his chest. His tongue curled against hers, and she made a sound deep in her throat, her breasts and loins tightening as if he had touched them.

Slowly Kell moved forward, backing her up until she was jammed against the cabinets. Rachel freed her mouth and gasped, "What brought this on?"

His mouth moved down to the curve of her jaw and explored the soft skin below her ear. "Must be all those love apples you've been feeding me," he murmured. "Stop turning your head away. Kiss me. Open your mouth." She did, her hands clenching his shirt, and he took her mouth in a long, deep, mind-drugging way that went on forever and had her standing on tiptoe to press against him. His hands slid down to her buttocks and cupped them, lifting her into even more intimate contact.

The kiss stripped away all pretense and left them clinging together in open passion, hungry for each other, straining to get even closer. Their passion had been building for days, feeding on the memory of intimate touches between them that normally would have come after the first questing kisses, but they had been thrown together in circumstances that had gotten the order mixed. She had seen and touched his hard, beautiful body while caring for him and soothing him. He had felt her in his hands and gotten used to the particular sweet scent of her even before he'd known her name. He had slept with her in his arms for four nights now, and their bodies had grown accustomed to each other. Nature had circumvented all the natural barriers that people threw up to protect their sense of privacy, forcing the two of them together in a hothouse atmosphere forged by circumstance.

The force of what she was feeling frightened her a little, and again she tore her mouth away from his, hiding her face in the warm curve of his throat. She had to slow this down before she went out of control. "You're a fast man," she gulped, trying to steady her voice.

He moved his hands from her buttocks to slide them up her back, holding her tightly. His mouth nuzzled her ear, and his voice was warm and dark. "Not as fast as I wanted to be."

Uncontrollable shivers were vibrating through her entire body, and her nipples were so tight that they ached. He held her even more tightly, crushing her breasts against his hard, muscle-layered body and rubbed his cheek against the top of her head, but the tender caress didn't last long against his hungry need for more. He dug his fingers into her hair and tilted her head back, his mouth once again taking hers, his tongue moving in the rhythm of making love. Rachel's entire body jolted when his other hand covered her breast, sliding inside her blouse to cup her warmly in his palm so he could rasp his callused thumb over her hardened nipple, simultaneously soothing the ache and creating a deeper one.

"I want to be inside you," he murmured, lifting his head to watch the way her nipple rolled under his thumb. "I've been going crazy, wanting you. Will you let me have you for the time we have left together?''

God, he was honest, and she had to swallow hard to keep from crying out at the pain. Even now, with their bodies fevered with need, he didn't make sweet promises he had no intention of keeping. He would be leaving; the best they could have would be temporary. Still, it would be so simple if she could just forget about the future and go with him now into her bedroom, but his honesty reminded her that she had to think about the future and the day when he would leave her.

Slowly she pushed against him, and he moved back, giving her the space she needed. With a shaking hand she pushed her hair back from her face. "It isn't something that's easy for me," she tried to explain, her voice shaking just like her hand. "I've never had a lover...only my husband."

His eyes were sharp, watchful, and he waited.

She made a helpless gesture. His honesty deserved her own. "I...care about you."

"No," he said sharply, deliberately. "Don't let it happen."

"Is it something I'm supposed to turn off, like a water faucet?" Rachel faced him, her gaze level.

"Yes. This is sex, nothing else. Don't fool yourself into thinking there can be anything more, because even if there were, there'd still be no future in it."

"Oh, I know that." She gave a tight little laugh and turned to look out the window over the sink. "When you walk out of here, that's when it ends."

She wanted him to deny it, but again that brutal honesty destroyed her hopes. "That's it. That's the way it has to be."

It would be useless to argue with him on that point; she

had known all along that he was solitary, a lone wolf. "It's that way for you, but I don't have that sort of emotional control. I think I love you—oh, damn, why try to hedge my bets?" Her voice was filled with helpless frustration. "I started loving you the minute I dragged you out of the ocean! It doesn't make sense, does it? But it won't stop just because you leave."

He watched her, accurately reading the tension in her slender back, the tightness of her hands. What had it cost her to confess that? She was the most direct woman he'd ever known, with no use for games or subterfuge. She was the only woman in all these years that he regretted leaving; just the thought of it twisted his guts, but he could handle that a lot easier than the knowledge that keeping her with him would jeopardize her life. She was too fine for him to carelessly endanger her for his own enjoyment.

He put his hands on her shoulders, kneading the tension from them. "I won't pressure you," he murmured. "You have to do what's best for you, but if you decide you want me, I'm here."

Decide she wanted him? She ached with wanting him! But he was giving her the space to decide for herself, rather than seducing her into bed as he knew he easily could; she had no illusions about her self-control where he was concerned. She put her hand on his, and their fingers entwined.

There was a thump as Joe left the shade under the steps and tore around the side of the house, and Kell's hand stiffened under hers, his head snapping around. Rachel went still, then shook herself and moved swiftly to the front door. She didn't have to tell him to stay out of sight; she knew that if she looked around he would already be hidden from view, moving silently through the house.

She opened the door and stepped out onto the front porch, and only then did she remember that Kell had partially unbuttoned her blouse. She rebuttoned it swiftly, looking around for whatever had set Joe off. Then she heard the car approaching down the private road; it wouldn't be Honey, since she had just left, and on the rare times Rafferty visited he rode his horse over rather than driving.

The car that pulled to a stop in front of the house was a pale-blue Ford, a government car. Joe was crouched facing it, snarling, his ears back. "Steady, steady," Rachel murmured to him, trying to see who was in the car, but the sun was glaring on the window and blocked her vision. Then the car door opened and a tall man got out, but he remained in the open door, looking at her over the top of the vehicle. Agent Ellis, his jacket off and dark sunglasses shading his eyes.

"Oh, hello," Rachel called. "Nice to see you again." The Southern ritual of greeting had its advantages, giving her time to gather her thoughts. Why was he here again? Had Kell been seen when he'd been outside? They had been careful, trusting Joe to warn them if anyone was near, but someone with binoculars might have seen him.

Tod Ellis gave her his bright college smile. "It's nice to see you again, Ms. Jones. I thought I'd check in with you, make sure everything's okay."

It was a pretty weak excuse for driving miles out of his way. Rachel stepped around Joe and walked out to the car in an effort to keep Ellis from looking toward the house. It wasn't likely that Kell would let himself be seen, but she didn't want to take any chances. "Yes, everything's okay," she said cheerfully, going around the car and standing at the door so he had to turn his back to the house in order to face her. "Hot, but okay. Did you ever find that man you were hunting?"

"No, not a trace. You haven't seen anything?"

"Not even at a distance, and Joe always lets me know if anyone's around."

The mention of the dog made Ellis jerk his head around for a quick look as if to check Joe's location; the dog was still standing in the middle of the yard, his eyes locked on the intruder, low growls still rumbling in his chest. Ellis cleared his throat, then turned back to Rachel. "It's a good thing you've got him, living way out here by yourself. You can't be too careful."

She laughed. "Well, actually you can. Look at Howard Hughes. But I feel safe with Joe guarding the place."

She couldn't be certain, because of the dark glasses shading his eyes, but she thought he kept looking at her legs and breasts. Alarm skittered through her, and she had to fight down the urge to check her buttons; had she buttoned the blouse straight? If not, it was too late now, and he had no reason to think she had been in the house, kissing the very man he was hunting.

Then abruptly he laughed, too, and took off his sunglasses, dangling them from his fingers. "I didn't come out here to check on you." He leaned his forearm on top of the open car door, his posture relaxed and confident. With his clean-cut good looks he was accustomed to approval from women. "I came to ask you out to dinner. I know you don't know me, but my credentials are respectable. What do you say?"

Rachel didn't have to fake her confusion; it was real. She had no idea how she should answer him. If she went out with him it would go a long way toward convincing him she knew nothing about Kell, but on the other hand, it might encourage Agent Ellis to come around again, and she didn't want that. Why were they still here, anyway? Why hadn't they moved farther down the coast in their search for Kell?

"Why, I don't know," she replied, stammering a little. "When?"

"Tonight, if you don't have other plans."

God, this was making her paranoid! If they had seen Kell, then this could be a ploy to get her out of the house so there would be no witnesses. If not, she might make him suspicious if *she* acted too suspicious. All this second-guessing could drive her crazy. Finally she went on her instincts. Agent Ellis hadn't tried to hide his male admiration for her the first time they'd met, so she was going to take his invitation at face value. If nothing else, she might be able to get some information from him.

"I think I'd like that," she finally said. "What did you have in mind? I'm not much of a party person."

He gave her his boyish grin again. "You're safe. I'm not into the punk scene, either. I'm too squeamish to stick safety pins through my cheeks. What I had in mind was a quiet restaurant and a good, thick steak."

And a roll in bed afterward? He'd be disappointed. "You're on," Rachel said. "What time?"

"Say, eight o'clock? It'll be sundown by then and cooling off, I hope."

She laughed. "I would say you get used to it, but all you do is learn to cope with it. The humidity is what gets you. All right, eight o'clock it is. I'll be ready."

He gave her a little salute and folded himself back under the steering wheel. Rachel walked back into the yard so she wouldn't get covered with dust when he drove off, and watched until the blue Ford was out of sight.

Kell was waiting for her inside, his eyes narrow and cold. "What did he want?"

"To ask me out to dinner," she replied slowly. "I didn't know what to say. Going out with him might keep him from being suspicious, or he could be asking me out just to get me out of the house. Maybe they've seen you. Maybe they just want to search."

"They haven't seen me," he said. "Or I wouldn't still be alive. What excuse did you give him?"

"I accepted."

Rachel had known he wouldn't be pleased, but she hadn't expected the reaction she got. His head snapped around, and his eyes burned with black fire, his usual cool remoteness shattered. "Hell, no, you're not. Get that idea out of your head, lady."

"It's too late. It might really make him suspicious if I made some weak excuse now."

He shoved his hands into his pants pockets, and in petrified fascination Rachel watched them ball into fists. "He's a murderer and a traitor. I've been doing a lot of thinking since I recognized him before they blew up my boat, tying together some details about things that went wrong when they shouldn't have, and Tod Ellis is connected in some little way to every one of those plans. You're not going out with him."

Rachel didn't back down. "Yes," she said. "I am. If nothing else, I may be able to pick up some information that will help you—"

She broke off with a gasp; he had jerked his hands out of his pockets and reached for her so rapidly that she hadn't had time to move back. His hard fingers closed on her shoulders in a grip that bruised, and he shook her slightly, his face hard and set with rage.

"Damn you," he whispered, the words barely audible as he pushed them between his clenched teeth. "When will you learn that this isn't something for amateurs to play with? You're in way over your head, and you don't have the sense to realize it! You aren't still in college playing a game of Assassination, sugar. Get that through your skull!

Damn it," he swore again, releasing her shoulders and running his hand through his hair. "You've been lucky so far that you haven't blundered around and really screwed things up, but how long do you expect that luck to last? You're dealing with a cold-blooded professional!"

Rachel stepped back from him, putting her hand up to rub her aching shoulder. Something inside her had gone very still at his attack; that stillness was reflected on her face. "Which one?" she finally asked quietly. "Tod Ellis...or you?"

She turned and walked away from him, going into the bathroom and closing the door; it was the one place in the house where he wouldn't follow. She sat down on the rim of the tub, shaking; she had wondered occasionally what it would be like if he slipped the tight rein of his control, but she hadn't wanted to find out like that. She had wanted him to lose control when he kissed her, touched her. Wanted him to shake with need and desire and bury his face against her. She hadn't wanted him to lose control in anger, hadn't wanted to hear what he really thought of her efforts to help. She had been terrified all along of doing something wrong that might jeopardize him; she had agonized over every decision, and he had dismissed her from the start as a bumbling amateur. She knew she didn't have his knowledge or expertise, but she had done the best she could.

It was doubly painful after the way he had kissed her and touched her, but now she remembered that even then he had retained his steely control. It had been she who trembled and yearned, not him. He hadn't even lied to her; he'd told her plainly that it was nothing more to him than casual sex.

Taking a deep breath, Rachel gathered herself together. Since she was in the bathroom she might as well shower now; that would give her straight, heavy hair time to dry naturally and she wouldn't have to do anything to it except give it lift and curve with the curling iron. She might be going out with Tod Ellis with all the enthusiasm of attending an execution, but she wouldn't let him think that she looked on it as anything other than a real date, and that meant taking pains with her appearance.

She stripped off and got in the shower, briskly shampooing her hair and bathing, not allowing herself the luxury of brooding. Self-pity wouldn't accomplish anything except wasting time, time that would be better spent considering how to conduct herself that night, how to be friendly without being encouraging. The last thing she wanted was for Ellis to ask her out again! If he did, she'd have to make up some excuse. She'd told Agent Lowell she was making a trip to the Keys; it had been pure fabrication, but perhaps she could use the lie as an excuse for packing, planning and so on.

She turned off the water and dragged a towel off the top of the shower door, then wrapped it around her head. Just as she started to slide the door open and step out of the tub she caught sight of Kell's blurred image through the frosted door, and she jerked her hand back from the door as if it had burned her.

"Get out of here," she breathed sharply, snatching the towel off her head and wrapping it around her body, instead. The frosted surface of the doors gave her some protection, but if she could see him, he could see just as much of her. Knowing that he had watched her bathe made her feel terribly vulnerable. How long had he been there?

She saw his hand reaching out, and she moved back against the shower wall as he slid the door open on its track. "You didn't answer when I called you," he said curtly. "I wanted to make certain you were okay."

Rachel lifted her chin. "That's not much of an excuse.

As soon as you saw I was taking a shower, you should have left.''

His eyes raked over her, from her wet, tangled hair to her glistening shoulders and down to her slim, bare legs, which had rivulets of water running down them. The towel covered her from breast to thigh, but it would take only a tug to bare her completely, and his black, searching eyes had a way of making her feel even more exposed than she was.

"I'm sorry," he said abruptly, finally lifting his gaze to her face. "I didn't intend to imply that you haven't been a help."

"You didn't imply any such thing," Rachel returned, her voice sharp. "You came right out and said it." She felt both insulted and hurt, and she wasn't in the mood to forgive him. After what he had said, he had a lot of nerve to stand there eyeing her the way he was doing!

Suddenly he moved, hooking his right arm around her waist and lifting her out of the tub. Rachel gasped, clutching at him for balance. "Watch out! Your shoulder—"

He stood her on the fuzzy bath mat, his face hard and unreadable as he looked down at her, his right arm still locked around her waist. "I don't want you going out with him," he finally rasped. "Damn it, Rachel, I don't want you taking any risks on my account!"

The towel was slipping, and Rachel grabbed for the ends to anchor it more securely. "Why can't you give me any credit for being an adult, able to accept responsibility for my own actions?" she cried. "You told me Tod Ellis is a traitor, and I believe you. Don't you think I have a moral responsibility to do what I can to stop him and to help you? I think the situation is critical enough to warrant the risk! It's my decision, not yours."

"You never should have been involved."

"Why not? You said yourself that you'll have to have help. You've sent other people into dangerous situations, haven't you?"

"They were trained agents," he snapped, goaded. "And, damn it to hell, I never lay awake at night burning to make love to any of them."

She fell silent, her eyes wide as they searched his. His expression gave away nothing but anger and a faintly startled look, as if he hadn't meant to say that. The arm around her waist had her arched against him, though she had wedged her arm between their bodies in an effort to hold the towel. Only her toes touched the mat. Her thighs were inside his slightly spread legs, his growing hardness nestled against the soft mound at the top of her thighs.

They said nothing, both of them very aware of what was happening. Their chests expanded and fell rapidly as their breathing quickened, and Rachel's knees grew weak as she felt him grow stronger and bolder.

"I'd kill him before I let him touch you," he muttered, the words wrenched from him.

She shuddered at the thought. "*I* wouldn't let him. Never." Staring up at him, she shuddered again, as if she'd been struck between the eyes. Tod Ellis had made her realize anew how much danger stalked Kell's heels. She wasn't guaranteed three weeks with him; she wasn't guaranteed tomorrow, or even tonight. For men such as Kell Sabin there was no tomorrow, only the present; it was the brutal truth that he could be killed, that tragedy and terror could strike without warning. She had already learned that lesson once; how could she have been so stupid as to forget? She had wanted things to be perfect, wanted him to feel as she felt, but life was never perfect. It had to be taken as it was, or it passed by without a second glance. All she had with Kell was right now, the eternal present, because the past is always gone and the future never comes.

His hands were flexing on her flesh, his fingers kneading her as if he were barely able to restrain himself from doing more. His face was rock hard as he stared down at her, his voice raw when he spoke. "I let you back away in the kitchen. By God, I don't think I can do it again. Not now."

Rachel's breath left her lungs at the look in his midnight eyes, the hard, almost cruel look of savage arousal. The skin was pulled tight over his high, prominent cheekbones, and his jaw and mouth were set. Her heart gave a sudden leap as she realized that he meant exactly what he'd said, and fear and excitement rushed through her veins in a dizzying mixture. Control was impossible for him now, and the primitive force of his hunger was burning in his eyes.

Her hands trembled on his chest as her entire body began quivering in reaction to the fiercely male intent that was plain on his face, the look of a predator who had scented female. Heat. Heat was rising in her body, melting her insides, turning them liquid. His hand at her back clenched the towel and pulled it free from the tuck at her bosom. It dropped to the floor in a damp heap. Naked, Rachel stood in his grasp, shaking and yearning and gasping for breath that wouldn't seem to go deep enough.

He looked down at her, and a low rumbling sound started in his chest, working up to the back of his throat. Rachel's thighs turned to water, and she swayed, her throat tight, her heart pounding. Slowly he lifted his hand and touched her breasts, high and round, soft, with small, tight brown nipples, filling his palm with her to discover anew the warm, velvety texture of her flesh. Then, just as slowly, his hand drifted downward, smoothing over the sleek delta of her stomach and the slope of her lower abdomen, his fingers at last sliding into the dark curls of her womanhood. She hung there, shaking wildly and unable to move, paralyzed by the hot river of pleasure that followed his questing touch. One finger made a bolder foray. Her body jerked wildly, and she whimpered as he touched and teased and explored.

His gaze lifted from the gut-wrenching contrast of his hard, sinewy hand cupping the soft, exquisitely female mound and drifted back up to her pretty breasts, then to her face. Her eyes were half closed, glazed with desire; her lips were moist and parted, her breath rushing in and out in gasps. She was a woman on the verge of complete satisfaction, and her look of sweet carnality exploded the slim hold he still had on himself. With a wild, deep sound he bent and hoisted her over his right shoulder, the blood pounding so wildly in his ears that he didn't hear her startled cry.

He made it to the bed in five long steps and dropped her across it, following her down, spreading her thighs and kneeling between them before she had recovered. Rachel reached for him, almost sobbing with need. He tore off his shirt and tossed it to the floor, then jerked at his pants until they were open, and he lowered himself onto her.

Her body arched in shock as he thrust into her, and she cried out at both the moment of pinching discomfort and the jolt to her senses and flesh as he filled her. He was... oh...

"Take it all," he groaned, demanded, pleaded. He hung over her, his face shiny with sweat, his expression at once tortured and ecstatic. "All of me. Please." His voice was hoarse with need. "Let yourself relax—yes. Like that. *More*. Please. Rachel. Rachel! You're mine you're mine you're mine...."

The rawly primitive chant washed over her, and she cried out again as he moved in and out of her, powerfully, their bodies writhing together. It had never been like this for her, so painfully intense that it was unbearable. She had never loved like this, knowing that the breath would still in her lungs and her heart stop beating in her chest if anything ever happened to him. If this was all he wanted of her, then she would give herself to him freely and fervently, branding him with the sweet burning of her own passion.

He rolled his hips against her with a heavy surge, and it was abruptly too much for her to bear, making her senses crest and shatter. She gasped and cried out, writhing beneath him in a shimmer of pure heat that went on and on until it caught him, too. She couldn't see, couldn't breathe, could only feel. She felt the heavy pounding of his thrusts as he drove himself into her, then the convulsive heaving of his body in her arms. His hoarse wild cries filled her ears, then became rough moans. Slowly he stilled, became silent. His body relaxed, and his heavy weight bore down on her, but she cradled him gladly, her hands still clutching his back.

Concern began to nudge her as sanity returned, bringing remembrance of the way he had lifted her onto his shoulder and the unrestrained wildness of his lovemaking. His head lay on her shoulder, and she twined her fingers into his coal-black hair, managing only a husky murmur as she said, "Kell? Your shoulder...are you okay?"

He levered himself onto his right elbow and looked down at her. Her clear gray eyes were dark with concern—for him, after he'd taken her with all the care and finesse of a bull in rut! There were her soft, trembling lips, but he hadn't kissed them, nor had he caressed her pretty breasts and sucked them as he'd done in his dreams. Love was in those eyes, love so pure and shining that it knotted his insides with pain and shattered a wall somewhere deep in his mind and soul, leaving him vulnerable in a way he'd never been before.

Now he knew what hell was. Hell was seeing heaven, bright and tender, but being on the outside of the gates, unable to enter them without risking the destruction of what you most treasured.

Chapter Nine

"Just who is this woman Ellis has gone so mad over?" Charles asked calmly, his pale-blue eyes never wavering as he watched Lowell. As always, Charles's manner was detached, but Lowell knew that he missed nothing.

"She lives in a little house close to the beach. Deserted area, nothing around for miles. We questioned her when we first started looking for Sabin."

"And?" The voice was almost gentle.

Lowell shrugged. "And nothing. She hadn't seen anything."

"She must be out of the ordinary to capture Ellis's attention."

After considering it a minute Lowell shook his head. "She's good-looking, but that's all. Nothing fancy. No makeup. Outdoorsy type. But Ellis hasn't stopped talking about her."

"It seems our friend Ellis doesn't have his mind completely on the job at hand." The comment was deceptively casual.

Again Lowell shrugged. "He thinks Sabin died when the boat blew up, so he's not putting a lot of effort into hunting him."

"What do *you* think?"

"It's a possibility. We haven't found any trace of him. He was wounded. Even if by a miracle he'd made it to shore, he'd have needed help."

Charles nodded, his eyes thoughtful as he waved Lowell away. He had worked with Lowell for many years now and knew him as a steady and competent, if uninspired, agent. He had to be competent to have survived. Lowell was no more convinced of Sabin's survival than Ellis was, and Charles wondered if he had allowed Sabin's reputation to override his own common sense. Common sense would certainly seem to indicate that Sabin had died in the explosion or immediately thereafter, drowning in the warm turquoise waters to become food for the denizens of the sea. No one should have survived that, but Sabin...Sabin was one of a kind, except for that blond devil with the golden eyes, who had disappeared and was rumored to be dead, despite the disquieting talk that had floated out of Costa Rica the year before. Sabin was more shadow than substance, instinctively cunning and damnably lucky. No, not lucky, Charles corrected himself. Skilled. To call Sabin "lucky" was to underestimate him, a fatal mistake too many of his colleagues had made.

"Noelle, come here," he called, barely raising his voice, but he didn't need to. Noelle was never far from him. It gave him pleasure to look at her, not because she was extraordinarily beautiful, though she was, but because he enjoyed the incongruity of such lethal skill housed in such a lovely woman. Her job was twofold: to protect Charles and to kill Sabin.

Noelle came into the room, walking with the grace of a model, her eyes sleepy and soft. "Yes?"

He waved his thin, elegant hand to indicate a chair. "Sit, please. I have been discussing Sabin with Lowell."

She sat, crossing her legs to best display them. The gestures that attracted unsuspecting males came naturally to her; she had studied and practiced too long for them to be anything else by now. She smiled. "Ah, Agent Lowell. Sturdy, dependable, if a little shortsighted."

"Like Ellis, he seems to think we're wasting our time in searching for Sabin."

She lit a cigarette and inhaled deeply, then blew smoke through her shapely lips. "It doesn't matter what they think, does it? Only what you think."

"I wonder if I *am* bestowing superhuman powers on Sabin, if I'm so wary of him that I can't accept his death," Charles mused.

Her sleepy eyes blinked. "Until we have proof of his death we can't afford to assume otherwise. It's been eight days. If hc somehow survived, he would now be recovered enough to start moving around, which should increase our chances of finding him. The most logical thing would be to intensify our search, rather than slacken it."

Yes, that was indeed logical; on the other hand, if Sabin had survived the explosion and somehow made it to shore, something that seemed impossible, why hadn't he contacted his headquarters for aid? Ellis's contact in Washington was completely certain that Sabin hadn't attempted to get in touch with anyone. That simple fact had convinced almost everyone that Sabin was dead...yet Charles couldn't convince himself. It was sheer instinct that prompted him to keep his men searching, waiting, poised to strike. He could not believe that it had been so easy to kill Sabin, not after all these years when attempt after attempt had failed. It was impossible to have too much respect for his capabilities. Sabin was out there, somewhere. Charles could feel it.

He was abruptly brisk. "You're right, of course," he told Noelle. "We will intensify the search, re-cover every inch of ground. Somehow, somewhere, we have missed him."

Sabin prowled the house, his savage mood reflected on his face. He'd done some hard things in his life, but none of them had been as difficult as having to watch Rachel get ready to go out with Tod Ellis. It went against every instinct he had, but nothing he'd said could change her mind, and he was helpless, handcuffed by circumstance. He couldn't afford to do anything that would focus attention on her; it would merely increase the danger she was in. If he'd been ready to move he would have gone that night rather than expose her to Ellis, but again he was stymied. He wasn't ready to move, and to move before he was prepared could mean the difference between success and failure, with his country's security at stake. He'd been trained for half his lifetime to put his country first, even at the cost of his own life. Sabin could have sacrificed himself without hesitation or even regret if it had been necessary, but the simple, terrible truth was that he couldn't sacrifice Rachel.

He had to do whatever he could to keep her safe, even if it meant swallowing his pride and possessive instincts. She was safe enough with Ellis as long as he had no reason to suspect her of anything. To jerk her out of the house and take her away before Ellis arrived to pick her up, as Kell had badly wanted to do, *would* arouse the man's suspicions. Kell knew the agent, knew that he was damned good at his job…too good, or he'd never have been able to hide his other activities for so long. He also had a good-sized ego; if Rachel stood him up it would make him furious, and he wouldn't let it pass. He would be back.

Patience, the ability to wait even in the face of great urgency, was one of Sabin's greatest gifts. He knew how to wait, how to pick his moment for optimum success, how to ignore danger and concentrate solely on timing. He could literally disappear into his surroundings, waiting, so much a part of the earth that the wild creatures had ignored him and the Vietcong had at times passed within touching distance of him without ever seeing him. His ability to wait was enhanced by his instinctive knowledge of when patience was useless; then he exploded into action. He explained it to himself as a well-developed sense of timing. Yes, he knew how to wait…but waiting for Rachel to come home was driving him crazy. He wanted her back safe in his arms, in bed. Damn, how he wanted her in bed!

He didn't turn on any lights in the house; he didn't think it likely that the house was being watched, but he couldn't take the chance. Rachel and Ellis might return early, and a lit house could trigger Ellis's suspicions. Instead he moved silently through the darkness, unable to sit still despite the ache in his shoulder and leg. His shoulder had been giving him hell since the afternoon, and he absently massaged it. A humorless smile quirked his lips. He hadn't felt a thing while he'd been making love to Rachel; his senses had been centered completely on her and the unbearable ecstasy of their bodies linked together. But since then the shoulder had been painfully reminding him that he was a long way from being healed; he'd been lucky he hadn't torn it open again.

Abruptly he swore and limped through the kitchen to the back door, so agitated that he couldn't remain inside the confines of the house any longer. As soon as Kell opened the back door he sensed Joe leaving his stakeout under the oleander bush, silently moving through the shadows, and he softly called to the dog in reassurance. Kell no longer feared being attacked; Joe had warily accepted his residency, but Kell didn't trust him enough to refrain from identifying himself before going down the back steps.

Automatically keeping himself in the shadows, Kell circled the house and investigated the pines, assuring himself that the house wasn't under surveillance. Joe padded along about ten feet behind him, stopping when Kell stopped and advancing when Kell moved on.

A new moon was just rising, a thin sickle of light on the horizon. Sabin looked up at the clear sky, so clear, like Rachel's eyes, that infinity seemed within his reach.

His heart twisted again, and his hand clenched into a fist. He whispered a curse into the night. She was too gallant, too strong, for her own good; why couldn't she play it safe and let him take all the risks? Didn't she know what it would do to him if anything happened to her?

No, how could she know? He'd never told her, and he never would, not at the expense of her safety. He'd protect her if it killed him. His mouth twisted wryly; it probably *would* kill him, not physically, but deep inside where he'd never let anyone touch him...until Rachel had slipped past all his defenses and seared herself into his mind and soul.

Of course, there was always the possibility that he wouldn't get out of this alive, anyway, but he didn't dwell on that. He had thought a lot in the past few days, considering and discarding options. His plans were made. Now he was waiting: waiting for his wounds to heal more completely; waiting until he was physically ready; waiting for Ellis and his pals to make some little mistake; waiting until he sensed the time was right...waiting. When the time came he would call Sullivan, and the plan would be put into action. He would rather have Sullivan with him than any ten other men. No one would ever be expecting the two of them to be working together again.

No, his only uncertainty was because of Rachel. He knew what he had to do to protect her, but for the first time in his life he dreaded it. Letting her go was one thing; living without her was another.

He stood there in the night and cursed whatever it was that made him different from other men: the extraordinary skill and cunning, the acute eyesight and athletic body, the extreme coordination between mind and muscle that, all combined, made him a hunter and a warrior. When his emotional aloofness was added to that it had made him a natural for the job he held, the perfect, emotionless soldier in the cold gray shadows. He couldn't remember ever being any different. He hadn't been a noisy, laughing child; he'd been silent and solitary, holding himself aloof even from his parents. He'd always been alone deep inside himself and had never wanted it any other way; perhaps he'd known, even as a child, how much it would hurt to love.

There. He'd let the words form in his thoughts, and even that was so painful that he flinched. He was too intense ever to love casually, lightly, to play the game of romance over and over. His emotional distance had been a defense, but Rachel had shattered it, and it hurt. God, how it hurt.

Rachel sat across from Tod Ellis, smiling and chatting and forcing herself to eat her seafood as if she enjoyed it, but it chilled her every time he gave her that toothpaste-ad smile. She knew what that smile concealed. She knew that he had tried to kill Kell; he was a liar, a murderer and a traitor. It took all her strength to continue acting as if she were having a pleasant time, but nothing could keep her thoughts from slipping back to Kell.

She had wanted nothing more than to continue lying in his arms that afternoon, her body limp and throbbing from his rough, fast, but intensely satisfying possession. She had forgotten what it was like…or perhaps it had never been like that before. Being married to B.B. had been warm and fun and loving. Being Sabin's woman would be like burning alive every time he touched her, going soft, hot and moist at his glance, his lightest touch. He wasn't easygoing and cheerful. He was a hard, intense man, the force of his personality radiating from him. He wasn't playful; she'd never heard him laugh, or even seen his rare smiles reach his eyes. But he had reached for her with such desperate, driving need that everything in her had responded immediately, and she had been ready for him, wanting him.

No, Kell wasn't a comfortable man to be around, or an easy man to love, but she didn't waste time railing against fate. She loved him, and accepted him for what he was. She looked at Tod Ellis and her eyes narrowed a little, because Kell was a lion surrounded by jackals, and this man was one of the jackals.

She put down her fork and gave him a bright smile. "How much longer will you be around here, do you think? Or are you permanently assigned to this area?"

"No, I move around a lot," he said, responding to her direct attention by flashing his smile once again. "I never know when I'll be reassigned."

"Is this sort of a special assignment?"

"It's more of a wild-goose chase. We've been wasting our time. Still, if we hadn't been searching the beach I never would have met you."

He'd been throwing out lines like that since he'd picked her up, and Rachel had been determinedly skirting them. He evidently thought he was a modern day Don Juan, and probably a lot of women found him attractive and charming, but, then, they didn't know what Rachel did about him.

"Oh, I'm certain you aren't hurting for casual dates," she said in an offhand manner.

He reached across the table and put his hand on hers. "Maybe I don't consider this a casual date."

Rachel smiled and removed her hand to pick up her wineglass. "I don't see how you could consider it anything else, considering you may be reassigned at any time. Even if you aren't, I'll be leaving on vacation soon and probably won't be back for the rest of the summer.''

He didn't like that; it put a small dent in his ego that she wasn't willing to hang around for as long as he was there. ''Where are you going?''

''The Keys. I'm going to stay with a friend and do some research in the area. I was planning to stay there until I have to come back to teach a night course in Gainesville when the fall quarter starts.''

Anyone else would have asked her about the course she was teaching; Ellis scowled at her and said, ''Is your friend male or female?''

Just for a moment she entertained the appealing idea of telling him to take a long walk off a short pier, but it wasn't her plan to antagonize him, not yet. She still wanted to get some information out of him if she could. So instead she gave him a cool look that told him he'd gone too far and said calmly, ''A woman, an old college friend.''

He wasn't stupid. Arrogant and conceited, but not stupid. He grimaced in a way that was meant to be charming, but left her cold. ''Sorry. I overstepped myself, didn't I? It's just that—well, from the moment I saw you, I was really attracted, and I want to get to know you better.''

''There doesn't seem to be much point in it,'' Rachel pointed out. ''You would be leaving soon, anyway, even if I hadn't planned my vacation.''

He looked as if he'd like to refute that, but he'd told her himself that he moved around a lot. ''We may be around for another couple of weeks,'' he said sulkily.

''Tying up loose ends?''

''Yeah, you know how it is. Paperwork.''

''Is it just you and Agent Lowell?''

He hesitated, habit too deeply ingrained in him to make it easy for him to talk in any detail about his work. Rachel held her breath, wondering if his ego would prompt him to try to make up for the ground he had lost by being too personal. After all, it was inherently flattering when someone asked about your work. It was a way of getting better acquainted, of asking innocent questions that still denoted interest. She was interested, all right, but not in Ellis.

"There are nine of us actively investigating," he finally said. "We were all chosen especially for this job."

Because they were unscrupulous? She gave him a wide-eyed, ego-stroking look. "It must be really big to have that many men working on it."

"As I said, we're the active investigators. We can call on about twenty other men for backup if necessary."

She looked suitably impressed. "But you think it's a dead end?"

"We haven't turned up anything, but the top man isn't satisfied yet. You know how it is. People behind a desk think they know more than the men in the field."

She sympathized with him and even made up a few tales to reciprocate, edging the conversation away from his work. If she probed too directly and too often it could rouse his suspicions. Talking to him made her feel unclean and anxious to get away from him, as far away as she could. The knowledge that he would try to kiss her, probably even try to talk her into bed, filled her with sick horror. There was no way she could tolerate his mouth on hers even for a moment. Even if he wasn't a total snake, which he was, she couldn't have kissed him; she was Kell Sabin's woman, a fact that had nothing to do with will or determination. It simply *was*.

She forced herself to chat for another hour, smiling at the appropriate moments and forcing down the increasing urge to gag. He was almost more than she could tolerate. Only the thought that Kell could use any information she got out of Ellis gave her the will to stay. When their dishes had finally been cleared away and they were taking their time over coffee, she put out another feeler. "Where are you staying? This isn't a tourist area, and motel rooms can be hard to find."

"We're actually spread out down the coast," he explained. "Lowell and I are sharing a room at this dinky little motel, Harran's."

"I know where it is," she said, nodding.

"We've been living off fast food since we got here. It's a relief to get a decent meal for a change."

"I imagine so." She pushed her coffee cup back and looked around the restaurant, hoping he'd get the message that she was ready to go. The sketchy details she'd gotten would have to be enough; she simply couldn't sit there with him any longer and pretend that she liked him. She wanted to go home and lock the door behind her, closing Tod Ellis and his cohorts out of her life. Kell was there, waiting for her, and she wanted to be with him, even though she was uneasy about his mood. He had been coldly silent when she left, his rage barely controlled. He had wanted her to play it safe and let all the risk fall on him, but Rachel could quit breathing more easily than she could stand by without doing anything while he was in danger. He wasn't used to his commands being ignored, and he didn't like it one little bit.

For his own reasons Ellis wasn't loath to leave a little early. Rachel imagined that he thought the remainder of the evening would be spent in a more physical manner. He would be disappointed.

She didn't talk much on the way home, both reluctant to have any more to do with Ellis than necessary and because her thoughts were increasingly taken with Kell, though he'd never been far from her mind all evening. Her heartbeat suddenly lurched and her blood skittered through her veins, making her feel flushed and dizzy. The fierce lovemaking they'd shared that afternoon should have clarified their relationship, even if only on that basic level, but it hadn't. Kell had looked at her so oddly afterward, as if she wasn't what he'd expected. Despite his anger with her when she refused to do what he told her, on some deep level he had seemed even more self-contained than ever. He was a difficult, unusual man, but she was so acutely sensitive to him that every faint nuance of his expression, which most people wouldn't notice at all, seemed to shout at her. Why had he looked at her like that, then withdrawn? Why did she feel farther from him now than she had before they had lain locked together in writhing heat?

Ellis turned onto the private road that ended at her house and a few minutes later pulled the car to a stop in front. The house was dark, but she hadn't really expected it to be any other way. Kell wouldn't advertise his presence by turning on lights.

They got out of the car, and as Ellis came around to her side they heard that low snarl. Joe, bless him, didn't miss anything.

Ellis visibly jerked, the sudden alarm starkly etched on his face in the ghastly light from the car's open door. He stopped in his tracks. "Where is he?" he muttered.

Rachel looked around but couldn't see the dog. He was black and tan, with the classic markings of a German shepherd, so his darkness made it difficult to see him. The snarls placed him slightly to her left, close to Ellis, but she still couldn't make him out.

Quickly she seized the opportunity. "Look, you stand still while I walk into the yard. He's behind you, so don't move any closer to him. When I'm out of the way, get in the car on this side and he probably won't bother you."

"That dog's vicious. You should have him chained," Ellis snapped, but he didn't argue with her instructions. He stood absolutely still while Rachel walked up into the yard, then sidled toward the open door on the passenger side of the car.

"I'm sorry," she apologized, hoping he couldn't hear the insincerity in her voice. "I didn't think. Still, he's good protection. He's never yet let a stranger walk into the yard."

Joe moved then, the movement betraying his position. Snarling steadily, he planted himself between Rachel and Ellis.

She wanted to laugh. There was no chance of even a good night kiss now, and from the look on Ellis's face he wanted nothing more than to be inside the car, with solid steel between him and the dog. Hastily he slid inside and slammed the door, then rolled the window down partway.

"I'll call you, okay?"

She made herself hesitate, rather than shouting out the "No!" she wanted to voice. "I'll be busy getting ready for my vacation. I have some work I have to finish before I leave. I really won't have much free time."

Now that he was safe from the dog his cockiness was returning. "You have to eat, don't you? I'll call you for lunch or something."

She planned on being busy, but she could handle him over the telephone. She didn't want him showing up here unannounced, but that wasn't likely as long as Joe was in residence.

She stood in the yard, watching the taillights as he drove off, then said, "Good boy," to Joe with obvious approval in her voice. Turning toward the house, she wondered why Kell didn't turn on a light for her now that Ellis was out of sight. She started to walk up to the porch but hadn't taken a full step, when a hard arm passed around her waist and jerked her backward.

"Have fun?" a low, angry voice whispered in her ear.

"Kell." She relaxed against him, pleasure flooding warmly through her at even this touch, despite his anger.

"Did he touch you? Kiss you?"

She had expected questioning, but not primarily about that. Kell's voice was rough, almost savage.

"You know he didn't," she replied steadily. "After all, you were out here watching."

"What about before?"

"No. Not at all. I couldn't stand the thought."

A great shudder passed through his body, an extraordinary response in a man as controlled as he normally was, but when he spoke his voice was level again. "Let's go inside."

He locked up while she went into the bedroom to put away her purse and slip out of her shoes; then he joined her in the bedroom. His black eyes were expressionless as he watched her slip the earrings out of her pierced lobes and put the jewelry away in a velvet-lined box. He'd been right; she slipped into stylish sophistication as easily as she puttered barefoot in the garden, and she was gut-wrenchingly sexy in either case.

His silent, unwavering stare was making her uneasy. "I did get some information," she finally offered, taking a nightgown from the dresser and darting a quick look at him. He looked...furious, somehow, though his face was rock hard and his eyes expressionless. His arms were folded across his bare chest; he wore only his jeans and running shoes, and he looked formidable.

He didn't ask, but she condensed it for him, anyway. "There are nine of them actively searching for you, but Ellis let it slip that they have a backup of about twenty more if needed. They're scattered, looking up and down the coast. Ellis and Lowell are staying at Harran's Motel. He thinks you're dead and that they're wasting his time, but the head man on the operation won't give up.''

That would be the mysterious "Charles." Sabin had known who had to be behind things from the moment he had recognized the red-haired woman, Noelle, on the boat. He had known it would be only a matter of time until they locked horns again. Charles was the head of an international terrorist organization that had been growing bolder and more challenging, while at the same time Charles himself had kept at a safe distance, protected by a web of technicalities and politics. Now he had come out into the open, to get Sabin. But he'd made one big mistake: his first attempt hadn't succeeded, and now Sabin knew that his own organization had been infiltrated. Charles couldn't afford to stop the search until Sabin was found, dead or alive.

When Kell didn't ask any questions Rachel shrugged and went into the bathroom to take off her makeup and change into her nightgown. His silence was unnerving; he probably used it as a weapon, to shake people off-balance and put them on the defensive. Well, she wasn't one of his minions; she was a woman who loved him.

Five minutes later she left the bathroom, her clothing draped over her arm. Sabin was sitting on the side of the bed, taking off his shoes. He kept his eyes on her while she hung her things in the closet, not looking away even when he stood to unzip his jeans.

"The nightgown is a waste of time," he drawled. "You might as well pull it off and put it back in that drawer."

Startled, Rachel looked around at him. He was standing by the bed, his hands on the fly of his jeans, and he was watching her with the concentrated attention with which a cat watches a mouse. The air around her suddenly sizzled with tension, and her throat went dry, forcing her to swallow. Slowly he slid down the zipper on his jeans, the denim spreading open in a vee to reveal bronzed skin and the vertical line of downy hair that arrowed down his lower abdomen into the thicker growth of hair just visible in his opened pants. The thick bulge beneath the denim clearly demonstrated his intention.

Her body leaped into immediate response, her heart beating faster and her breath racing in and out of her lungs. It had been like that from the beginning, and she had no more control over it now than she'd had then. He wanted her; that was more than obvious. But he didn't *want* to want her, and the knowledge hurt.

She swallowed again, pushing the closet door shut and leaning against it. "It's silly," she said, trying for a wry tone but failing miserably. Her voice was taut and shaking. "After this afternoon you'd think I'd be more comfortable about going to bed with you, but I'm not. I don't know what...what we have, if anything. I thought it would be clearer, but it isn't. What do you want from me?" She made a brief, dismissive gesture. "Other than sex."

Silently Kell swore. He was so good at holding people away from him that now, when he desperately wanted Rachel as close as he could get her for what time they had left, she still thought he was pushing her away. They had so little time together that the thought of not grabbing for every moment with her was unbearable, and he didn't know how to make her see that. Perhaps it was better if she didn't see it; perhaps it would be easier for her if she never knew how tempted he was to forget all his rules and priorities. But he had to have her, had to stockpile memories against the empty days in the future when she wouldn't be there. Even now she wasn't playing games, wasn't trying to hide behind lies to protect her pride. She was so honest that she deserved at least a fraction of the same honesty from him, no matter how it hurt. But the pain wasn't only hers.

He looked at her and said, "Everything. That's what I want. But I can't have it."

She quivered, and tears welled in her eyes. "You know you can have anything you want. All you have to do is reach out and take it."

Slowly he walked up to her and put his hand on her shoulder, sliding his fingers under the strap of her nightgown and stroking his rough fingertips over her warm, satiny skin. "At the risk of your life?" he asked in a low voice. "No. I couldn't live with that."

"You make it sound like a concrete fact that anyone close to you is a target. Other agents—"

"Other agents aren't me," he interrupted quietly, his black eyes level on hers. "There are several renegade governments and terrorist groups that have a bounty on my head. Do you think I'd ask any woman to share that sort of life with me?"

She managed to smile through her tears. "Don't try to tell me you live like a monk. I know there have been women—"

"No one close. No one special. No one who could be used or threatened in an attempt to get at me. I've tried it, honey. I was married, years ago before it got as bad as it is now. She was wounded in an attempt on my life. Being a smart woman, she got the hell away from me as fast as she could."

Not so smart, Rachel thought. She knew that she never would have let that drive her away from him. Her throat was so tight that she was almost choking on her words as she stared up at him, the tears finally overflowing and rolling down her cheeks. "It would be worth it, to be with you," she whispered. "I'd take the chance."

"No," he said, shaking his head. "I won't let you. *I* won't take the chance, not with your life." With one thumb he rubbed away the tears tracking her face.

"Isn't that my decision to make?"

He moved both his hands up to cup her face, sliding his fingers into her thick straight hair and tilting her face closer to his. "Not when you don't have any real idea of the danger involved. You pulled a little stint as an investigative reporter, and you notice more than is good for you, but you're as innocent as a baby when it comes to knowing what my work is really like. There *are* agents who live fairly normal lives, but I'm not one of them. I'm one of a very small minority. My existence isn't even admitted publicly."

She had gone pale, her face very still. "I know more about the risks involved than you think."

"No. You know the movie versions, the cleaned up, romanticized, glamorized crap."

Rachel suddenly jerked her head away from his touch, her hands clenched into fists. "You think so?" she rasped, her voice rough with pain. "My husband was killed by a car bomb meant for me. There was nothing cleaned up, romanticized, or glamorous about that. He died in my place! Ask me what I know about someone else paying the price for a risk I chose to take!" Tears began falling again, and she dashed them away, glaring fiercely at him. "Damn you, Kell Sabin! Do you think I *want* to love you? But at least I'm willing to take the chance, rather than run away from it the way you do!"

Chapter Ten

She was crying, and it was like taking a punch in the gut to watch her. Rachel simply wasn't a weepy person, and she was trying hard not to cry, but the tears kept rolling down her face as she faced him, and she kept angrily dashing them away. Slowly Kell reached out and brushed her hair away from her damp face, then eased her into his arms and pressed her head against his uninjured shoulder. "Whatever happens, I can't risk you," he said in a low, tortured voice.

Hearing the finality in his voice, she knew that there was no convincing him otherwise. He would go, and when he did it would be forever. Desperately she clung to him, inhaling deeply to draw the scent of him into her body, her hands trying to memorize the way it felt to touch him. All she had was this.

He tilted her chin up and bent his head then slanted his mouth over hers, the pressure hard and hungry, even a little angry, because they had so little time when forever wouldn't suffice. She sighed and opened her mouth to his probing tongue, her fingers flexing on his muscular back, and as always there was that strong, immediate response to him that tightened her breasts and sent twinges of pleasure through her loins. He sensed it, cupping her bottom in his rough hands and lifting her into grinding contact with his own throbbing flesh while his mouth continued to take hers.

He wanted to wipe out the pain he'd seen in her eyes;

he wanted to savor her, take his time with her, as he'd been unable to do that afternoon. Sabin couldn't remember ever before losing control like that, not even when he'd been a young boy on the prowl, driven by a rapacious sexuality. But with Rachel his responses were so extreme that he'd exploded only moments after entering her; she had reached her peak, too, but he knew that he'd rushed her, hurt her with his too-powerful penetration. She was so tight that accommodating him hadn't been easy for her. He wasn't going to let it be that way again; he was going to take his time with her, until she was truly ready for him and trembling on the brink.

She was trembling in his arms, the salty taste of her tears on his tongue. Silently he led her to the bed, leaving the light on because he wanted to see every nuance of her expression while he made love to her. He paused to push his jeans off, and Rachel watched him, her hands automatically lifting to her nightgown.

Quickly he stayed them. "No, leave your gown on for now." Perhaps it would be easier for him if he couldn't see her stretched out naked and waiting for him. He was caught in his own delicious dilemma, wanting to watch her as he made love to her, as he made her ready to receive him, yet knowing that the sight of her naked body would push him closer to the edge than he wanted to be right now. Just thinking about her was torture enough. His loins were heavy and throbbing, his all-too-accurate memory reminding him just how it had felt to be sheathed inside her.

"Why?" Rachel asked huskily when they were lying on the bed and he was leaning over her with an expression on his face that would have frightened her if she hadn't trusted him completely.

He smoothed his hand over her breasts, the motion deliberately slow as the thin cotton slid across her nipples, bringing them to tingling prominence. "Why the gown?" he clarified.

It was hard to talk when her breath kept catching. "Yes."

"Because I'm inciting myself to riot."

No, it was she who was being incited, tantalized. Everywhere his lightly trailing fingers went they left behind a delicious tingle as her aroused nerve endings pleaded for more. Sometimes he merely brushed her with his fingertips, while at others he stroked her with the flat of his palm, the contact almost hard. And he kissed her: her mouth, her ears, the line of her jaw, the arch of her throat, the exquisitely tender hollow above her collarbones. Finally her breasts knew the warm, moist pressure of his mouth and the probing of his tongue. It was all the more maddening because he didn't remove her gown; even when his mouth closed hotly on her extended nipple and sucked at it with a strength that made her cry out, it was with the thin barrier of cotton between his mouth and her flesh. In frustration she tried to unbutton the two buttons that closed the top of the gown, to give him access to her bareness, but he stopped her and captured her hands, pinning them to the pillow above her head and anchoring them there with his strong right hand.

"Kell!" she protested, writhing to escape, but he was incredibly strong, despite his half-healed wounds, and she couldn't wrest herself free. "You've got a cruel streak in you!"

"No," he murmured against her breast, licking her nipple through the wet fabric. "I only want to make you feel good. Don't you like this?"

There was no way she could deny it; he could easily read the signs of arousal in her body. "Yes," she admitted, panting. "But I want to touch you, too. Let me—"

"Umm, not yet. You make me feel too much like a teenager, ready to go off like a Fourth of July rocket. I'm going to make it good for you this time."

"It was good before," she said, and moaned as his left hand trailed down to the juncture of her thighs, rubbing delicately. Rachel's breath caught, and her hips lifted blindly to his hand.

"I was too rough, too fast. I hurt you."

She couldn't deny it, but the discomfort hadn't been unexpected, and pleasure had swiftly followed. She started to tell him that, but the words were strangled in her throat. The gown had been pushed between her legs by his exploring hand, stretched tightly across her femininity. With one finger he probed the soft cleft, found and stroked her most sensitive flesh. Rachel's body jolted with pleasure, and a low whimper came from her throat.

His touch was firm but tender, with just the right amount of pressure. Slowly her head rolled back and forth on the pillow between the frame of her arms, and her back arched. If he had tantalized her before, this was torture, the sweetest torture imaginable. Hot coils wound inside her, heat spreading throughout her body until she was flushed and damp. Her breasts were so tight that they ached. Kell knew exactly when she couldn't stand it any longer and bent to suck strongly at her nubbed flesh, wringing another soft, wild sound from her throat.

Then his hand was on her bare thigh, under the nightgown, and the relief of feeling skin on skin was so intense that she jerked again.

"Easy," he breathed, and she held herself as still as she could while his warm, hard hand slowly moved upward, stroking her thigh. Her legs were parted already, in aching need, and she strained toward him.

His palm barely brushed her, then moved to her other

thigh and stroked until she thought she would go mad. "You just wait!" she both threatened and promised, hissing the words through her tightly clenched teeth.

He laughed aloud, a low, rough sound of masculine triumph. Dimly she realized that it was the first time she'd heard him laugh. "I'm looking forward to it," he said, his voice strained. He was hot and damp, too, his eyes glittering with barely controlled passion, his face taut, with hectic color on his cheekbones and his lips. "Are you ready, love? Let me see." He touched her, and then the light, teasing touches ceased completely. He parted her soft flesh and slid two long fingers into her. Rachel gave a thin, high cry, her hips heaving as she trembled on the verge of ecstasy.

"Not yet," he breathed. "Not yet. Hold on, honey. I'm not going to let you go just yet. Not until I'm inside you."

His low, rough words washed over her shaking, twisting body. Crying a little, tormented by those long, probing fingers as he brought her to moist readiness, she tried again to free her hands, and this time he let them go.

"Now," he crooned, pulling the nightgown up. Rachel lifted herself up to aid in the removal of the frustrating garment, pulling it over her head herself and throwing it across the room. Kell's face tightened even more as he stared down at her naked body, at her flushed, glowing skin. Briefly his eyes closed, and he ground his teeth together as a heavy surge in his loins threatened his self-control.

Carefully he rolled to his back, favoring his shoulder, and guided her astride him. "Slow and easy," he muttered, his eyes glittering like black fire as he positioned himself for her. "Let's go easy, a little at a time."

"I love you," Rachel whispered achingly, closing her eyes at the probing of his flesh against her. She braced her hands on his chest, her fingers flexing in the mat of curly hair, and slid onto him. He made a guttural sound and arched beneath her, his hands clenching on the sheet. "I love you," she said again, and another low animal sound came from him as his control shattered and he grabbed for her hips, grinding her in a rotating motion against him.

"Rachel," he groaned, shaking. His body was taut and straining beneath her.

She moved on him, rising, sliding, falling. Now it was her turn, and she did a primeval dance of passion, slowing whenever it seemed that her motions would take either of them past the point of no return. She was no longer so painfully empty; she was filled with him, an intense satisfaction in itself. Time became elastic, expanded, then disappeared altogether. She forgot everything but Kell, and she gave herself to him in a way she'd never known would be possible. He had become irrevocably hers when she pulled him from the surf, and she was irrevocably his, perhaps by the same power. For as long as she lived, she would be his.

She was crying again, but this time she was oblivious to the tears raining down her face. "I love you," she choked, then abruptly she crested, surging against him while her soft inner quivering made the world explode, then fade away and there were only the two of them, straining together, until he cried out hoarsely and heaved beneath her. Later, as she slept in his arms, he lay awake staring into the night, and though his face was as blank as usual, there was a look of desperation in his eyes.

"Let's drive into town," he said the next morning after breakfast.

She drew a deep breath, her hands stilling for a moment before she resumed washing the last plate. She handed it to him to dry, feeling the dread rising in her chest to choke her. "Why?"

"I need to make a phone call. I'm not going to do it from here."

Her throat was so tight she could scarcely speak. "You're going to call the man you think you can trust?"

"I *know* I can trust him," Kell replied briefly. "I'm staking my life on it." Even more than that, he was staking Rachel's life. Yes, he trusted Sullivan completely.

"I thought you were going to wait until you had recuperated." When she turned to look at him, her eyes were shadowed with a stark pain that twisted the knife inside him once more.

"I was, until Ellis came around again. It'll take Sullivan a few days to check out some things for me and get things organized. I don't want to push it any longer than that."

"Sullivan? That's the man?"

"Yes."

"But you just got your stitches out yesterday," she protested urgently, lacing her fingers together to keep from wringing her hands. "You're still weak, and you can't—" She bit her lip, halting her own desperate flow of words. Arguing wouldn't change his mind. And how could she tell him he was too weak, when he had made love to her twice during the night and woken her that morning when he slid into her again? She was both stiff and sore, and every step she took reminded her of his strength and endurance. He wasn't at his own personal peak of strength, but even so, he was probably stronger than most men.

She closed her eyes, hating her own weakness for trying to hold on to him when she'd known from the first that she couldn't. "I'm sorry," she said quietly. "Of course you can. We'll go now, if you want."

Kell watched her silently; if there was any one moment that revealed the strength of the woman, it was now, and it only made the leaving harder. He didn't want to call

Sullivan; he didn't want to hurry the day when this would have to end. He wanted to stretch time to its utmost limits, to spend the hot, lazy days lying on the beach with her, getting to know every minute facet of her personality and making love to her whenever they wanted. And the nights...those long, warm, fragrant nights, spent tangled together on the damp, twisted sheets. Yes, that was what he wanted. Only the sure knowledge that she was in increasing danger could force him to make that call to Sullivan. His instinct told him that time was running out.

He was silent so long that Rachel opened her eyes and found him looking at her with that intent way of his. "What I want," he said deliberately, "is to make love again."

That was all it took, just that look of his and the words, and she felt herself growing warm and moist as her body automatically tightened, but she knew that she wouldn't be able to comfortably accept him. She looked at him with poignant regret. "I don't think I can."

He touched her cheek, his hard, rough fingers stroking the contours of her face with incredible tenderness. "I'm sorry. I should have realized."

She gave him a smile that wasn't as steady as she wished. "Let me change clothes and brush my hair, and we'll leave."

Because she wasn't the type to linger in front of a mirror, they were on their way in five minutes. Sabin was alert, his dark eyes noting every detail of the countryside and examining every car they met. Rachel found herself watching the rearview mirror in case they were being followed.

"I need a phone booth off the main drag. I don't want to be seen by six hundred people on their way to buy groceries." The words were terse, his attention on the traffic.

Obediently she searched out a phone booth next to a service station on the edge of town and parked the car next to it. Kell opened the door, then shut it again without getting out. He turned to her with a smile of real amusement on his lips. "I don't have any money."

His smile relieved the tension inside her, and she chuckled as she reached for her purse. "You could use my credit card number."

"No. If anyone checked it could lead them to Sullivan."

He took the handful of change she gave him and went into the phone booth, closing the door behind him. Rachel watched as he fed coins into the slot, then looked around to see if anyone else was watching him, but the only other person in sight was the man at the service station, and he was sitting in a chair in the front office, leaning back against the wall with the front legs of the chair off the ground while he read a newspaper.

Kell was back in only a few minutes, and Rachel started the car as he slid onto the seat and slammed the door. "That didn't take long," she said.

"Sullivan doesn't waste words."

"He'll come?"

"Yeah." Suddenly he smiled again, that rare, true smile. "His biggest problem is getting out of the house without his wife following him."

The humor, on that particular subject, was unexpected. "She doesn't understand about his job?"

He snorted. "It isn't his job—he's a farmer. And it'll make Jane madder than hell that he didn't take her with him."

"Farmer!"

"He retired from the agency a couple of years ago."

"Was his wife an agent, too?"

"No, thank God," he said with real feeling.

"Don't you like her?"

"It's impossible not to like her. I'm just glad Sullivan has her under control on that farm."

Rachel gave him a dubious glance. "Is he any good? How old is he, anyway?"

"He's my age. He retired himself. The government would have been glad to keep him another twenty years, but he got out."

"And he's good?"

Kell's dark eyebrows lifted. "He's the best agent I ever had. We trained together in Nam."

That reassured her; even more than her dread at his leaving, she feared the danger he would have to face. Not a hint of it would ever surface in any newspaper, but there would be a small war in the nation's capital. Kell wouldn't rest until his section was clean again, even at the cost of his own life. The knowledge ate at her. If she could, if he would let her, she would go with him and do whatever she could to protect him.

"Stop at a drugstore," he instructed, swiveling in his seat to check behind them.

"What do you want at a drugstore?" She looked at him again and found him watching her with faint amusement.

"Birth control. Or haven't you realized what a chance we've been taking?"

"Yes, I'd realized," she admitted in a low voice.

"You weren't going to say anything or do anything about it?"

Her hands tightened on the steering wheel until the knuckles were white, and she concentrated on the traffic. "No."

Just that one, calmly uttered word had the power to jerk his head up, and she felt his gaze burning on her. "I don't want to get you pregnant. I can't stay, Rachel. You'd be alone, with a baby to raise."

She braked for a red light and turned her head to meet his gaze. "It would be worth it, to have your baby."

His jaw tightened, and he swore under his breath. Damn, he was hard again just at the thought of getting her pregnant, of her bearing his child and nursing it at her pretty breasts. He wanted to. He wanted to take her with him and go home to her every night, but he couldn't turn his back on his job and his country. Security was critical, now more than ever, and his services were invaluable. It was something he had to do; endangering Rachel was something he couldn't do.

Her gray eyes were dark with mingled love and pain. "I won't make it easy for you to leave me," she whispered. "I won't hide what I feel and wave you off with a smile."

His profile was hard and unreadable as he turned back to watch the road; he didn't answer, and when the light changed to green again she drove carefully to the nearest drugstore. Without speaking, she took a twenty from her purse and handed it to him.

His hand clenched on the crisp bill, and he looked like murder. "It's either this or abstinence."

She drew a deep breath. "Then I suppose you'd better go in, hadn't you?"

No, she wasn't making it any easier; she was making it so difficult that it was tearing him apart. Damn it, he'd give her a baby every year if things were different, he thought savagely as he went into the drugstore and made his purchase. Maybe he was too late; maybe she was already pregnant. Only the naive or the careless could discount the possibility.

He left the cash register and had started for the door, when Rachel came through it, her face strained, her eyes wide and urgent. Without hesitation he turned and walked several aisles over to intently examine a high stack of insulated beverage coolers. Rachel walked past, to the cosmetic department. Sabin waited, and a moment later the door opened again. He caught a glimpse of sandy hair and ducked his own head down, automatically reaching behind his back for the pistol, but his waistband was empty. The pistol was in the car. His eyes narrowed, and a cold, deadly look settled over his features; moving silently, he began trailing Ellis.

Rachel had seen the blue Ford driving down the street and had known immediately that it was Ellis; her only thought had been to warn Kell before he walked out of the drugstore and let Ellis see him. If Ellis had been following them it was already too late, but she was fairly certain that wasn't the case. This was just an unhappy coincidence; it had to be. She had pretended not to see him, getting out of the car and walking into the drugstore as if she'd just driven up herself. She had heard a car door close behind her just as she went inside, and she knew Ellis would be there in a few seconds. Kell had taken one look at her face and detoured; now all she had to do was get rid of Ellis, even if she had to get back in the car and drive away without Kell. She could circle back to pick him up.

"I thought it was you. Didn't you hear me call?" Ellis asked behind her as she surveyed the array of lipsticks.

She jerked around, pretending that he'd startled her. "Tod! You scared me!" she gasped, holding a hand to her chest.

"Sorry. I thought you knew I was behind you."

He seemed to be thinking a lot this morning; she hoped it didn't strain him too much. She gave him an abstracted smile. "I've got so much on my mind I'm just walking around in a daze. I'm trying to get everything together for my trip, but I left my shopping list at home, and it's driving me crazy trying to remember everything."

He looked at the display, his easy grin flashing. "I guess lipstick is essential."

"No, but lip balm is, and I thought it would be here." Condescending mongrel! She wondered how he'd look if she told him to shove off. The problem with someone with an enormous ego was that any slight sent them around the bend, hell-bent on revenge. Still, she couldn't keep the tartness out of her voice, and he looked at her in surprise.

"Is something wrong?"

"I've got a vicious headache," she muttered. She caught sight of Kell, moving just behind Ellis; his face was set, his eyes narrowed and cold, and he moved like a stalking panther. What was he doing? He was supposed to stay out of sight until she got rid of Ellis, not attack the man! All the color drained from her face as Ellis peered at her.

"You do look sick," he finally admitted.

"I think it was too much wine last night." She turned on her heel and marched down the aisle, away from Kell. Damn the man! If he wanted to jump Ellis, he'd have to chase him down to do it! She didn't stop until she got to the insect repellent section; she grabbed a bottle and scowled as she read the directions on the back.

Ellis was still right behind her. "Do you think you'd feel like going out tonight?"

Rachel ground her teeth in frustration. She couldn't believe he was that thick-skinned. It was an effort to take a deep breath and answer calmly. "I don't think so, Tod, but thanks for asking. I really feel rotten."

"Sure, I understand. I'll call you in a day or so."

From somewhere she dredged up enough control for a wan smile. "Yes, do that. Maybe I'll feel better then, unless this is some sort of virus."

Like most people, he backed off a little at the mention

of anything contagious. "I'll let you get back to your shopping, but you really should go home and take it easy."

"That's good advice. I just might do that." *Would he never leave?*

But still he lingered, chatting, being so obviously charming that she wanted to gag. Then she saw Kell again, silently working his way around behind Ellis, his eyes never wavering from his prey. Desperately she grabbed her stomach and said clearly, "I think I may throw up."

It was really amazing how fast Ellis retreated, looking at her warily. "You'd better go home," he said. "I'll call you later." The last words were said as he went out the door. She waited until he got in the Ford and drove off before she turned to look at Kell as he walked up to her.

"Stay in here," she said curtly. "I'll drive around the block to make certain he's gone."

She walked off before he could say anything. She was seething, and driving around the block would give her time to cool down. It made her furious that he would take that sort of risk right now, when he wasn't a hundred percent physically fit. When she was in the car she leaned her head on the steering wheel for a moment, shaking. What if Ellis had seen Kell go into the drugstore and had just been playing it cool, making sure it was Kell so he could report back to his superiors? She didn't think so, unless Ellis was much more cunning than she'd given him credit for, but even the possibility was horrifying.

Shaking, she started the car and circled the block, looking up and down all the streets for a blue Ford parked anywhere. She didn't just have to look for Ellis; she had to look for Lowell, too, and she had no idea what he might be driving. And how many other men were in this area now?

Returning to the drugstore, she pulled up close to the

door and Kell came out, sliding into the car beside her. "See anyone?"

"No, but I don't know what kind of cars the others might have." She pulled into traffic, heading in the opposite direction from the one Ellis had taken. That wasn't where she wanted to go, but she could always cut back.

"He didn't see me," Kell said quietly, hoping to ease some of the tension evident in her face.

"How do you know? He could have decided to report you and wait for backup, catch you out later rather than trying something in the middle of a crowded drugstore."

"Relax, honey. He's not that smart. He'd try to take me himself."

"If he's so stupid, why did you hire him?" Rachel shot back.

He looked thoughtful. "I didn't. Someone else 'acquired' him."

Rachel glanced at him. "One of the two men who knew where you were?"

"That's right," he said grimly.

"That narrows it down for you, doesn't it?"

"I wish it did, but I can't afford to take that for granted. Until I know for certain, both of them are suspects."

It made sense; if he had to err, it would be on the side of caution. He couldn't afford even one mistake.

"Why were you trailing him like that? Why didn't you just stay out of sight until I'd gotten rid of him?" she demanded, her knuckles showing white again.

"If he had seen me, it could have been his plan to grab you for bait, to draw me out. I wasn't going to let that happen." The quiet, calm way he said it made Rachel shiver, as if the air had suddenly turned cold.

"But you aren't up to something like that yet! Your leg could give out on you, and your shoulder is so stiff you can barely move it. What if you'd torn everything open again?''

"It didn't happen. Anyway, I didn't anticipate a fight, just one good crack at him.''

His male arrogance made her want to scream; instead she ground her teeth together. "It didn't occur to you that something could have gone wrong?''

"Sure, but if he'd grabbed you, I wouldn't have had any choice, so I wanted to be in position."

And he was willing to do whatever was necessary, despite his stiff shoulder and lame leg. He was one of a rare breed, able to see the cost and still be willing to pay it, though he would do everything he could to tip the scales the other way.

She was still pale, her eyes shadowed, and he reached over to slide his hand down her thigh. "It's all right," he said gently. "Nothing happened."

"But it could have. Your shoulder—"

"Forget my damned shoulder, and my leg. I know how far I can push them, and I don't go into anything unless I think I can win."

She was silent for the remainder of the drive, until she parked the car under the tree. "I think I'll go for a swim," she said tightly. "Want to come along?"

"Yes."

Joe came up to her car door as always, his dark eyes trained on her even though he remained just out of touching distance, and he walked beside her as she went up the steps to the porch. He accepted Kell, but if the two of them were outside he was never far from Rachel. He was one warrior who was content to stay, she thought wistfully, then resolutely pushed away the creeping self-pity. Life would go on, even if it was without Kell. It hurt to think about it, and she didn't want to, but she knew that she would survive somehow, though her life had been irrevocably changed by the time she had spent with him, quiet days punctuated by moments of sheer terror.

She changed into her sleek black bathing suit and Kell put on his denim shorts, and after grabbing a couple of towels, they walked through the pines down to the beach. Joe followed them and lay down in the scant shade of a clump of sea oats. Rachel dropped the towels on the sand and pointed out to the bay, where the water was rising and breaking over the submerged rocks. "See the line where the water breaks? That's where the rocks are. I'm pretty sure you hit your head on one of them that night. The tide was just starting to come in, so the water was low." She pointed again. "I dragged you out here."

Kell looked at the beach, then turned and stared up the slope, where the pines were standing tall and straight, a thicket of wooden sentinels. She had somehow dragged him up that slope and gotten him into the house, a feat that he couldn't imagine when he looked at her slender body. "You damn near killed yourself getting me up there, didn't you?" he asked quietly.

She didn't want to think about that night, or what it had cost her physically. Part of it had already been blocked from her brain; she remembered that she'd been in pain, but the exact nature of the pain escaped her. Perhaps adrenaline was responsible for both her strength that night and the selective amnesia that followed. She looked at him for a long moment, then turned and walked into the sea. He watched until the water reached her knees, then pulled the pistol out of his waistband and carefully laid it on a towel, covering it with the other to keep the blowing sand out of it. Then he dropped his shorts and walked naked into the water after her.

Rachel was a strong swimmer, having spent most of her

life living on the Gulf, but Kell stayed even with her despite his stiff shoulder. At first, when she realized he was in the water, she had started to protest that he shouldn't get his wounds wet, but she swallowed the words. After all, he had swum with open wounds, and the exercise would be good therapy. They swam in the bay for half an hour before he decided that he'd had enough, and Rachel returned to the beach with him. It wasn't until the water reached his waist that she realized he was nude, and the familiar quiver shook her insides as she watched him wade out of the water. He was so lean and hard and perfect, darkly tanned and roped with muscle, even his tight buttocks. She watched as he moved the pistol and lay down on one of the towels, his glistening body offered to the sun.

She left the water, too, bending over to wring out her hair. When she straightened again she found him watching her. "Take off the bathing suit," he said softly.

She looked out to sea, but there were no boats in sight. Then she looked at him again, lying there like a bronzed, naked statue, except that she'd never seen a statue in a state of arousal. Slowly she reached up for the straps on her shoulders and drew them down, and immediately she felt the heat of the hot sun kissing her wet breasts. A slight breeze suddenly kicked up, whispering across her nipples and making them pucker. Sabin's breath caught in his chest, and he held his hand out to her. "Come here."

She pushed the bathing suit down and off, then walked to the towels. He sat up and reached for her, drawing her down beside him and stretching her out. Amusement was twinkling in his dark eyes as he looked down at her. "Guess what I forgot to bring."

She began to laugh, the sound pure and deep in this world where only the two of them existed.

"Ah, well, you're too sore for that, anyway," he mur-

mured, sliding his hand over her breasts and bringing her
nipples to tingling awareness. "I'll just have to…impro-
vise."

He leaned over her, his shoulders so broad that they
blocked out the sun, and his mouth burned on hers, then
down on her body.

He was very good with improvisations. He lingered over
her as if she were a willing, sun-kissed sacrifice offered up
for his delectation, until her body finally arched to his rapacious mouth and she cried out in intolerable pleasure, her
cry rising to the white inferno of the sun.

Chapter Eleven

Rachel didn't let herself think about time, though she knew they had only a few more days at the most, however long it took this Sullivan to make his arrangements and travel down to meet Kell. She lived completely in the present, reveling in his company whatever they were doing. He began helping her gather the vegetables from the garden, and he worked some with Joe, gaining more of the dog's trust and showing Rachel how highly trained Joe was. After the first swim they also spent a lot of time down at the bay; they swam every morning and again in the afternoon, after the worst of the heat was over. It was marvelous therapy, and every day he got stronger, his shoulder more flexible and his limp improving. He also did other exercises, continually working to bring his body back up to par, and she could only watch in amazement. She was athletic and strong herself, but her endurance was nothing compared to his. He was often in pain; she sensed it, even though he never said anything, but he ignored it as if it weren't there. Ten days after she'd found him he was gingerly jogging around the house, his thigh tightly wrapped to brace the injured muscle. After a moment of anger Rachel joined him and jogged along beside him, ready to catch him if his leg gave out and he fell. It wouldn't have done any good to yell at him, because it was important for him to be able to meet whatever demands might be placed on him when he left.

And whatever they did, they talked. He was reticent about himself, both naturally and as a result of his training, but he did have a lot of fascinating inside details about the political and economic considerations of governments around the world. He probably also knew more than anyone would want him to know about military forces and capabilities, but he didn't talk about those. Rachel learned as much about him from his omissions as she did from the subjects he would talk about.

No matter what they did, whether weeding the garden, jogging around the house, cooking a meal or arguing politics, desire ran between them like an invisible current, linking them together in a state of heightened awareness. Her senses were filled with him; she knew his taste, his smell, his touch, every nuance of his deep voice. Because he was normally so expressionless she watched him closely for each small movement of his brows or twitch of his lips. Even though he was relaxed with her and smiled more often, sometimes teasing her, his laughter was rare, and therefore doubly treasured, the occasions pressed into her memory. Their desire couldn't be quenched by lovemaking, because it was more than a physical need. She immersed herself in him, knowing that she had only the present.

Still, physical desire couldn't be denied. Rachel had never been so thoroughly enjoyed before, even in the early days of marriage. Kell had a strong sexual appetite, and the more he made love to her, the more they both wanted it again. He was exquisitely careful with her until she became more accustomed to him, his lovemaking both sophisticated and earthy. There were times when they lingered, savoring each sensation like sexual gourmets until the tension was so strong that they exploded together. There were also the times when their loving was fast and hard, when there was no foreplay because their need to be together was too urgent.

The third day after he'd called Sullivan, Kell made love to her with barely controlled violence, and she knew that he was thinking this might be the last day they had together. She clung to him, her arms tight around his neck when he lay on her in heavy, damp exhaustion. A lump lodged in her throat, and she squeezed her eyes tightly shut in an effort to deny the march of time. She couldn't bear to let him go.

"Take me with you," she said thickly, unable to let it lie, to simply let him walk away from her. Rachel was too much of a fighter to let him go without trying to change his mind.

He stiffened, then withdrew from her to lie on his back beside her, his forearm thrown up to cover his eyes. The ceiling fan whirred overhead, wafting a cool breeze across their overheated skin and making her feel a little chilled without the heat of his body pressed over her. She opened her eyes to stare at him, her gaze burning with desperation.

"No," he finally said, and left it at that, the single word filled with a finality that almost broke her heart.

"Something could be worked out," she pressed. "At worst we could see each other occasionally. I'm mobile. I can work anywhere—"

"Rachel," he interrupted tiredly. "No. Leave it." He took his forearm down from his eyes and looked at her. Though his expression changed very little, she could tell that he was annoyed by her persistence.

She was too desperate to stop. "How can I leave it? I love you! This isn't a game I'm playing, that I can just pick up my marbles and go home when I get tired of it!"

"Damn it, I'm not playing games, either!" he roared, bolting upright in the bed and seizing her arm to shake her, finally goaded past his limits. His eyes were hot and narrowed, his teeth clenched. "You could be killed because of me! Didn't it teach you anything when your husband died?"

She went pale, staring at him. "I could be killed driving into town," she finally said shakily. "Would that make me any less dead? Would you grieve any less?" Suddenly she stopped, wrenching her arm free and rubbing it where his fingers had bitten into her flesh. She was so white that her eyes burned darkly in her colorless face. Finally she said with an attempt at lightness, "Or would you grieve at all? I'm being rather presumptuous, aren't I? Maybe I'm the only one involved here. If so, just forget everything I've said."

Silence stretched between them as they faced each other on the bed; her face was strained, his grim. He wasn't going to say anything. Rachel inhaled sharply at the pain squeezing her insides. Well, she'd asked for it. She'd pushed him, fighting to change his mind, to get a commitment from him, and she had lost...everything. She had thought that he cared for her, loved her, even though he'd never said anything about love. She had put it down to his natural reticence. Now she had to face the unpleasant truth that it was his brutal honesty that had kept him from saying he loved her. He wouldn't spout pretty words that he didn't mean just to soothe her feelings. He liked her. She was a reasonably attractive woman, and she was convenient; he was highly sexed. The reason for his attentions was obvious, and she'd made a complete fool of herself.

The worst of it was that even facing the hard, unpalatable reality didn't stop her from loving him. That was another reality, and she couldn't wish it away.

"Sorry," she mumbled, scrambling off the bed and

reaching for her clothes, suddenly embarrassed by her nudity. It was different now.

Sabin watched her, every muscle coiled tightly. The look on her face ate at him, the abrupt embarrassment, the sudden extinguishing of the light in her eyes as she fumbled with her clothing in an attempt to cover herself. He could let her go. She might get over him more easily if she thought he had just used her sexually, without returning any of her emotion. Emotion made Sabin uneasy; he wasn't accustomed to it. But damned if he could stand that look on her face! Maybe he couldn't give her much, but he couldn't leave with her thinking she'd been nothing more than a sexual convenience.

Rachel was out of the room before he could catch her, and then he heard the screen door slam. Going to the door, he saw her disappearing into the pines with Joe right beside her, as usual. He cursed steadily as he jerked on his pants and started after her. She wasn't going to be inclined to listen to him now, but listen she would even if he had to hold her down.

When Rachel reached the beach she kept walking, wondering how she was going to find the courage to go back to the house and act as if everything were normal, as if she weren't a shriveled knot of pain inside. Still, it was probably only for one more day; she could manage that. She could endure it for twenty-four hours. Part of her was glad that it could be measured in hours; then she could forget about a stiff upper lip and cry until the tears were all gone. But the rest of her screamed silently at the thought of not seeing him again, no matter what he felt—or didn't feel—for her.

A pastel pink shell was half-hidden by a clump of seaweed, and she paused to push the seaweed aside with her foot, hoping to find something beautiful to lighten her heart.

But the shell was broken, most of it gone, and she kept walking. Joe left her side, trotting up the beach to do his own exploring; he had been changed by Kell's arrival, too, for the first time allowing a man to touch him and learning to accept someone other than Rachel. She watched the dog, wondering if he would miss Kell, too.

A warm hand closed on her shoulder, bringing her to a halt. Even without looking around she knew it was Kell; she knew his touch, the rasp of his roughened fingertips. She felt him at her back, tall and warm, so intense that her skin tingled whenever he was near. All she had to do was turn around and her head would fit right into the hollow of his shoulder, her body would fit into his arms, but he wouldn't allow her to fit into his life. She didn't want to treat him to tears and hysterics, and she was very much afraid she would if she turned around, so she kept her back to him.

"This isn't easy for me, either," he said roughly.

"I'm sorry," she broke in, wanting to make a quick end to it. "I didn't mean to start a scene, or put you on the spot. Just forget it, if you can."

His hand tightened on her shoulder, and he turned her around, sliding his other hand into her hair and tilting her face up so he could see her eyes. "Don't you see that it couldn't work between us? I can't leave my job. What I do...it's hard and it's ugly, but it's necessary."

"I haven't asked you to give up your job," she said, her face proud.

"It's not the damn job I'm worried about!" he shouted, his dark face furious. "It's you! God, it would tear my guts out if anything happened to you! I love you." He paused, took a deep breath, and continued more quietly. "I've never said that to anyone before, and I shouldn't be saying it now, because there's no use in it."

The wind whipped her hair around her face as she stared up at him, her gray eyes fathomless. Slowly his fist loosened in her hair and he moved his hand down to her neck, rubbing his thumb over the fluttering pulse at the base of her throat. Rachel swallowed. "We could try it for a little while," she whispered, but he shook his head.

"I want to know that you're safe. I *have* to know that, or I can't function the way I should. I can't make a mistake, because if I did it could mean that people died, good men and women. And if you were kidnapped—" He stopped, his face almost savage. "I'd sell my soul to keep you safe."

Rachel felt herself shattering on the inside. "No, it can't be like that. No negotiation—"

"*I love you,*" he said harshly. "I've never loved anyone before in my life, not my parents, any of my relatives, or even my wife. I've always been alone, different from everyone else. The only friend I've ever had is Sullivan, and he's as much of a lobo as I am. Do you really think I could sacrifice you? Sweet hell, woman, you're my one chance in a lifetime—" He broke off, a muscle in his jaw twitching as he stared at her. "And I don't dare take it," he finished quietly.

She understood, and she wished she didn't. Because he loved her, he didn't trust himself not to betray his country if she were kidnapped and used as a weapon against him. He wasn't like people who had loved before and would love again; he was too remote, too chillingly alone. For whatever reason, whatever particular chemistry and circumstance, he loved her, and it was the only time in his life he would ever love a woman. Living with him would make her vulnerable to attack; merely loving her would make him vulnerable, because for a man such as he, love was something both wonderful and terrible.

He took her hand, and they walked silently back to the

house. It was time for lunch; Rachel went into the kitchen with the intention of trying to busy herself cooking so she wouldn't be able to think. Kell leaned against the cabinets and watched her, his black eyes burning her flesh. Suddenly he reached out and caught her hand, removing the pot from her grasp and setting it back on the countertop. "Now," he said gutturally, pulling her toward the bedroom.

He stripped down her shorts but didn't take the time to remove her shirt; nor did he take the time to shed his pants, merely opening them and shoving them down. They didn't make it to the bed. He took her on the floor, so desperate to be inside her, to sheathe himself in her and eliminate all distance between them, that he couldn't wait. Rachel clung to him as he pounded into her, every inch of her flesh, every cell, branded by his possession. And even then they both knew it wouldn't be enough.

Late that afternoon she walked out to the garden to gather a few fresh peppers to add to the spaghetti sauce she was cooking. Kell was taking a shower, and Joe, oddly, was nowhere in sight. She started to call him, but decided that he must be asleep under the oleander bush, taking refuge from the heat. The temperature had to be pushing a hundred, and the humidity was high, prime conditions for a thunderstorm. With her hand full of peppers she crossed the small backyard to the house. Later she could never decide where he came from; there had been no one in sight, and no place for him to hide. But as she went up the back steps he was suddenly there behind her, his hand clamping over her mouth and jerking her head back. His other arm went around her in almost exactly the same movement Kell had used when he had jumped her from behind, but instead of a knife this man carried a gun clutched in his fist; it glinted in the sun with a dull blue sheen.

"Don't make a sound and I won't hurt you," the man

murmured in her ear, his voice easy on consonants and pure liquid on the vowels. "I'm looking for a man. He's supposed to be in this house."

She clawed at his hand, trying to scream a warning even though Kell might still be in the shower and wouldn't be able to hear her. But what if Kell did hear her? He could be shot trying to help her. The thought paralyzed her, and she sagged against the man, struggling to organize her mind and think of something she could do. "Shhh, that's right," the man said in that low, soft voice that made chills run over her body. "Open the door now, and we'll go in nice and easy."

She didn't have any choice but to open the screen door. If he had wanted to kill her he already would have, but he could still easily knock her unconscious, and the end result would be the same: she would be unable to help Kell if the opportunity arose. The man pushed her up the back steps with his big body, holding her so securely against him that she couldn't struggle. She stared at the gun in his hand. If he tried to shoot Kell, she could hit his arm, throw off his aim. Where was Kell? She tried to listen for the shower, but her thundering heartbeat made a roaring in her ears that blotted out sound. Was he dressing? Had he heard the back door close? Even if he had, would he think anything of it? They relied on Joe to let them know if anyone was close by. Hard on the heels of that thought came another one, and pain welled in her again. Had he killed Joe? Was that why the dog hadn't come around the house when she went out to the garden?

Then Kell walked out of the bedroom, wearing only his jeans and carrying his shirt in his hand. He stopped, his face very still as he looked first at the man holding her, then at her terrified eyes above the hand clamped over her mouth. "You're scaring her to death," he said in a cool, controlled tone.

The hand over her mouth loosened, but the man didn't completely release her. "Is she yours?"

"She's mine."

Then the big man let her go, gently setting her away from him. "You didn't tell me anything about a woman, so I wasn't taking any chances," he said to Kell, and Rachel realized who he was.

She held herself very still, fighting for control and taking slow, deep breaths until she thought she could speak without her voice trembling. "You must be Sullivan," she said with admirable calm as she gradually relaxed her clenched hands.

"Yes, ma'am."

She didn't know what she'd expected, but it wasn't this. He and Kell were so much alike that it staggered her. It wasn't the way he looked, but they both had the same stillness about them, the same aura of power. He had sun-streaked, shaggy hair, and his eyes were as piercing and golden as an eagle's. A scar cut across his left cheekbone, testimony to some past battle. He was a warrior, lean and hard and dangerous...like Kell.

While she had been looking at him, he'd been giving her the same treatment, studying her while she struggled for control. One corner of his mouth kicked up in an almost-smile. "Sorry for scaring you, ma'am. I admire your self-control. Jane would've kicked me in the shins."

"She probably did," Kell commented, his tone still cool, but now with an undercurrent of amusement.

Sullivan's dark brows snapped down over his golden eyes. "No," he said dryly. "That wasn't where she kicked me."

That sounded like a fascinating story, but though Kell

still looked amused, he didn't pursue it. "This is Rachel Jones," he said, holding out his hand to her in a quiet command. "She dragged me out of the ocean."

"Glad to meet you." Sullivan's drawl was soft and raspy as he watched Rachel immediately go to Kell in response to his outstretched hand.

"I'm glad to meet you, Mr. Sullivan...I think."

Kell gave her a brief, comforting touch, then began pulling on his shirt; it was an action that still caused him some difficulty, as his shoulder was stiff and sore. Sullivan looked at the tender, red, newly formed scar tissue where the bullet had torn into Kell's shoulder. "How much damage?"

"I've lost some flexibility, but there's still some swelling. Part of it may return as the swelling goes down."

"Did you get it anywhere else?"

"Left thigh."

"Will it hold up?"

"It'll have to. I've been jogging, loosening it up."

Sullivan grunted. Rachel sensed the man's reluctance to talk freely in front of her, the same ingrained caution that characterized Kell. "Are you hungry, Mr. Sullivan? We're having spaghetti."

That wild-animal gaze turned on her. "Yes, ma'am. Thank you." The soft slurring of his drawl and the grave courtesy of his manners made such a contrast to the fierceness of his eyes that she felt off-balance. Why hadn't Kell warned her?

"I'll finish while you two talk, then. I must have dropped the peppers when you grabbed me," she said. She started toward the door, then turned back, distress in her eyes. "Mr. Sullivan?"

He and Kell were walking into the living room, and Sullivan stopped, looking back at her. "Ma'am?"

"My dog," she said, a faint trembling in her voice. "He's always there when I go outside. Why didn't he—"

Understanding was in those wild golden eyes. "He's all right. I've got him tied up in that pine thicket. Had a helluva time outsmarting him. That's a nice animal."

Relief made her weak. "I'll go untie him, then. You didn't…hurt him in any way?"

"No, ma'am. He's about a hundred yards down, just to the left of that little trail."

She ran down the trail, her heart thudding; Joe was right where Sullivan had said he would be, tied securely to a tall pine, and the dog was furious. He even snarled at Rachel, but she talked softly to him and approached him at a slow, measured pace, calming him before she knelt beside him to untie the rope around his neck. Even then she kept talking, giving him small, quick pats, and the snarls diminished in his throat. Finally he accepted a hug from her, and for the first time gave her a welcoming lick. A lump rose in her throat. "Come on, let's go home," she said, getting to her feet.

She collected the peppers from where she had dropped them on the back steps and left Joe prowling around the house. She washed her hands and began preparing the sauce, listening to the quiet rumble of the men's voices from the living room. Now that she had met Sullivan she understood Kell's confidence in him. He was…incredible. And Kell was even more so. Seeing them together made her realize anew the caliber of the man she loved, and she reeled under the shock of that realization.

It was almost an hour before she called them to the table, and the sun was a fierce red ball low on the horizon, a reminder that now her time with Kell was truly running out. Or was it already gone? Would they be leaving soon?

Deliberately, to get her mind off her fears, she kept the

conversation going. It was remarkably difficult, with both men being the way they were, until finally she hit on the right subject. "Kell told me that you're married, Mr. Sullivan."

He nodded, a curious lightening of his expression making him seem less formidable. "Jane is my wife." He said it as if everyone knew Jane.

"Do you have any children?"

There was no mistaking the look of intense pride that came over the hard, scarred face. "Twin sons. They're six months old."

For some reason Kell was looking amused again. "I didn't know twins ran in your family, Grant."

"They don't," Sullivan growled. "Or in Jane's, either. Even the damn doctor didn't know. She took everybody by surprise."

"That's not unusual," Kell said, and they looked at each other, grinning.

"The hell of it is, she went into labor two weeks early, in the middle of a snowstorm. All the roads were closed, and I couldn't get her to a hospital. I had to deliver them." For a moment there was a look of desperation in his eyes, and a faint sheen of perspiration broke out on his forehead. "Twins," he said faintly. "Damn. I told her not to ever do that to me again, but you know Jane."

Kell laughed out loud, his rare deep laugh making pleasure shimmer through Rachel. "Next time she'll probably have triplets."

Sullivan glared at him. "Don't even think it," he muttered.

Rachel lifted a forkful of spaghetti to her mouth. "I don't think it's Jane's fault that she had twins, or that it snowed."

"Logically, no," Sullivan admitted. "But logic flies out the window when Jane walks in the door."

"How did you meet her?"

"I kidnapped her," he said offhandedly, leaving Rachel gasping, because he offered no other explanation.

"How did you get away from her?" Kell asked, provoking another glare.

"It wasn't easy, but she couldn't leave the kids." Sullivan leaned back in his chair, an unholy light entering his eyes. "You're going to have to go back with me to explain."

Kell looked alarmed, then resigned; finally he grinned. "All right. I want to see you with these babies."

"They're already crawling. You have to watch where you step," the proud father said, grinning in return. "Their names are Dane and Daniel, but beats the hell out of me which one is which. Jane said we can let them decide when they get older."

That was it. The three of them looked at one another, and Rachel gulped helplessly. Kell made a rough choking sound. In a perfectly choreographed move three forks were laid down on the table and three people held their heads and laughed until they hurt.

Charles read the hastily gathered intelligence report on Rachel, frowning as he rubbed his forehead with one thin finger. According to both Agents Lowell and Ellis, Rachel Jones was a good-looking but otherwise ordinary woman, even though Ellis was enamored of her. Ellis was enamored of women in general, so that wasn't unusual. The problem was that the report painted her as anything but ordinary. She was a well educated, well traveled, multitalented woman, but again the problem went even deeper than that. She had been an investigative reporter of extraordinary talent, nerve and perseverance, which meant that she was more knowledgeable than the ordinary person about things that were usually kept from public knowledge. According to her record she had been very successful in her field. Her husband had been murdered by a car bomb meant for her when she began investigating a powerful politician's connection with illegal drugs; rather than backing down, as many people would have done, this Rachel Jones had kept after the politician and not only proved that he was involved with drug smuggling and dealing, she had proved that he was behind her husband's death. The politician was now serving a life sentence in prison.

This wasn't the rather unsophisticated woman Lowell and Ellis had described. What particularly troubled Charles was why she had projected such an image; she had to have a reason, but what was it? Why had she wanted to deceive them? For amusement, or had there been a more serious motivation?

Charles wasn't surprised that she had lied; in his experience most people lied. In his profession it was necessary to lie. What he didn't like was not knowing *why*, because the why of something was the heart of it.

Sabin had disappeared, possibly dead, though Charles couldn't convince himself of that. No trace of him had been found, not by Charles's men, a fishing trawler, a pleasure boater, or any law enforcement agency. Even though Sabin's boat had exploded there should have been some identifiably human remains—if Sabin had been on the boat. The only explanation was that he had gone overboard and swum for shore. It almost defied belief to think that he could actually have made it in his wounded condition, but this was Sabin, not some ordinary man. He *had* made it to shore, but where? Why hadn't he surfaced yet? No one had found a wounded man; no unaccounted for gunshot wounds had been reported to the police; he hadn't been admitted to any of the hospitals in the area. He had simply disappeared into thin air.

So, on the one hand he had Sabin, who had vanished. The only possibility was that someone was hiding him, but there were no clues. On the other hand, there was this Rachel Jones, who, like Sabin, was not ordinary. Her house was in the prime search area, the area where Sabin would have most likely made it to shore. Neither Lowell nor Ellis thought she had anything to hide, but they didn't know everything about her. She had projected a false image; she was more familiar than could have been suspected with undercover agents and tactics. But what reason could she have for acting like less than what she was...unless she had something to hide? More to the point, did she have some-*one* to hide?

"Noelle," he said softly. "I want to talk to Lowell and Ellis. Immediately. Find them."

An hour later both men were sitting across from him. Charles folded his hands and smiled absently at them. "Gentlemen, I want to discuss this Rachel Jones. I want to know everything you can remember about her."

Ellis and Lowell exchanged looks; then Ellis shrugged. "She's a good-looking woman—"

"No, I am not interested in her looks. I want to know what she has said and done. When you searched the beach in her area and went up to her house, did you go inside?"

"No," Lowell replied.

"Why not?"

"She's got this damned big guard dog who hates men. He won't let a man in the yard," Ellis explained.

"Even when you took her out to dinner?"

Ellis looked discomfited, as if he disliked admitting that a dog had scared him off. "She came out to the car. When

I took her home the dog was there waiting, ready to take my leg off if I moved in the wrong direction.''

"So no one has been inside her house."

"No," they both admitted.

"She denied any knowledge of seeing a man, a stranger?"

"There's no way Sabin could have gotten anywhere near that house without the dog having him for breakfast," Ellis said impatiently, and Lowell nodded in agreement.

Charles tapped his fingertips together. "Even if she took him into the house herself? What if she found him? She could have tied the dog up, then gone back for Sabin. Isn't this possible?"

"Sure, it's possible," Lowell said, frowning. "But we didn't find any sign of Sabin making it to shore, not even a footprint. The only thing we noticed was where she dragged shells up from the beach on a tarp—" He stopped, his eyes meeting Charles's.

"You fools!" Charles hissed. "Something had been dragged up from the beach and you didn't check it out?"

They looked uncomfortable. "She said it was shells," Ellis muttered. "I noticed that she did have some shells on the windowsills."

"She didn't act like she had anything to hide," Lowell put in, trying to gloss things over. "I ran into her the next day while she was shopping. She stopped to talk, about the heat and things like that..."

"What did she buy? Did you look in her cart?"

"Ah, underwear and, uh, women's things. When she checked out I saw a pair of jogging shoes. I noticed them because—" Suddenly he went a sickly shade.

"Because?" Charles prompted dryly.

"Because they looked too big for her."

Charles glared at them, his eyes cold and deadly. "So.

She dragged something up from the beach, something you didn't investigate. Neither of you has been inside the house. She was buying shoes that were too big for her, possibly men's shoes. If Sabin has been under our noses all this time and he's escaped due to your bungling, I personally promise you that your future won't be pleasant! Noelle!'' he called.

She appeared immediately in the door. ''Yes, Charles?''

''Call everyone in. We may have found Sabin.''

Both Lowell and Ellis looked sick, and both fervently hoped that this time they *didn't* find Sabin. ''What if you're wrong?'' Ellis asked.

''Then the woman may be frightened and upset, but nothing more. If she doesn't know anything, if she hasn't helped Sabin, then we have no reason to harm her.''

But Charles smiled when he said it, his eyes cold, and Ellis couldn't believe him.

The sun had set, and twilight had brought out a loud chorus of frogs and crickets. Ebenezer Duck and his flock waddled around the yard, reaping the late afternoon harvest of insects, and Joe lay on the porch. Kell and Sullivan were now at the table, drawing diagrams and discussing plans; Rachel tried to work on the manuscript, but her mind kept wandering. Kell would be leaving soon, and dull misery throbbed inside her.

The flock of geese suddenly scattered, honking wildly, and Joe gave a single bark before he lunged off the porch. Kell and Sullivan acted as one, ducking away from the table and running soundlessly, on the balls of their feet, to the living room windows. Rachel bolted out of her office, her face pale, though she tried to be calm. ''It's probably just Honey,'' she said, going to the front door.

''Honey?'' Sullivan asked.

"The veterinarian."

A white sedan pulled up in front, and a woman got out. Sullivan peered out the window and all the color washed out of his face. Resting his head on the wall, he swore quietly and at length. "It's Jane," he groaned.

"Hell," Kell muttered.

Rachel opened the door to dart out and catch Joe, who was planted in the middle of the yard. But before Rachel could get out the door, Jane had walked around the car and into the yard. "Nice doggie," she said cheerfully, patting Joe on the head as she passed.

Sullivan and Kell came out on the porch behind Rachel. Jane put her hands on her hips and glared at her husband. "Since you wouldn't bring me with you, I decided to follow you!"

Rachel liked Jane Sullivan on sight. Anyone who calmly petted Joe, then faced Grant Sullivan's fury without blinking an eye, was someone Rachel would like to know. The two women introduced themselves, while Sullivan stood with his arms folded across his chest, his golden eyes shooting fire as he watched his wife from beneath lowered brows. "How did you find me?" he rasped, his voice low and almost soundless. "I made sure I didn't leave a trail."

Jane sniffed at him. "You didn't, so I did the logical thing and went where you weren't, and found you." Turning her back on him, she welcomed Kell with an enthusiastic hug. "I knew it had to be you. No one else could have dragged him away. Are you in trouble?"

"A little," Kell said, his black eyes filled with amusement.

"I thought so. I came to help."

"I'll be damned," Grant snapped.

Jane gave him a cool look. "Yes, you may be. Sneaking out and leaving me with the babies—"

"Where *are* they?"

"With your mother. She thinks I'm doing her a favor. Anyway, that's what took me so long to get here. I had to take the twins to her. Then I had to figure out what you'd do if you were trying to keep anyone from knowing where you were."

"I'm going to turn you over my knee," he said, and he

looked as if the thought gave him immense satisfaction. "You're not getting out of it this time."

"You can't," she said smugly. "I'm pregnant again."

Rachel had been enjoying the spectacle of Grant Sullivan driven to frustration by his pretty, dark-eyed wife, but now she felt almost sorry for him. He went pale.

"You can't be."

"I wouldn't bet on that," Kell put in, enjoying this turn of events as much as Rachel.

"The twins are just six months old," Grant croaked.

"I know that!" Jane replied, her face indignant. "I was there, remember?"

"We weren't going to have any more for a while."

"The thunderstorm," she said succinctly, and Grant closed his eyes. He was really white by now, and Rachel was moved to pity.

"Let's go inside, where it's cooler," she suggested, opening the screen door. She and Kell went inside, but no one followed them. Rachel peeked out the door; Jane was wrapped in her husband's muscular arms, and his blond head was bent down to her dark one.

Oddly, that sight added a little more to Rachel's inner pain. "They made it," she whispered.

Kell's arms slid around her waist, and he pulled her back against him. "He isn't in it now, remember? He was retired before they ever met."

Rachel wanted to ask why he couldn't retire, as well, but kept herself from voicing the question. What had been right for Grant Sullivan wasn't right for Kell Sabin; Kell was one of a kind. Instead she asked, "When do you leave?" She should have been proud that her voice was so steady, but pride didn't mean anything to her at this stage. She would have begged him on her knees if she thought it would work, but his dedication was more than lip service.

He was silent for a moment, and she knew she wouldn't like the answer, even though she was expecting it. "Tomorrow morning."

So she had one more night, unless he and Sullivan planned to spend most of it working out the details of their objective.

"We're turning in early," he said, touching her hair, and she twisted in his arms to meet his midnight eyes. His face was remote, but he wanted her; she could tell it by his touch, by something fleeting in his expression. Oh, God, how could she ever stand to watch him leave and know that she'd never see him again?

Jane and Grant came inside, and Jane's face was radiant. Her eyes widened with delight when she saw Rachel in Kell's arms, but something in their expressions kept her from saying anything. Jane was nothing if not intuitive. "Grant won't tell me what's going on," she announced, and crossed her arms stubbornly. "I'm going to follow you until I find out."

Kell's black brows lifted. "And if I do tell you?"

Jane considered that, looking from Kell to Grant, then back to Kell. "You want to negotiate, don't you? You want me to go back home."

"You *are* going back home," Grant said quietly, steel in his voice. "If Sabin wants to fill you in, that's up to him, but this new baby gives me twice the reason to make sure you're safe on the farm, instead of risking your neck chasing after me."

There was a glint in Jane's eyes that made Rachel think Sullivan would have a fight on his hands, but Kell forestalled that by saying, "All right, I think you deserve to know what's happened, since Grant's involved in it now. Let's sit down, and I'll fill you in."

"On a 'need to know' basis," Jane guessed accurately, and Kell gave her his humorless smile.

"Yes. You know there are always details that can't be discussed, but I can tell you most of it."

They sat around the table, and Kell sketched in the main points of what had happened, the implications and why he needed Grant. When he had finished Jane looked at both the men for a long time, then slowly nodded. "You have to do it." Then she leaned forward, planted both hands on the table and bent an uncompromising look on Sabin, who met it squarely. "But let me tell you, Kell Sabin, that if anything happens to Grant, I'll come after you. I didn't go through all that trouble to get him for anything to happen to him now."

Kell didn't respond, but Rachel knew what he was thinking. If anything happened it wasn't likely that he would survive, either. She didn't know how she knew what was in his mind, but she did. Her senses were locked on Kell, and his slightest gesture or change of tone registered on her nerves with the force of an earthquake on the most sensitive seismograph.

Grant stood up, drawing Jane up to stand beside him. "It's time we got some sleep, since we're leaving so early in the morning. And you're going home," he said to his wife. "Give me your word."

Now that she knew what was involved, Jane didn't argue. "All right. I'll go home after I pick up the twins. What I want to know is when I can expect you back."

Grant glanced at Kell. "Three days?"

Kell nodded.

Rachel got to her feet. In three days it would be over, one way or the other, but for her it would end in the morning. In the meantime she had to make sleeping arrangements for the Sullivans, and she was almost grateful to have something that would occupy her time, if not her mind.

She apologized to Jane for the lack of an extra bed, but it didn't seem to bother Jane at all. "Don't worry about us," Jane soothed. "I've slept with Grant in tents, caves and sheds, so a nice living room floor isn't any hardship to us."

With Jane's help Rachel gathered quilts and extra pillows for a pallet, taking them from the top of her closet and stacking them on Jane's arms. Jane eyed her shrewdly. "You're in love with Kell, aren't you?"

"Yes." Rachel said the one word steadily, not even thinking of denying it. It was a fact, as much a part of her as her gray eyes.

"He's a hard, unusual man, but top quality steel has to be hard to be top quality. It won't be easy. I know. Look at the man I chose."

They looked at each other, two women with a world of knowledge in their eyes. For good or ill, the men they loved were different from other men, and they would never have the security most women could expect.

"When he leaves tomorrow, it's over," Rachel said, her throat tight. "He won't be back."

"He *wants* it to be over," Jane clarified, her brown eyes unusually somber. "But don't say that he won't be back. Grant didn't want to marry me. He said it wouldn't work, that our lives were too different and I'd never fit into his world. Sound familiar?"

"Oh, yes." Her eyes and voice were bleak.

"I had to let him go, but in the end he came after me."

"Grant was already retired. Kell won't retire, and the job is the problem."

"It's a big problem, but not insurmountable. Loving

someone is hard for men like Grant and Kell to accept. They've always been alone.''

Yes, Kell had always been alone, and he was determined to keep it that way. Knowing and understanding his reasons didn't make living with them any easier. She left Jane and Grant to bed down in the living room, and Kell followed her into the bedroom, closing the door behind him. She stood in the middle of the room with her hands tightly clenched, her eyes shadowed as she watched him.

"We should have left tonight," he said quietly. "But I wanted one more night with you."

She wouldn't let herself cry, not tonight. No matter what happened she would wait until tomorrow, until he was gone. He turned out the light and came to her in the darkened room, his rough hands closing on her shoulders and pulling her against him. His mouth was hard, hungry, almost hurting her as he kissed her with savage need. His tongue probed at hers, demanding a response that was slow in coming, because the pain was so great inside her. He kept on kissing her, sliding his hands over her back and hips, cradling her against the warmth of his body, until finally she began to relax and yield to him.

"Rachel," he whispered, unbuttoning her shirt to find her naked breasts and cup them in his warm palms. Slowly he circled her nipples with his thumbs and enticed them to hardness; the warmth, the tightening sense of excitement and anticipation began to intensify inside her. Her body knew him and responded, growing heavy and moist, readying her for him because she knew he wouldn't leave her unsatisfied. He slid the shirt off her shoulders, pinning her arms to her sides with the fabric while he lifted her, arching her over his arm and thrusting her breasts up to him. Deliberately he put his mouth over her nipple and sucked at her, the strong motion drawing hot tingles from her sensitive flesh. She made a faint, gasping sound of pleasure as the sensations swept from her breasts into her lower abdomen, where desire was pulling at her.

Her head swam, and she had the sudden sensation of falling, which made her clutch at his waist. It wasn't until she felt the coolness of the bed beneath her that she realized he had been lowering her to its surface. Her shirt was caught beneath her, with the sleeves trapped and twisted midway between her elbows and wrists, effectively pinning her arms while her upper torso lay bare for his marauding lips and tongue to savor. He looked down at her with a tortured, hungry expression in his eyes, then bent and buried his face between her breasts, his hands squeezing them together around his face as if he wanted to lose himself in the scent and feel of her satiny flesh.

She moaned as her body throbbed in need, and tried futilely to wrest her arms free. "Kell." Her voice was high, strained. "Let me get my arms out."

He lifted his head and appraised the situation. "Not yet," he murmured. "Just lie there and let me love you until you're ready for me."

She made a rough sound of frustration, trying to roll to one side so she could free herself, but Kell subdued her, his hard hands holding her flat on her back. "I *am* ready," she insisted before his mouth came down on hers and stifled any further protests.

When he raised his head again it was with hot satisfaction stamped on his taut features. "Not like you will be." Then he bent to her breasts again, not stopping until they were wet and gleaming from his mouth and her nipples were red and achingly tight. Gently he bit the undercurve of her breast, using his teeth just enough to let her feel them but not enough to bring pain.

"Let's get you out of these." The strain was evident in

his voice, too, as he tugged at the fastening of her shorts. It came free, and the zipper rasped quietly as he slid it down. His hand went inside the opened shorts, burrowing under her panties to find the warm, moist, aching flesh he sought. "Ah," he said in quiet satisfaction as his fingers explored her and found her ready, indeed. "You liked that, didn't you?"

"Yes." All she could do was whimper the word.

"You'll like it better when I'm inside you," he promised huskily, and slid her panties and shorts down her hips and thighs, but not off. He left them just above her knees, and her legs were trapped as effectively as her arms. Slowly he ran his hand over her, from her breasts down over her flat belly, to linger at her naked loins.

She writhed under his probing fingers, her heart thundering in her chest and interfering with the rhythm of her breathing. "Don't you even *think* it," she cried, her hands clutching at the sheet beneath her. He was looking at her in a way that told her he liked holding her helpless while he teased her and enjoyed her body. He was more than a little uncivilized, his instincts swift and primeval.

He gave a low, rough laugh. "All right, love. You don't have to wait any longer. I'll give you what you want." Swiftly he stripped her, even of the shirt that bound her arms, and took off his own clothes, then settled his weight onto her. Rachel accepted him with a sigh of painful relief, her arms wrapping around him as he spread her legs and entered her. She reached her peak quickly, convulsing in his arms, and slowly he built her to pleasure again. He couldn't get enough of her that night, returning to her over and over, as if time slowed when they were locked together in love.

It was shortly before dawn when she woke up for the last time, lying on her side with her back to him, snuggled into the warm curve of his chest and thighs, just as they had slept every night since he'd regained consciousness. This was the last time he would hold her like this, and she lay very still, not wanting to wake him.

But he was already awake. His hand moved slowly over her breasts, then down to her thighs. He raised her leg, draping it over his thigh, and slid into her from behind. His hand flattened against her stomach to brace her as he began moving in and out of her. "One last time," he murmured into her hair. Dear God, it was the last time, and he didn't think he could stand it. If he had ever been happy in his life it had been during these too short days with Rachel. This would be the last time her soft body would sheathe his hardness, the last time her breasts would fill his hands, the last time he would ever see the misty look of passion in her lake-gray eyes. She trembled beneath his hands, biting her lips to keep from crying out as the pleasure built within her. When the time came he clasped her to him, holding himself deep within her while she turned her face into the pillow to stifle the sounds she made, then he thrust deep and hard and shuddered with his own release.

The room was growing light now, the sky glowing with the pink pearl of approaching sunrise. He sat up in the bed and looked down at her, her body damp and glowing like the sky. Perhaps this last time had been a mistake, because he hadn't taken his usual precautions, but he couldn't regret it. He couldn't have tolerated any separation of their bodies.

Rachel lay exhausted on the pillows, watching him with her heart in her eyes. Her body still throbbed from his lovemaking, and her pulse was only gradually slowing. "You may never come back," she whispered. "But I'll wait here for you, anyway."

Only the slight jerking of a muscle beside his mouth revealed his reaction. He shook his head. "No, don't waste your life. Find someone else, get married and have a houseful of kids.''

Somehow she managed a smile. ''Don't be a fool,'' she told him with aching tenderness. ''As if there could be anyone else after you.''

They were ready to leave, and Rachel was so stiff inside that she thought she would shatter if anyone touched her. She knew there would be no goodbye kisses, no final words to burn into her memory. He would simply leave, and it would be finished. He wasn't even taking the pistol with him, which would give him an excuse to contact her again to return it. The pistol was registered to her; he didn't want anything that could be traced back to her in case things didn't go as planned.

Sullivan had hidden his rental car somewhere down the road; Jane was going to drive them to it, then return to their farm. Rachel would be left alone in a house that echoed with emptiness, and she was already trying to think of ways to fill the time. She would work in the garden, mow the lawn, wash the car, maybe even go swimming. Later she would go out to eat, see a movie, anything to postpone coming back. Perhaps by then she would be so tired she would be able to sleep, though she didn't hold out much hope for that. Still, she'd get by, because she had no choice.

''I'll let you know,'' Jane whispered, hugging Rachel.

Rachel's eyes burned. ''Thank you.''

Grant opened the door and walked out onto the porch, which brought Joe to his feet, and snarls filled the air. Calmly Grant surveyed the dog. ''Well, hell,'' he said mildly.

Jane snorted. ''Are you afraid of that dog? He's as sweet as can be.''

Kell followed them onto the porch. "Joe, sit," he commanded.

There was the peculiar, high-pitched CRACK! of a rifle being fired and the wood exploded on the post not two inches from Kell's head. Kell turned and dove for the open door just as Rachel leaped for him, and he knocked her sprawling. Almost simultaneously Grant literally threw Jane through the door as another shot exploded, then he covered her with his body.

"Are you all right?" Kell asked through clenched teeth, anxiously looking Rachel over even as he lashed out with one foot and kicked the door shut.

She'd banged her head on the floor, but it wasn't anything serious. Her face white, she clutched at him. "Yes, I'm f-f-fine," she stammered.

He rolled to his feet, crouching to stay below the windows. "You and Jane lie down in the hall," he ordered tersely, getting the pistol from the bedroom where he'd left it.

Grant had helped Jane to a sitting position, brushing her hair out of her face and giving her a swift kiss before he pushed her toward Rachel. "Go on, move," he snapped, drawing his own pistol from his belt.

There was another shot, and the window closest to Grant shattered, raining shards of glass all over him. He cursed luridly.

Rachel stared at them, trying to gather her thoughts. They were armed only with pistols, while whoever was shooting at them had a rifle, stacking the deck against Kell and Grant. A rifle had the advantage of accuracy over a greater distance, allowing their assailant to shoot from outside the range of the pistols. Her .22 rifle didn't have much power, but it did have a greater range and accuracy than the pistols, and she crawled into the bedroom to get it, as well as what ammunition she had. Thank God Kell had told her to buy those shells!

"Here," she said, crawling back into the living room and sliding the rifle toward Kell. He glanced around, his fist closing over the weapon. Grant was moving through the house, checking to make certain no one was coming up on them from behind.

"Thanks," Kell said briefly. "Get back in the hall, honey."

Jane was crouched there, staring at her husband with an odd fury in her chocolate eyes. "They shot at you," she growled.

"Yep," he confirmed.

She was fuming like a volcano about to blow, muttering to herself as she dragged the nylon overnighter she'd brought to her, unzipping it and throwing clothing and makeup to one side. "I'm not putting up with this," she said furiously. "Damn it, they shot at him!" She produced a pistol and shoved it into Rachel's hand, then dug back into the bag. She dragged a small case out of it, about the size of a violin case, and threw it at Grant. "Here! I don't know how to put the thing together!"

He opened the case and glared at Jane even as he began snapping the rifle together with swift, practiced movements. "Where the hell did you get this?"

"Never mind!" she barked, tossing a clip of ammunition to him. He fielded it one-handed and snapped it into place.

Kell glanced over his shoulder. "Got any C-4 or grenades in there?"

"No," Jane said regretfully. "I didn't have time to get everything I wanted."

Rachel crawled to the side window, cautiously lifting her head to peek out. Kell swore. "Get down," he snapped. "Stay out of this. Get back in the hall, where it's safer."

She was pale, but calm. "There are only two of you, and four sides to the house. You need us."

Jane grabbed Grant's discarded pistol. "She's right. You need us."

Kell's face was set like granite. This was exactly what he'd wanted most to avoid, one of his worst fears coming true. Rachel's life was being threatened because of him. Damn! Why hadn't he left last night, as he should have? He'd let sexual desire override his common sense, and now she was in danger.

"Sabin!" The voice came from the pine thicket.

He didn't answer, but his eyes narrowed as he surveyed the thicket, trying to find the speaker. He wasn't going to answer and reveal his position; let them find out the hard way.

"Come on, Sabin, don't make it any harder than it has to be!" the voice continued. "If you surrender, I give you my word none of the others will be harmed!"

"Who is that joker?" Grant grunted.

"Charles Dubois, alias Charles Lloyd, alias Kurt Schmidt, alias several other names," Kell murmured.

The names meant nothing to Rachel, but Sullivan's brows lifted. "So he finally decided to come after you himself." He looked around. "We're not in a good position. He's got men all around the house. There aren't that many of them, but we're hemmed in. I checked the phone—it's dead."

Kell didn't have to be told that their situation wasn't good. If Dubois used the rockets on the house, as he had on the boat, they were all as good as dead. But then again, he was trying to take Kell alive. Alive, he was worth a lot of money to a lot of people who would pay anything to get their hands on him.

He tried to think, but the cold fact was that there was no

way out of the house. Even if they waited until nightfall and tried to sneak out, there was little available cover to use except for the bushes, which were right against the house. Away from the house, it was open for a good distance in all directions. That meant it would be difficult for anyone to catch them unawares, but it also meant the same thing in reverse. Even if he walked out and surrendered, it wouldn't save the others. There was no way Dubois would let any witnesses live. He knew it, and Sullivan knew it; he could only hope Rachel and Jane didn't realize quite how hopeless the situation really was.

A glance at Rachel dispelled that idea. She knew, all right. That had been the problem from the first; she was too aware, with no veil of ignorance to shield her. He wanted to take her in his arms and hold her head on his shoulder, assure her that it would be all right, but with those clear, level gray eyes on him, he couldn't lie to her, even to give her momentary comfort. He never wanted any lies between them.

There was a shot from the bedroom, and all the color washed out of Grant's face, but before he could move Jane called him. "Grant! Is the kneecap where I'm supposed to shoot these people?"

If anything, he went even whiter, swearing long and low.

"Well, it doesn't matter," she added philosophically. "I missed, anyway. But I hit his gun, if that counts."

"Sabin!" the man yelled again. "You are testing my patience! This cannot go on much longer. It would be such a pity if the woman was harmed."

"Woman," instead of "women." Then Kell realized that Rachel hadn't gone out on the porch; they had seen Jane and thought she was Rachel. They were both slim and had dark hair, though Jane was taller and her hair was a little longer, but at a distance no one would have noticed.

It didn't give him much of an advantage, but it might help that Dubois would be underestimating the number of armed people.

"Sabin!"

"I'm thinking!" Kell yelled, keeping his head away from the window.

"Time is a luxury you can't afford, my friend. You know you can't win. Why not make it easy on yourself? The woman will go free, I promise you!"

Dubois's promises weren't worth the air it took to make them, and Kell knew it. Time. Somehow he had to buy a little time. He didn't know what he was going to do, but every extra second gave chance an opportunity to step in. Timing was always critical, and if he could stall Dubois it might throw the man off in some way.

"What about my other friend?" he yelled.

"Of course," Dubois lied smoothly. "I have no quarrel with him."

Grant's lips twisted back in a feral grin. "Sure. There's no way he didn't recognize me."

What a coup it would be for Dubois to capture both Sabin and the Tiger, the big tawny warrior with the wild, golden eyes who had ranged the jungle with Sabin and later been his prime agent. Each was legendary in his own right; together they had been incredible, so attuned that they acted as one man. Sullivan had had a run-in with some of Dubois's men a few years back; no, Dubois wouldn't have forgotten that, considering how Sullivan had made a fool of him.

A movement in the trees suddenly caught Kell's attention, and his black eyes narrowed. "See if you can get him to say something else," he told Grant, sliding the barrel of the .22 just a fraction of an inch outside the broken window and keeping his eyes fixed on the spot in the trees.

"Come on, Dubois," Grant yelled. "Don't play games. I know you recognized me."

Kell's finger tightened slightly on the trigger as silence reigned; was Dubois really surprised to find out they knew who he was? It was true that he had always operated from the background rather than risk his own safety, but Kell had been after him for years now, ever since Dubois had begun selling his services as a terrorist.

"So it *is* you, Tiger."

There it was again, that slight movement. Kell sighted down the barrel and gently squeezed the trigger. The report of the rifle echoed in the small house, drowning out any cry of pain, but Kell knew he hadn't missed. He also didn't know if he'd hit Dubois or someone else.

A hail of bullets tore into the house, shattering all the windows and gouging long splinters out of the walls and window frames, but the steel reinforced doors held. "Guess he didn't like that," Kell muttered.

Grant had ducked to the floor, and now his head came up. "You know, I never liked that nickname worth a damn," he drawled, then swung his rifle up. It was an automatic, and he fired it in the three-shot bursts of a well-trained soldier, making good use of his firepower without wasting his ammunition. Pistol shots came from both the bedroom and Rachel's office; then all hell broke loose again. They were tearing the house up, and cold fear filled him, because Rachel was caught in this barrage.

"Rachel!" he yelled. "Are you all right?"

"I'm okay," she answered, and her calm voice made him ache.

"Jane!" Grant yelled. No answer. "Jane," he yelled again, his face gray as he started for the bedroom.

"I'm busy!"

Grant looked as if he might explode, and despite everything Kell found himself grinning. Better Grant than him. Still, Jane's life was in jeopardy, too, and the thought of anything happening to her was almost as hard to bear as the thought of anyone hurting Rachel.

There was another lull, and Grant pulled out his empty clip and slapped another one into place.

"Sabin, my patience is at an end," Dubois called, and Kell grimaced. Damn, it hadn't been Dubois he'd hit.

"You haven't made the right offer yet," he yelled in return. Anything to buy time.

Jane crawled out of the bedroom, her hair all mussed and her eyes big. "I think the cavalry is coming," she said.

The two men ignored her, but Rachel scrambled to her side. "What?" she asked.

"Men on horseback," Jane said, waving her hand toward the bedroom. "I saw them, coming from that way."

Rachel felt like crying or laughing, but she couldn't make up her mind which. "It's Rafferty," she said, and now she had their attention. "My neighbor. He must have heard the shots."

Grant crouched low and ran through the kitchen to the back, where he could see. "How many?" Kell asked.

"Twenty or so," Grant said. "Damn, they're riding right into automatic fire. Start shooting and draw Dubois's fire!"

They did. Rachel crept up to a window, held the heavy pistol out it and fired until it was empty, then reloaded with shaking hands before emptying it again. Kell was making judicious use of the .22, and Jane was revealing remarkable skill herself. Had they given Rafferty enough time to get behind Dubois and his men? If they kept shooting, they might hit their rescuers.

"Hold it," Kell ordered. They lay flat on the floor with their heads covered while the walls were shredded by bullets. The light fixture crashed to the floor, sending glass flying. Grant cursed, and they looked over to see blood streaming down his face from a cut on his cheek. Jane gave a thin, high cry and made a move toward him, despite the continuing gunfire; Kell grabbed her and wrestled her to the floor.

"I'm all right," Grant yelled. "It's just a little cut."

"Stay close to the floor," Kell told Jane, then let her go, knowing that she'd fight him like a wildcat if he tried to keep her from Grant.

Then, suddenly, it was quiet except for a few scattered shots, and they were abruptly halted, too. Rachel lay on the floor, hardly daring to breathe, the acrid smell of burned gunpowder filling her nostrils and even her mouth. Kell put his hand on her arm, his black eyes drifting over her pale features as if he would burn her into his memory.

"Hey!" a deep voice roared. "Rachel, are you in there?"

Her lips trembled, and tears suddenly blurred her eyes. "It's Rafferty," she whispered, then lifted her head to call, "John! Is it all right?"

"Depends," the answer came. "These bastards here don't think it's all right."

Kell slowly climbed to his feet and pulled Rachel to hers. "He sounds like my kind of man."

Rachel felt like the survivor of a shipwreck as she walked out on the porch with Kell supporting her. Grant and Jane followed, with Jane dabbing at the cut on Grant's cheek, crying a little as she fussed at him. Without the arm around her waist, Rachel was sure she wouldn't have been able to stand.

She gave a ghostly cry when she saw three of the geese lying in the yard, blood on the white of their feathers, but there was no way she could make a sound when she saw

Joe lying on his side at the edge of the porch. Kell turned her into his arms, pressing her face into his shoulder.

Big John Rafferty, armed with a hunting rifle and surrounded by his men, who were likewise armed, herded about fifteen men before him. Rafferty's eyes were fierce and narrow under his dark brows as he prodded a slim, gray-haired man before him. "We heard the shooting and came to see what was going on," John drawled. "I don't like riffraff shooting at my neighbor."

Charles Dubois was white with rage, his eyes fastened on Sabin. Beside him was Noelle, her beautiful eyes full of boredom.

"It isn't over, Sabin," Dubois hissed, and Kell gently put Rachel aside, handing her over to Grant. Kell had business to attend to, and explaining it to the law, then keeping it quiet would take some doing.

"It's over as far as you're concerned," he said briefly.

Beside Charles, Noelle smiled her slow, sleepy smile, then suddenly wrenched free; because she was a woman, the cowhand behind her hadn't been holding her securely. And, somehow, she had a gun in her hand, a small, ugly revolver.

Rachel saw it, and everything moved in slow motion. With a cry she tore free of Grant's arm, hurling herself toward Kell. A man grabbed for Noelle's arm, and the pistol exploded just as Rachel hit Kell, knocking him away. She cried out again at the burning pain in her side; then there was only blackness filling the world.

_____ *Chapter Thirteen*

Sabin leaned against the wall in the hospital waiting room, his nostrils filled with the sharp smell of antiseptic and his dark face cold and remote, even though there was scream-ing hell in his eyes. Behind him were Jane and Grant, wait-ing with him. Jane was huddled over, her expressive face pale and full of misery; Grant prowled the confines of the room like some great cat.

No matter how he tried, Kell couldn't get the picture of Rachel, lying on the ground awash in her own blood, out of his mind. She had looked so small and fragile, her eyes closed and her face paper white, crumpled like a child's discarded doll, one slender hand lying palm up. He'd fallen to his knees beside her, oblivious to the scuffle and shots going on behind him, and a low, rough sound had exploded from his chest. Her name had echoed in his mind, but he hadn't been able to voice it.

Then, incredibly, her eyes had opened. She was dazed and in pain, but those clear, clear eyes had fastened on him as if he were her lifeline, and her trembling lips had fash-ioned his name. It wasn't until then that he'd realized she was alive. Seeing her take the bullet meant for him had been a nightmare come true, and he still hadn't recovered. He didn't expect ever to recover.

Yet he had managed to rip her clothing away from the ugly wound in her side and apply rough first aid, with Jane kneeling beside him and helping. Grant had taken over with the others, doing what was necessary, making certain that no hint of what had happened was leaked.

Dubois was dead, Noelle critically wounded and not expected to survive. Ironically, it had been Tod Ellis who had shot them. During the ensuing scuffle after Noelle had shot Rachel, Ellis had pulled free and grabbed a rifle. His motives were murky. Perhaps he had wanted to get rid of Dubois so no one would know the extent to which Ellis had helped him; perhaps, in the end, he hadn't been able to stomach what he'd done. Or perhaps it had been because of Rachel. Sabin could identify with that last reason; he could gladly have killed Dubois and that treacherous bitch with his bare hands for what they'd done to Rachel.

Honey Mayfield had been fetched to take care of Joe, and she thought he would make it. Rachel would need something, someone to hold on to, even if it was just a dog. Her house had been so badly damaged that it would take weeks to restore it; her pets had been shot, her life turned upside down, she herself wounded, and the man she loved was the cause of it all. Cold, piercing agony filled his chest. He'd nearly cost her her life, when he would have died himself rather than have her suffer this. He'd known the danger, yet he'd stayed, unable to tear himself away from her. This once he'd let his heart overrule his mind, and it had almost killed her. Never again. God in heaven, never again.

He would stay only until she was out of surgery and he knew she would be all right; there was no way he could leave until he knew, until he'd seen her again and touched her. But then he and Grant would have to leave. The situation was critical; he had to get to Washington before the news of this leaked back and the traitor, or traitors, could cover their tracks.

"Jane," he said quietly, not turning around. "Will you stay?"

"Of course," she responded without hesitation. "You know you didn't have to ask."

It had been all he could do to get the local authorities to cooperate; if it hadn't been for one of the deputies, a man named Phelps, who knew Rachel, the whole thing would have blown sky-high. But Phelps had known what to do, and he'd done some long, hard talking to get the lid put on this. Rafferty had guaranteed the silence of his men, and Kell doubted that there was a one of them who would dare cross Rafferty.

The surgeon entered the waiting room, his lined face tired. "Mr. Jones?"

Kell had identified himself as Rachel's husband and signed the release forms for her to be treated to speed things up. Legality be damned. Every minute had meant the loss of more blood for her. He straightened away from the wall, his entire body taut. "Yes?"

"Your wife is doing fine. She's in recovery now. The bullet nicked her right kidney. She lost a lot of blood, but we got some back in her, and her condition is stabilizing. I had doubts about saving the kidney, but there was less damage than I'd anticipated. Barring complications, I don't see any reason she won't be home in about a week."

The relief was so great that all he could do was croak, "When can I see her?"

"Probably in about an hour. I'm going to keep her in ICU overnight, but it's just precautionary. I don't think that kidney's going to start bleeding again, but if it does, I want her there. I'll have a nurse come for you when they get her moved."

Kell nodded and shook the doctor's hand; then he stood rigidly, unable to relax even now. Jane came to stand beside him, slipping her hand into his bigger one and squeezing it comfortingly. "Don't tear yourself apart over this."

"It was my fault."

"Really? When were you put in charge of the world? I must have missed the headlines."

He sighed wearily. "Not now."

"Why not now? If you don't snap out of this you're not going to be in any shape to do what needs doing."

She was right, of course. Jane might not get where she was going by the same route the rest of the world would take, but in the end she was usually right on the money.

When at last they let him see Rachel, he was braced for the shock; he'd seen too many wounded people not to know that the paraphernalia of hospitals often made it seem worse. He knew about the machines that would be hooked up to her, monitoring her vital signs, and he knew there would be tubes running into her body. But nothing could have prepared him for the blow of walking into the room—and then she opened her eyes and looked at him.

Incredibly, a weak smile spread over her bloodless lips, and she tried to hold out her hand to him, but her arm was anchored to the bed with tape, while an IV needle fed a clear liquid into her vein. For a moment Kell was frozen in place, and his eyes closed on the burning sensation that filled them. It was almost more than he could do to walk around the bed and lift her other hand to his cheek.

"It...isn't that bad," she managed, her voice almost soundless. "I heard...the doctor...say so."

God, *she* was trying to reassure *him*! He choked, rubbing her hand against his temple. He'd have given his own life to have spared her this, and he was the cause of it.

"I love you," he muttered hoarsely.

"I know," she whispered, and went to sleep. Sabin hung over her bed for several more minutes, memorizing every line of her face for the last time. Then he straightened, and his face settled into its usual hard, blank mask. Walking briskly from the room and down the hall to where Grant and Jane waited, he said tersely, "Let's go."

Rachel walked the beach as she did every afternoon, her eyes on the sand as she automatically looked for shells. Joe roamed in front of her, periodically coming back as if to check on her, then going off on his own pursuits again. For weeks after she'd collected him from Honey, Joe had been almost paranoid about letting her out of his sight, but that stage had long passed. For Joe, it was as if the events of the summer had never happened.

It was early in December, and she wore a light jacket to protect her from the cool wind. The fall quarter at the college in Gainesville was finished except for the final exams, but she had enough to keep her busy. She'd worked like a Trojan in the months since July, finishing her manuscript well ahead of schedule and immediately diving into another one. There had been the class to teach, and the increasing number of tourists after the slow days of broiling summer heat had kept the two souvenir shops doing a booming business, which meant she had to drive down at least twice a week, sometimes three times.

The scar on her right side was the only reminder of what had happened in July. That, and her memories. The house had been repaired, new Sheetrock hung and painted because the damage had been too great to simply plaster over. The windows had new frames, and she had a new light fixture in the living room, as well as new furniture and new carpeting, because she'd given up hope of ever getting the glass out of the old. The house looked normal, not as if anything had ever happened that had taken weeks to repair.

Her recovery had been uneventful, and relatively short.

Within a month she had been going about her normal activities, trying to salvage some of the vegetables in the garden, which had become overgrown from neglect. Still, the pain from her wound had given her some idea of what Kell had gone through exercising his leg and shoulder to regain his mobility, and it staggered her.

She hadn't heard from him, not a word. Jane had stayed with her until she was released from the hospital, and had relayed the information that things had gone well in Washington. Rachel didn't know if Jane knew more but wasn't saying, or if that was all she'd been told. Probably the latter. Then Jane had left, too, to collect the twins and rejoin Grant at the farm. By now she would be round with pregnancy. For a time Rachel had thought she might be pregnant, too, from that last time Kell had taken her, but it had turned out to be a false alarm. Her system had simply gone awry from shock.

She didn't even have that. She had nothing but her memories, and they never left her alone.

She had survived, but it was only that: survival. She had gotten through each day without finding any joy in it, though she hadn't expected joy. At best, she would eventually find peace. Maybe.

It was as if part of her had been torn away. Losing B.B. had been terrible, but this was worse. She had been young then, and perhaps she hadn't been as capable of loving as deeply as she was now. Grief had matured her, had given her the depth of feeling with which she loved Kell. There wasn't a minute of the day that she didn't miss him, that she didn't live with pain because he wasn't there. She couldn't even find out about him from Jane; no information was available on Kell Sabin, ever. He had returned to his gray world of shadows and been swallowed up by them, as if he'd never been. Something could happen to him and she would never know.

That was the worst, the not knowing. He was there, but unreachable.

Sometimes she wondered if she'd dreamed it, that he'd come to her in the hospital and bent over her with his heart in his eyes as she'd never seen him before and whispered that he loved her. When she had awoken again she had expected to see him, because how could a man look like that and then walk away? But he had done exactly that. He'd been gone.

Sometimes she almost hated him. Oh, she knew all his reasons, but when she thought about it, they just didn't seem good enough. What gave him the right to make decisions for her? He was so damn arrogant, so certain that he knew best, that she could have shaken him until his teeth rattled.

The fact was that she had recovered from her wound, but she wasn't recovering from losing Kell. It ate at her day and night, taking away her joy in living and extinguishing the light in her eyes.

She wasn't pining away—she was too proud to let herself do that—but she was merely existing in limbo, without plans or anticipation. Walking the beach, staring out at the incoming waves, Rachel faced the fact that she had to do something. She had two options: she could try to reach Kell, or she could do nothing. To simply give up, to do nothing, went against her grain. He had had time to change his mind and come back, if he'd been going to, so she had to accept that he wasn't going to do it...not without incentive. If he wouldn't come to her, she'd go to him.

Just making that decision made her feel better than she had in months, more alive. She called to Joe, then turned and walked briskly up the beach toward her house.

She had no idea how to reach him, but she had to start somewhere, so she called telephone information to get the number of the agency in Virginia. That was easy enough, though she doubted it would be that simple to get put through to Kell. She called, but the operator who answered the phone denied that anyone by that name worked there. There was no listing for him. Rachel insisted on leaving a message, anyway. If he just knew she had called, perhaps he'd call back. Maybe curiosity wouldn't let him ignore the message.

But days went by and he didn't call, so Rachel tried again and received the same answer. There was no record of a Kell Sabin. She began contacting all the people she had done business with years ago when she was a reporter, asking for advice on how to get through to someone protected by the secrecy of the intelligence network. She sent messages to him through five different people, but had no way of knowing if any of them actually reached him. She continued to call, hoping that eventually the operator would get so frustrated that she'd hand the message on to someone.

For a month she tried. Christmas came and went, as well as the New Year celebrations, but the focus of her life was on somehow contacting Kell. It took a month for her to admit that either there was no way of getting a message to him, or he'd gotten them and still hadn't called.

To give up again, after trying so hard, hurt almost more than she could bear. For a while she'd had hope; now she had nothing.

She hadn't let herself cry much; it had seemed pointless, and she had really tried to pick herself up and keep going. But that night Rachel cried as she hadn't cried in months, lying alone in the bed she'd shared with him, aching with loneliness. She had offered him everything she had and was, and he'd walked away. The long night hours crawled by, and she lay there with her eyes wide and burning, staring at the darkness.

When the phone rang the next morning she still hadn't slept, and her voice was dull when she answered.

"Rachel?" Jane asked hesitantly. "Is that you?"

With an effort Rachel roused herself. "Yes. Hello, Jane, how are you?"

"Round," Jane said, summing it up in one word. "Do you feel like coming up for a visit? I warn you, I have ulterior motives. You can chase the boys while I sit with my feet up."

Rachel didn't know how she could bear to see Jane and Grant so happy together, surrounded by their children, but it would have been small of her to refuse. "Yes, of course," she forced herself to reply.

Jane was silent, and too late Rachel remembered that nothing got by Jane. And being Jane, she went right to the heart of the matter. "It's Kell, isn't it?"

Rachel's hand tightened on the receiver, and she closed her eyes at the pain of just hearing his name spoken. So many people had denied his existence that it stunned her for Jane to bring up the subject. She tried to speak, but her voice broke; then suddenly she was weeping again. "I've tried to call him," she said brokenly. "I can't get through. No one will even admit that they know him. Even if they're giving him my messages, he hasn't called."

"I thought he'd give in before now," Jane mused.

By that time Rachel had gotten herself under control again, and she apologized to Jane for crying all over her. She bit her lip, promising herself that it wouldn't happen again. She had to accept his loss and stop mourning.

"Look maybe I can do something," Jane said. "I'll have to work on Grant. Talk to you later."

Rachel hung up the phone, but she didn't let herself dwell on what Jane had said. She couldn't. If she got her hopes up again only to have them dashed, it would destroy her.

Jane went in search of Grant, and found him in the barn, working on the tractor. It was cold, but despite the chill he was working in only his shirt sleeves, and they were rolled up to his elbows. Two chubby little boys with white-blond hair and amber eyes, snugly bundled against the chill, played at his feet. Grant had started taking them out with him, now that she was so big with pregnancy that it was hard for her to chase after two rambunctious toddlers.

When he saw her he straightened, a wrench in his hand. Swiftly his gaze went over her, and despite her bulk a certain gleam entered his eyes.

"How do I get in touch with Kell?" she asked, getting right to the point.

Grant looked wary. "Why do you want to get in touch with Kell?"

"For Rachel."

Consideringly, Grant eyed his wife. Kell had had his private phone number changed soon after he'd returned home, and Grant had made certain Jane hadn't discovered it since then. It was too dangerous for her to know things like that; she had a positive genius for attracting trouble.

"What about Rachel?"

"I just talked to her. She was crying, and you know Rachel never cries."

Grant looked at her in silence, thinking. Not many women would have done what Rachel had. She and Jane weren't ordinary women, and though they went about things differently, it was the basic truth that they were both strong women. Then he looked down at the little boys playing happily in the hay, crawling over his feet. Slowly a grin cracked his hard face. Kell was a good man; he deserved some of this happiness.

"All right," he said, putting the wrench aside and leaning down to scoop the twins into his arms. "Let's go into the house. I'll put the call through. There's no way in hell I'm letting you get his number."

Jane stuck her tongue out at him, but followed him to the house with a big grin on her face.

Grant didn't take any chances; he made her wait in the next room while he made the call. When he heard the line ringing he called her, and she raced in to grab the receiver from his hand. It took three more rings before the phone was picked up on the other end and a deep voice said, "Sabin."

"Kell," she said cheerfully, "This is Jane."

There was dead silence for a moment, and she stepped into the breach. "It's about Rachel."

"Rachel?" His voice was guarded.

"Rachel Jones," Jane said, rubbing it in. "Don't you remember her? She's the woman in Florida—"

"Damn it, you know I remember. Is something wrong?"

"You need to go see her."

He sighed. "Look, Jane, I know you mean well, but there's no point in talking about it. I did what I had to do."

"You need to go see her," Jane repeated.

Something in her voice got through to him, and she heard the sudden sharpness that edged into his tone. "Why? Is something wrong?"

"She's been trying to get in touch with you," Jane said evasively.

"I know. I got the messages."

"Then why haven't you called her?"

"I have my reasons."

He was the most stubborn, noncommittal man she'd ever met, except for Grant Sullivan; they were two of a kind. Still, even stone could be worn away by dripping water, so she didn't give up. "You should have called her."

"It wouldn't do any good," he said sharply.

"If you say so," Jane returned just as sharply. "But at least Grant married me when he found out I was pregnant!" Then she slammed the phone down with a satisfying bang, and a pleased smile spread over her face.

Kell paced his office, running his hand through his black hair. Rachel was pregnant, carrying his baby. He counted the months; she would be six months along, so why had she waited so long before trying to contact him? Had something gone wrong? Was she sick? In danger of losing the child? Was something wrong with the baby?

The worry ate at him; it was even worse than what he'd gone through every day since he'd left her in the hospital. The want and need hadn't lessened; if anything, they had grown stronger. But every time the temptation to call her began undermining his common sense, his memory would dredge up the picture of her lying on the yard with her blood soaking her clothing, and he knew he couldn't live if his very presence put her in that sort of danger again. He loved her more than he'd known a human being could love; he'd never loved before, but when he'd fallen, he'd gone over hard. It pervaded his bone and tissue; he was never allowed to forget even for a moment. When he slept it was with the memory of holding her in his arms, but more often he lay awake, his body hard and aching for her softness to surround him.

He couldn't sleep; his appetite had suffered; his temper was shot to hell. He couldn't even have sex with other women, because the simple fact was that other women didn't even tempt him enough to arouse him. When he closed his eyes at night he saw Rachel, with her straight dark hair and clear, lake-gray eyes, and he tasted her on his tongue. He remembered her directness, her honesty, and the games played by women who tried to attract him did nothing other than turn him off.

She was going to have his baby.

The messages he'd been getting had been driving him crazy, and a dozen times he'd reached for the telephone. The messages had all been the same, short and simple. *"Call me. Rachel."* God, how he'd wanted to, just to hear her voice again, but now those messages took on more meaning. Had she just wanted to let him know that he was going to be a father, or was it more urgent than that? *Was something wrong?*

He reached for the telephone and actually dialed the number, but slammed the receiver down before her phone could begin ringing. Sweat broke out on his forehead. He wanted to see her, to make certain that everything was all right. He wanted to see her, just once, heavy and rounded with his child, even if he was never given anything else in this life.

It was raining the next day when he drove down the narrow private road that led toward the beach and Rachel's house. The sky was low and gray, sullenly pouring rain as if it would never stop. The temperature was in the forties, but that seemed almost warm after the twenties he had left behind in Virginia, and the weather report on the radio had promised clear skies and a warming trend for the next day.

He had arranged for a flight to Jacksonville, then caught a commuter plane to Gainesville, where he rented a car. It was the first time he'd ever walked out of the office like that, but after what had happened last summer, no one questioned him. It wouldn't have done much good if they had; once Sabin decided to move, he moved.

He stopped the car in front of the house and got out, ducking against the rain. Joe was braced in front of the steps, snarling, and it was so much like before that a tight smile tugged at Kell's mouth. "Joe, heel," he said. The dog's ears perked forward at that voice and the command, and with a small bark he bounded toward Kell, his tail actually wagging.

"That's quite a greeting," Kell murmured, leaning down to rub the dog's head. "I just hope Rachel is as glad to see me." After he'd ignored all of her messages she might well slam the door in his face. Despite the chill he felt himself starting to sweat, and his heart was slamming against his ribs. He was so close to her; she was just on the other side of that door, and he was shaking with anticipation, his loins hardening. Damn, that was just what he needed.

He was getting soaked, so he sprinted across the yard and leaped onto the porch with one bound, disdaining the steps. He knocked on the frame of the screen door, then impatiently did it again, harder.

"Just a minute."

He closed his eyes at her voice, then heard her footsteps approaching the door, and opened them again, not wanting to miss even a second of looking at her. She opened the door, and they faced each other silently through the screen. Her lips moved, but no sound emerged. He tried to see her through the screen, but there were no lights on in the living room, and the dim, gray day didn't help much. All he could really see was the pale oval of her face.

"May I come in?" he finally asked quietly.

Without a word she pushed the screen door open and moved back for him to enter. He stepped inside, closed the wooden door behind him and reached to flip the light switch, flooding the room with light. She stood before him, small and fragile and very slim. She was wearing tight jeans and a baggy black sweatshirt; her hair was longer and pulled back from her face on each side with two big tortoiseshell clips. She was pale, her face strained.

"You're not pregnant," he said in a tight voice. Had she lost the baby?

She swallowed, then shook her head. "No. I'd hoped I would be, but it didn't happen."

Her voice, so low and well remembered, made him shudder inside with pleasure, but her words brought him up short. "You haven't been pregnant?"

Now she looked confused. "No."

His fists knotted. He didn't know which was worse, the realization that Jane had lied to him, or disappointment that Rachel wasn't pregnant, after all. "Jane told me you were pregnant," he ground out, then abruptly remembered her exact words, and a bark of laughter burst out even through his anger. "Hell, no, she didn't. What she said was 'At least Grant married me when he found out I was pregnant!'" he told her, mimicking Jane. "Then she hung up on me. She's so slick that I didn't catch it until now."

Rachel had been watching him, not even blinking as she drank in his appearance. He was thinner, harder, that black fire of his even more intense. "You came because you thought I was pregnant?"

"Yes."

"Why bother now?" she asked, and bit her lip to stop it from trembling.

Well, he'd asked for that. He looked at her again. She had lost weight, and her eyes were listless. It startled him, hit him hard. She didn't look like a happy woman, and all he'd ever wanted was for her to be safe and happy. "How are you?'' he asked, concern deepening his voice to a rumble.

She shrugged. "Well enough, I suppose."

"Does your side bother you?"

"No, not at all." She turned away, going toward the kitchen. "Would you like a cup of hot chocolate? I was just going to make some."

He took off his coat and tossed it over a chair before following her. It gave him an overpowering sense of déjà vu to lean against the cabinets and watch her fiddle with pots and measuring cups. Abruptly she stopped and bent her head down to rest it against the refrigerator door.

"It's killing me without you," she said in a muffled voice. "I try, but I just don't care anymore. One day with you is worth more to me than a lifetime without you."

His fists clenched again. "Do you think it's easy for me?" His voice rasped the air like a rusty file. "Don't you remember what happened?"

"I know what can happen!" she screamed, whirling on him. "But I'm an adult, Kell Sabin! The risk is mine to take if I think it's worth it! I accept that every time I get in my car and drive to town. A lot more people are killed on the highways every year than by terrorists or assassins. Why don't you forbid me to drive, if you really want to protect me?"

His eyes burned on her, but he didn't say anything, and his remote silence goaded her. "I can live with the risks you take in your job," she continued. "I don't like it, but that's your decision to make. If you can't give me the same right, then why are you here?"

Still he stared at her, frowning. The hunger for her was growing in him, like an obsession. He wanted her, more than he wanted his next breath. He could either live with her, or live without her, and the past six months had shown him just how poor the quality of life was without her. The flat, unvarnished truth was that life wasn't worth living if he couldn't have her. Once he accepted that, his thoughts moved ahead. He'd have to take steps to make *certain* she was safe; he'd have to make changes and adjust, something he hadn't done before. It was odd how simple it looked all of a sudden, just because he admitted to himself that he had to have her. God bless Jane for getting his attention and giving him an excuse for coming down; she had known that once he saw Rachel again he wouldn't be able to leave.

He faced Rachel across the kitchen. "Can you really take it, the risks I take and the times I'll be gone when you won't know where I am or when to expect me?"

"I already have," she said, lifting her chin. "What I need to know is that you'll come back to me when you can."

Still he watched her, his eyes narrow and piercing. "Then we might as well get married, because God knows I've been a wreck without you."

She looked stunned; then she blinked. "Is that a proposal?"

"No. It was basically an order."

Slowly tears filled her gray eyes, making them glitter like diamonds, and a smile began to brighten her face. "All right," she said simply.

He did what he'd been hungering to do; he crossed the floor to her and took her in his arms, his mouth fastening hungrily on hers while his hands rediscovered the sleek curves of her body. Without another word he lifted her and carried her into the bedroom, tossing her across the bed just as he'd done the first time he'd made love to her. Swiftly he pulled her jeans down and off, then shoved the sweatshirt up to reveal her pretty round breasts. "I can't take it slow," he whispered, jerking his pants open.

She didn't need for him to take it slow. She needed *him*, and she held her arms out to him. He spread her thighs and mounted her, controlling himself just long enough to slow his entry so he wouldn't hurt her, and with a low cry of pleasure Rachel took him into her body.

They lay in bed the rest of the day, making love and talking, but mostly just holding each other and reveling in the other's nearness. "What happened when you got back to Washington?" she asked sometime during the afternoon.

He lay on his back with one muscular arm thrown above his head, drowsy after making love, but his eyes opened at her question. "I can't tell you too much," he warned. "I won't ever be able to talk a lot about my work."

"I know."

"Tod Ellis talked, and that helped. Grant and I set a trap, and one of my superiors walked into it. That's about all I can tell you."

"Were there others in your department?"

"Two others."

"They almost had you," she said, shuddering at the thought.

"They would have had me, if it hadn't been for you." He turned his head on the pillow and looked at her; the glow was back in her eyes, the glow that only he could produce. He never wanted to see that light go out. He reached out to touch her cheek. "I was disappointed that you weren't pregnant," he said softly.

She laughed. "I may be after today."

"Just in case," he murmured, rolling onto her.

She caught her breath. "Yes, by all means, just in case."

———————————————————————— *Epilogue*

They sat on the porch of the big farmhouse where Grant and Jane lived, enjoying the warmth of the late summer sunshine. Kell was leaning back in his chair, his booted feet propped on the railing, and Grant was sprawled in a position of total relaxation. Both men looked sleepy after the heavy meal they had just eaten, but nevertheless two pairs of alert eyes monitored the children playing in the yard while Rachel and Jane were in the house. Presently the two women joined their husbands on the porch, sitting down in big rockers.

Kell straightened abruptly as Jamie, who was no more than a toddler, fell down in the yard, but before he could open his mouth the four little boys crowded around her, and Dane—or Daniel?—helped her up, brushing the dirt from her chubby little legs. The five children looked unusual together, with the three Sullivan boys almost white haired, they were so blond, while both Brian and Jamie were dark, with black hair and eyes. Jamie was the queen of that particular crowd, ruling everyone with her big eyes and dimples. She was going to be small, while Brian had his father's build.

The children ran shrieking toward the barn, with Dane and Daniel each holding one of Jamie's hands, and Brian and Craig behind them. The four adults watched them go. "Can you believe," Kell said thoughtfully, "that we're in our forties and have five preschoolers between us?"

"Speak for yourself," Rachel returned. "Jane and I are still young."

Kell looked at her and grinned. He still didn't have any gray in his hair, and neither did Grant. They were both hard and lean, and more content with their lives than they had ever been before.

It had all worked out rather well. Married to Rachel, and quickly aware that there was indeed a baby on the way, Kell had accepted a promotion and was no longer such a prime target. He was still in a position to use his knowledge and expertise, but at much less risk to himself. It had been a trade-off, but one that was worth it. He glanced over at Rachel. Oh, yes, it had definitely been worth it.

"You never did tell me," Jane said idly, rocking in her chair as if she hadn't a care in the world. "Did you forgive me for lying to you about Rachel being pregnant?"

Grant chuckled, and Kell stretched out even more, closing his eyes. "It wasn't much of a lie," Kell said peacefully. "She was before the next day was out. By the way, how did you get my number?"

"I called you for her," Grant confessed, putting his booted feet up on the railing, too. "I thought some of the good life was just what you needed."

Rachel's eyes met Kell's, and they smiled at each other. It was nice to have such good friends.